Cutter's Reach

The sweeping saga of a family caught up in an epic struggle of empires, with the fate of North America hanging in the balance.

With a flintlock rifle and a dream, Abel Cutter blazed a trail into the wild Allegheny forests to establish a settlement for others who wanted only to be left alone to grow their crops and raise their families – a place called Cutter's Reach.

But France and England, with their Indian allies, are girding for war to secure their claim to America's first frontier, and Cutter's Reach turns out to be of strategic importance to both.

Reunited with his son, raised as a Tuscarora Indian, and his daughter, now wed to a British lieutenant, Cutter and his followers are willing to fight to live in peace. But the vengeful son of a man Cutter killed years ago takes advantage of the rising war fever to unleash an army of bloodthirsty Hurons and Canadian trappers determined to kill every man, woman and child at Cutter's Reach.

American Blood (Falconers 3)
Apache Shadow (Apache 2)
Apache Storm (Apache 1)
Apache Strike (Apache 3)
Battle of the Teton Basin (High Country 3)
Christmas in the Lone Star State
Cutter's Reach
Falconer's Law (Falconer 1)
Flintlock (Flintlock 1)
Frontier Road (Ethan Payne 1)
Gone to Texas (Flintlock 3)
Green River Rendezvous (High Country 2)
Gun Justice (Westerners 1)
Gunmaster (Westerners 2)
Gunsmoke on the Sierra Line
High Country (High Country 1)
Killer Gray
Last Chance (Ethan Payne 3)
Lobo Riler
Mountain Courage (Mountain Man 3)
Mountain Honor (Mountain Man 5)
Mountain Massacre (Mountain Man 2)
Mountain Passage (Mountain Man 1)
Mountain Renegade (Mountain Man 6)
Mountain Vengeance (Mountain Man 4)
Promised Land (Falconer 2)
Revenge in Little Texas
Robbers of the Redlands
Showdown at Seven Springs
Texas Blood Kill
Texas Bound

CUTTER'S REACH

JASON MANNING

TABLE OF CONTENTS

PART ONE

Late Winter 1753

CHAPTER 1

A bel Cutter woke with a fearsome headache.

His head had ached many times before, whether it was from being thrown by an occasional horse or bludgeoned with a pistol barrel. There was the time when he had taken a glancing blow from a Huron tomahawk and lived to tell the tale. While a young man in Scotland he had fancied himself a pugilist for a time and was often matched against men bigger and stronger and better than he, although some declared that none had more grit. The problem then had been his refusal to accept defeat, his stubborn insistence that he wasn't done so long as he breathed. But then, as a youth he had always felt he had something to prove. He had proven he wasn't particularly skilled with his fists but he was much admired for his endurance and sheer will.

He had long been prone to imbibing too much in the way of strong spirits, particularly heather ale when he had lived in the old world. But no hangover was as profound as those resulting from imbibing too much of Josiah Taney's buttered rum. The owner of The Axe 'n' Ale, the one and only grog shop in Cutter's Reach, Taney made his notoriously potent rum as most on the frontier did, except in one respect. Like others, he started with two quarts of rum mixed with sugar water, cinnamon, and a hand-sized lump of lard, all tossed into a bucket for mixing. But while most rum-makers were content to then fill the bucket with hot water when hot cider wasn't readily available, Taney adamantly refused to this practice. As a result, he went to great lengths to always have cider on hand. As a result, his buttered rum was much sought after, not least by Cutter himself.

Cutter pried his eyes open long enough to discover that the room was slowly spinning. One didn't recover quickly from consuming a large quantity of Taney's specialty. The butter was the culprit. He knew from experience that he would feel the effects most of the day no matter what he tried to do to mitigate them, and quite possibly wouldn't be right as rain until the next day.

Lying flat on his back, he raised his arms and used the heels of his palms to massage his temples. This didn't deter the demon that crouched in his skull banging with fearsome glee on some very large drums. Cutter groaned, rubbed his face, then let his arms fall to his sides, accepting defeat.

His right hand brushed something warm, smooth and round. He reluctantly opened his eyes and slowly turned his head to see a thick and tousled mane of long blonde hair on the pillow beside his. He moved the back of his hand over the perfect slope of the woman's rump to the small of her back. She made a soft, sleepy sound and rolled over, throwing an arm over his bare, bushy chest. In so doing, the quilts that covered them both, sheltering them from the nearly frigid cold, were dislodged enough so that he could glimpse her proud young breasts and the seductive curve of her narrow waist and half-covered hip.

He groaned when there came a loud rapping of knuckles on the door. "Damn your eyes whoever you are," he growled hoarsely.

"Tis I, Josiah. I'll be needin' my girl, Cap'n. If you be done with her, that is." Taney's voice was laced with sarcasm.

Cutter sighed, pried his eyes open again and reached over to gingerly finger mussed golden curls away from the lovely, heart-shaped face of the woman who lay so close beside him. His nostrils flared as he deeply inhaled her scent, which he found intoxicating in its own right. His gray-blue eyes softened with affection, while the expression on his sun-browned, square-jawed face was one of regret.

"For the love of all that's holy," whined Taney from the other side of the door. "The sun be nearly over the trees and I have customers. She needs to collect some eggs and do some cooking and wait on the men. I can't do everything myself!"

"A minute," said Cutter gruffly.

He rolled over on his side, which pushed the quilts down further over her hips. She made a soft whimpering sound, unplucked brows furrowing a bit as she snuggled more tightly into him, drawn even in sleep to the warmth of his body. Even so he hesitated to pull the covers up, admiring every inch of her. Matilda Armstrong was a pleasure to look at, slender but shapely in all the right places. He looked for a moment, then brought the quilts up to her neck. A little smile teased the corners of her compliant lips, a smile not haunted by the ghost of melancholy that would be there if she were awake.

Matty had lost her parents and a brother to typhoid when she was a Dorset lass in her fifteenth year. She had come to the colonies with a man who made a good living selling the contracts of indentured servants to others for a tidy profit. The man was very pleased with what he received for Matty.

The buyer of her contract had been a Boston man named Henry Herron, a shipwright who carried her with him when he migrated to the Allegheny River valley, where he laid claim to some land a half-day's journey downriver from Cutter's Reach. Hudson hoped to prosper by building river craft. By that time Cutter's Reach was not the only settlement on the river, and Hudson surmised that valley would be well-populated by settlers in the next decade or two as good land became less and less available back east.

A couple of years later, Herron's life was taken by the oft-times treacherous river that the Delaware Indians called *Alligewineck* and which Cutter could hear running deep and strong from where he lay. A Shawnee hunting party discovered the corpse downriver, washed up on a sandy shoal. Knowing Herron, they had hurried upriver, making for the dead man's cabin to loot and burn it and, with luck, seize his pretty servant for their own. But Matty had been lucky and slipped away before they could take hold of her, making her way to Cutter's Reach.

Herron had visited the settlement now and then, so Taney knew Matty, knew what she was. Since Herron hadn't lived long enough to realize his entrepreneurial dream, he had become indebted to Taney, among others in the settlement. Taney removed all the potential rivals for Matty's services, paying off Herron's debts before turning to Cutter and requesting that she be indentured to him.

Cutter had traveled to the site of Herron's cabin in hopes of finding the shipwright's will, if such existed, but the cabin and everything in it had been consumed by fire. Since Herron had never spoken of family elsewhere, and he had not officially made Matty his wife, his property—which included Matty—would not be inherited, and since Taney had paid the money Herron had owed to others in Cutter's Reach the tavern owner had a legitimate claim to Matty's services. Being among other things the man who was called upon to make legal judgments, Cutter had reluctantly approved Taney's demand for three years of service from the girl.

All this had occurred the previous summer, and in the months since Matty had often shared Cutter's bed, a fact known to just about everyone in the community, now over a hundred-and-thirty men, women and children. So it came as no surprise to Cutter that Taney was now fuming outside his bedroom door. After all, the outer door, in the common room of the blockhouse, one floor down, was kept unlocked. No doubt he had come straight here after discovering that Matty's wood-and-canvas camp bed, located in the shed behind The Axe 'n' Ale, had not been slept in that night.

"Cap'n, please!" groaned Taney plaintively. "This be costing me coin!"

The tavern offered more than strong spirits. There were a few beds in a common room upstairs for visitors to Cutter's Reach. And while visitors were few and far between at this time of the year, Taney also offered a good breakfast, and there were enough single men in the settlement who regularly took advantage of this fact. Then, too, the opportunity to be waited on by a woman as fetching as Matty Armstrong was another inducement.

Cutter was aware that Matty was another draw for Taney, as occasionally she was paid to sleep with male customers. She was allowed to keep any coin given her for this service. Even though Taney sometimes encouraged this activity, he didn't wish to profit from it. The Delaware girl who had preceded Matty had done the same, and more often, and for free. Cutter assumed that while The Axe 'n' Ale was a brothel in fact if not nme, Taney didn't wish to think of his place as a brothel, nor that he be seen as a procurer. It was a fine line but Cutter was well aware that self-delusion often required fine lines.

Matty's brows furrowed as she stirred, her lissome body moving against him in a way that awakened his desire. He considered growling at Taney to cease and desists and then waking his bedmate in the most passionate way possible. But then an errant thought occurred to him—and not for the first time—that Matty was but a few years older than his own daughter.

"Hell," he muttered and moved the quilt aside in such a way that it didn't expose another inch of Matty's skin to the winter chill. He rose and swayed a moment as the room seemed to spin around him, yet managed to pull on his buckskin breeches nonetheless. Moving to the hearth, he stirred the embers of last night's fire and added a log, using a bellows to get a new blaze well-started and stood there a moment, leaning against the mantel, to warm himself.

He listened to the sounds signifying that Cutter's Reach was awake and stirring. There was the distant ringing of a hammer on an anvil. Richard Severing, the blacksmith, was always at work before the sun had fully risen. He heard as well the creak and groan of a wagon trundling past the blockhouse and the stentorian voice of Francis Colyer calling "Open the gate!" Colyer, no doubt accompanied by one or more of his three grown sons, was heading out of the compound to gather lumber, as he did every morning unless that it was a day of rain or snow, in order to sell or trade what he had harvested. Most of the others were more than willing to get their wood from the Colyers, usually by trade, since they had more than enough chores to keep them busy from first light to last. In the background a few dogs were barking, a man and a woman were laughing, and children were playing.

The blockhouse had not a single window, but plenty of narrow gun loops. Wondering how far along the morning was, Cutter moved to one of these narrow, horizontal embrasures on the eastern wall, pulled free the thick leather hinges that held a heavy wooden flap over the embrasure. He winced as sunlight stabbed at his eyeballs like the point of a knife.

Eyes narrowed, he looked across the rooftops of other structures within the confines of the palisades, and to gaze at the river and forests beyond, as well. Cutter's Reach stood on flat ground atop s steep bank that rose as high as twenty feet on this side of the river. At the base of this bank, fortified by nature with the massive roots of ancient trees and rocks large and small, was a narrow strip of sand, then the broader expanse of the river, here at the great bend about a hundred yards wide at this time of year, and wider with the spring thaw still a month or two away, when the river could rise at times to within ten feet of the stockade's stout walls. On the opposite bank, the verdant forest stood thick on a slope, with tall trees growing right to the river's edge, their stately canopies arching over the water. The river itself was swift, with deep channels in three places, and two stretches of rapids where it was quite shallow. The current quickened as it swept around the bend, making a crossing nearly impossible even in summer. Even this time of year one could sometimes see fish jumping in the shallows—smallmouth bass, brown trout, walleye and the northern pike, while the sturgeon and catfish more often remained hidden in the depths of the channels.

Stately oaks mingled with towering pine trees grew along the river in the shelter of the valley, the former producing a profuse canopy that overhung the water. On the slopes beyond, many of the hemlocks and beech trees had lost their leaves, but in the spring and summer the canopy of the forest was a blanket of green up the gradual slopes of the foothills and then growing profusely on the steep lower slopes of the mountains that cradled the river itself, mountains with majestic cliff faces of gray granite stone. In the fall the riot of color produced by deciduous trees in the valleys was a sight to behold.

It was a view that seldom failed to put Cutter in a good humor, not wholly because of its beauty and majesty, but also because the Allegheny was embraced by those steep mountains that, with precious few passages, shielded him from the tumult of civilization. For a moment, standing there, he felt content and free of worry.

"Cap'n!" Taney began rapping on the door. His tone had changed from plaintive to perturbed.

Two long strides took Cutter to the door. He threw it open, scowling.

"Stop pestering me, damn you! She'll be out in a moment."

He slammed the door shut, instantly regretting his outburst, and thought to blame his foul temper on the throbbing headache. But when he turned away from the door and saw Matty propped up on one arm, knuckling sleep out of her eyes, the quilts having fallen down round her waist to reveal more of her nubile body, he knew that wasn't the only or even the main reason. He resented the tavern keeper's claim on Matty Armstrong's time. He had to fight the urge to keep her in his bed through the morning, Josiah's claim be damned. But to do so would just make her day harder, by shortening the time she would have to do all the chores that lay ahead of her.

She looked at him with a sleepy, pensive smile. "I had better go," she murmured, in a way that made clear she preferred not to.

Cutter nodded and in approaching the bed, passed by the chair across which her garments had been strewn in the midst of the passionate haste with which she had thrown herself at him the night before. She tossed aside the covers and stood on the opposite side of the bed from him, closer to the warmth of the crackling fire. He gazed at her slender form as though he had never seen her naked before, even though he had admired, caressed and kissed every inch of her.

First she put on a clean but threadbare shift, and then the plain dress dyed a pretty shade of elderberry blue. Cutter marveled that she could keep her clothes so clean and well-mended in spite of the hard and often dirty work she did from sunrise to sunset and sometimes beyond. She tightened the dress around her narrow waist with a belt of braided hemp and then turned to him, running fingers through tousled golden curls and said, "I must look a mess."

"A wonderful mess," he replied, as he took over combing her thick tresses with his long, thick fingers. She gazed at him with blue eyes wide and soft lips parted slightly, begging to be kissed. He couldn't resist. His kiss was hard, plundering, hungry, and it left her breathless.

"When I'm with you," she murmured, once the kiss was over, "I forget what I am."

She smiled another pensive smile. There was a pervasive melancholy in her. Acquainted with her past, Cutter wasn't surprised. The only time he didn't sense it was when they made love. She was a wild, passionate, joyous and uninhibited lover.

Her words struck him deep and left him momentarily speechless. He pulled on a woolen shirt and crossed the room to open the door.

Taney was leaning against the wall opposite the door, arms crossed, a disgruntled expression on his dyspeptic face. He was a short, bony, grizzled man wearing a canvas apron over his homespun clothes. Cutter stood aside to let Matty pass through the door. Taney frowned at her. She gave him a tentative, apologetic smile which became big and warm when she turned it on Cutter before hurrying down the short hallway to the stairs and started down them. Instead of following her, Taney pushed off the wall and faced Cutter.

"I would consider offering her contract to you," he said, "but at present there is no one around with which I could replace her. Yes, I could likely get me another Indian girl for trade goods, but Matty is a hard worker, diligent in her duties." He glanced past Cutter at the mussed bed and added, "Most of the time."

"I don't believe in owning other people," said Cutter.

"Well, I just thought... I mean you do spend a lot of time with her, Cap'n. You appear to favor her company. And you *are* alone."

Taney saw something in Cutter's eyes that made him think he had perhaps said too much, and he nervously turned for the stairs.

"Wait."

Taney turned back, wary. Like everyone else in Cutter's Reach, he knew that Abel Cutter had an explosive temper. He seldom let unleashed it but the tavern keeper knew that when it came to women it wasn't uncommon for a man to take leave of his senses.

Halfway down the narrow stairs, Matty stopped and turned, too, wide-eyed and breathless, looking past Taney at the man whose bed she had shared the night before.

As for Cutter, he realized that if he was ever going to make his claim on Matty this was the time. If he let this pass, then in the future he would have to approach Taney as a supplicant, a situation that the tavern keeper would likely take full advantage of.

"You paid nothing for her, Josiah, you simply laid claim to Herron's contract in return for paying off most of his debt. I will pay you a hundred pounds, in Spanish dollars and New York bills of credit. Then I will declare her contract fulfilled and she will be free to work for you, if she wishes, for wages."

Astonished, Taney's eyes widened, glittering with greed. "A hundred pounds! You have that on hand, Cap'n?"

I wouldn't make the offer if I didn't."

The tavern keeper thoughtfully rubbed his chin. Cutter assumed the tavern keeper was calculating whether he could get even more than what was already a very generous offer.

"She is most valuable to me, you know," said Taney. "And I have a year and a bit remaining on her contract."

"A hundred and twenty, then."

"I will work for you for free, Mister Taney," promised Matty.

"But she'll not be sleeping with your guests," added Cutter. "For ten or twenty dollars in trade goods you can get yourself a willing and winsome Indian girl for that."

Aware that Matty was gazing at him, Cutter managed to refrain from glancing her. Instead he kept his steely gray gaze locked on Taney. The tavern keeper's head had been swiveling from one to the other of them and back, but now he stared wide-eyed at Cutter. He knew the founder of The Reach as well as anyone, and could tell that the Cap'n was not in the mood to take no for an answer.

"A hundred and twenty, and the deal is done," he murmured. "I will bring you her contract later today, if you would have the bill of sale done that quickly."

"It will be done." Cutter stuck out a hand. Taney glanced at it with a measure of caution, then shook it quickly. Cutter's big paw engulfed his and didn't let go for a moment.

Cutter's narrowed steelcast eyes were piercing, and he gave a curt nod. "Then we have an accord."

When Taney nodded, Cutter let go his hand. The tavern keeper understood. He was not to change his mind or back out of the deal that had just been struck. Cutter Cutter was not just the founder of The Reach. He was its lord. His power was absolute, but he seldom took advantage of the fact. Taney didn't want to test the man's restraint. He hastily turned to go down the steps, saying to Matty, "Let's be off, girl. We have customers waitin'!"

Matty continued down the steps and at the bottom, just before she stepped out of Cutter's sight, she looked back up at him and smiled, eyes glistening with tears of happiness and gratitude. For once he saw nary a hint of melancholy in her smile.

CHAPTER 2

When Cutter heard the blockhouse door close he sighed and went down to the common room. It was early February, and while there had not been a hard freeze or heavy snowfall for weeks here on the upper Allegheny it was still plenty cold. He moved to the big stone hearth and, as he had done in his bedroom, stirred the embers to life, added a few pieces of wood, and used the wood-and-leather bellows to induce a crackling fire.

Standing there a moment warming his hands, he looked glumly around a room illuminated by the firelight that cast dancing shadows into the corners. There was his cluttered desk, the old chart cabinet beside it, the three sturdy chairs made of joined walnut and worn, padded, leather upholstery arrayed in front of the fireplace, the bear skins on the floor, the framed maps on the walls, the doors leading to a store room and the magazine. Near the door through which Matty and Taney had passed were several guns racked on the wall, a British "Brown Bess" musket, the breechloading flintlock he had used many years ago, now replaced by a Pennsylvania long rifle, a blunderbuss pistol otherwise known as a dragon, and a Scottish broadsword that had been in his family for nearly a hundred years. Upstairs were two rooms with the narrow central hallway. It had been a single room until the birth of his eldest child, his son Joshua.

The blockhouse had been built by his hand with help from his friends Fen MacGregor and Guy Rimbeau. He could relate the provenance of every scar left by arrow, tomahawk and musket ball on its outer walls. This had been his home for more than a quarter of a century. He had fought and bled for it. His children had been born here. It had become the centerpiece of the largest settlement in western Pennsylvania, so large that it extended now beyond the stout stockade that had been erected a twenty years ago. The blockhouse was not just his home but had always been the settlement's seat of government, and the last stand on a couple of occasions when Indians had attacked prior to the erection of the stockade walls.

But in recent years it had felt more like a coffin then a home.

It was little wonder, then, that for a while that morning Cutter gazed into the fire and did some soul searching. Was it love or lust or loneliness that had compelled him to insist that Taney sell him Matty Armstrong's contract? There was no question that he had used his standing as the cock of the roost to intimidate the tavern keeper.

Taney was right. He was alone. Even the sounds of the thriving settlement that bore his name had not made him feel less isolated of late. He had staked his claim here with a young Tuscaroran woman and a couple of trapping partners, at the big bend on the northern stretch of the river. He and his friends had established a thriving trade with various tribes. He had nurtured this place, had defended it and bled for it, and occasionally he had ruled with an iron fist. But as the settlement grew larger, older and stronger—like his son and daughter—it seemed that it needed him less and less.

These days Cutter's Reach had its own minister, a Congregationalist, and while there were plenty of residents who were inclined to cling to Anglican beliefs, the Harvard-educated Pastor Dunleavy's gentle persistence in his belief that all God-fearing residents, regardless of their denominational preference, was a legitimate part of the Body of the Church, had won over nearly everyone. He was a young man, kind and considerate beyond measure, and had won the trust of nearly all of the settlers. Now it was no longer up to Cutter, who felt himself singularly unqualified for the task, to perform baptisms, preside over marriages, or conduct services at gravesites.

Rarely was he called upon to settle legal disputes, as had often been the case in the early days. Now there was a former Albany magistrate, one Hiram Hoxley, who was better able to apply established common law to matters involving contracts and property and all the day-to-day litigation that was bound to arise among so many folks. These days Cutter was called upon only on the rare occasions when some crime required force or the threat thereof.

The settlement had a physician, as well. Dr. Edward Lyman had showed up ten years ago, without wife or children or very many belongings. He had remained tight-lipped about his past ever since, but no one could deny that he knew his trade. His skills had saved more than a few lives. As a consequence, Cutter's crude but usually effective frontier medicine was seldom in demand anymore.

Cutter felt a stirring of resentment but set it aside, angry with himself for indulging in self-pity, for feeling as though he was owed something. He had never intended to preside over the westernmost English settlement of the northern colonies. He had never given much weight to the strategic position of his home with respect to the empire-building designs of France and England. It wasn't just blockhouse and stockade and guns that made the location so desirable from a defensive perspective. Geography played a major role. So it was that Cutter's Reach was of strategic importance, being so close to the passage between Lake Erie and Lake Ontario, and the proximity of French forts—Presque Ile, le Boeuf and Niagara.

He realized now that he should have anticipated all of this, considering the location he had chosen. Cutter's Reach stood on a triangular point of land at the big bend of the northern Allegheny River, sheltered by the river itself on the northeast and the northwest, with a very gradual incline up to the wooded slopes to the south on the third. To the south, the thick woods had been pushed back by piecemeal cutting and burning over the years, until the edge of the forest was several hundred paces up the gentle slope. That slope had been increasingly cultivated over the years as the settlement's population increased. Cutter knew now that he should have anticipated the popularity of the site—there was ample water and timber and fertile soil here, and the weather was reasonably mild.

All he had set out to do was find a place far removed from people and politics. The Scottish people had suffered under the heel of the English crown. They had been cheated, treated with contempt, and shown little mercy when they had rebelled under such treatment. He had come to America to be free of all that, only to find a similar system of power and privilege in the civilized and cultivated coastal areas. And so he had headed west with his friend Fen MacGregor—he had met fellow trader Guy Rimbaud later—to live free and make a new beginning.

There had been a time when only a stubborn resilience and a willingness to resort to extreme actions had kept Cutter's Reach alive. In those days the fighting prowess and sheer force of will exhibited by him and his friends had been the difference maker. Many a settlement had been established on the frontier and many had met with disaster, but his had thrived and grown beyond all expectations. And as it grew bigger and stronger it came to rely less on him.

Cutter shook his head and pulled on a long, fur-lined leather coat that was as weathered and scarred as his craggy, square-jawed face. He chided himself for wallowing in self-pity. It was time to stop living in the past. The times and circumstances changed. Maybe he would head west again. Only memories held him here. He could head west and start all over, and take Matty with him. It would be a new beginning for them both. A new adventure.

But he needed to share the notion with her. It was only right, since on the frontier the odds of dying on any given day were fair to good.

He left the blockhouse and went around a corner to the outhouse, speaking to his two hounds, Laddie and Bretta, neither of whom had spent a single day inside. They preferred to live under the open sky, regardless of the season, even if it meant being on a long, thick ropes when they weren't accompanying their owner outside the stockade where they could run free. Considering their rough and tumble ways, they had to be restrained inside the stockade. It wasn't that they would attack a man or woman without provocation, but any animal would be fair game, which meant other dogs, pigs and even chickens were not safe. Cutter often took them out into the woods, when he was hunting or just escaping the hustle and bustle of The Reach, which he sometimes felt the need to do.

After relieving himself, Cutter made his way to The Axe'n'Ale, nodding in response to greetings sent his way by those who passed by. The tavern door swung open as he reached for it and Fen MacGregor emerged.

Fen belched, rubbing his prodigious belly, before looking up to see who stood in his way. His scowling, bearded face brightened. Grinning, he slapped Cutter's shoulder with a meaty paw.

"Reckon you're the reason I had to settle for the vile mush ol' Taney cooked up this mornin' from yesterday's scraps," he said in a deep and gravelly voice. "But can't say as I blame you. Reckon you and that winsome wench of his was the beast with two backs last night. Tell me I'm wrong. No, wait. Tell me all about it." He reached down and grabbed his crotch. "My stomach is happy but I'm not yet awake from the belt down."

"The hell I will. What did he feed you?"

"I don't rightly know. I don't *want* to know! Some sort of gruel. Tasted a mite over-ripe. I et it anyhow. I was hungry as a church mouse, ye ken."

"Over-ripe." Cutter chuckled. "Kind of like you smell, Fen. You would do well to grab a cake of lye soap and make your way to the river."

Fen raised an arm and sniffed one armpit and then the other. He was a big bear of a man, but there was plenty of grit and muscle on his frame. He had been christened Fenrir, after the giant wolf of Norse legend, and Cutter thought that it was an appropriate name for his old friend.

Fen's bushy brows furrowed. "I don't smell no different now than I have all these years ye've known me."

"True enough, but some things you never get used to. I recall that time a bunch of Hurons looking for trouble found our sign and commenced to tracking us, and we holed up in that swatch of fallen trees north of Katarakow Point. They started searching for us then caught a whiff of you and must of thought there was a passel of skunks in the timber and went on their way."

Fen grunted. "Wish you'd stop tellin' that tall tale. You know well as I that they went away 'cause they couldn't get to us without havin' to climb over all them tree trunks. Had they tried we would've picked 'em off. Well, I would've anyway, being far and away the best shot." He grinned. Cutter knew this because he caught a glimpse of yellow, crooked teeth through an opening in the thicket of his friend's bushy brown beard.

"Sounds like we need to head out and have a little shooting contest, so as to remind you that the only reason you and your scalp haven't parted company is because of me."

Cutter looked past Fen as Guy Rimbeau came around the corner of the tavern. The tall, thin Acadian was grinning, having heard the last part of the exchange between his friends.

"*Sacre bleu!*" Guy threw up his arms in a melodramatic gesture of mock exasperation. "The two of you are at it again! Allow me to negotiate a truce, which as you both know is one of my many exemplary talents. Truth be told, you *are* the best marksman of the three of us, Fen. But you are also the worst smelling individual this nose has ever been downwind of." He touched his hawkish proboscis. "But give Cutter credit where it is due. It was he that had us take our stand in those fallen timbers, which saved our bacon, as you English say. Otherwise, our scalps would be hanging to this day in Huron lodges."

Fen's eyes narrowed menacingly. "How come you insult us by callin' us English!"

Cutter laughed, aware that Guy had done just that so to make Fen's hackles rise. Being in the company of his two oldest living friends improved his mood immensely.

He had met and befriended Fen before they boarded the ship that had carried them both to Boston from Ulster, which many Scots, including Cutter's parents, had tried to colonize northern Ireland at the behest of the English crown. But as time passed the Irish grew stronger and pushed back, with both laws and weapons. As a result, the Scots had been persecuted mercilessly. Cutter had traveled with part of his family, including his parents. Fen had been traveling alone. His father was the victim of cold-blooded murder. He had vowed vengeance but his mother prevailed on him to sail to the colonies instead, convincing him that she simply couldn't bear seeing him buried alongside his father. Fen had brought his hatred for the Irish with him, and he was none too fond of the English, either, as he felt that the Crown had abandoned the Scottish colonizers to their own devices. And rightly so. These dislikes burned hot in him to this day.

Guy Rimbaud's grandparents had been among the French colonists who had settled in Acadia, a colony separate from New France. As a result, Guy had been raised to distrust the Quebecois French and, himself a trader, had become the subject of much animosity from some of the established traders in Quebec. This was due to his good relations and successful business arrangements with various Indian tribes. Ironically, many British colonists mistrusted the Acadians, erroneously considering them no different from the French in Quebec and the remainder of New France.

At first Cutter and Guy had been de facto rivals for the furs which Indians traded for trade goods—clothing, blankets, trinkets, knifes and hatchets, even muskets, shot and powder. They had both vied for the attention of a certain winsome Tuscaroran maiden named Jequara. Guy had agreed to help Cutter and Fen build the blockhouse for the sole reason of wooing Jequara, who had been given to

Cutter in return for muskets. But as charming as Guy was, the maiden had fallen in love with Cutter. To his credit, Guy had made his home at The Reach, telling Cutter that he did so "in case the *belle fille* comes to her senses someday." But the truth of it was that he had come to like Abel Cutter, and to realize they profited more as a team rather than competing traders.

The fact that Cutter had always been his own man, without fealty to either the French or the British—he didn't trust the former and as a Scotsman wasn't fond of the latter—was the glue that sealed the friendship of the trio. They were fiercely loyal to one another.

Fen frowned as he listened to Guy weighing in on the matter of their escape from the Hurons. He relished a good argument as much as anyone, but when the Acadian was finished with his reminiscence the buckskin-clad giant merely shrugged, much to the surprise of the others.

"Aye, mayhap ye be right," he said begrudgingly, mollified by Guy's concession that he was in fact the best marksman of the three of them. "But I sure do hate missing a good fight!"

"As much as you hate missing a good bath, it seems," observed Guy with a mischievous gleam in his eye.

"First Abel and now you!" roared Fen, his cheeks red as ripe tomatoes.

Guy pretended to be alarmed, cringing with melodramatic flair. This had Fen fuming even more, since he knew the Acadian feared him not at all. Guy relished picking on Fen and Cutter was certain that in spite of his bluster Fen would not have harmed a hair on the Acadian's head. Cutter threw his head back and laughed. Regardless of how angry or depressed he became, he found that being in the presence of these two almost always improved his mood.

In appearance they were different as night from day. Where Fen was brawny and broad-shouldered and stood over six feet tall, with a thick beard and a mane of graying, curly black hair, Guy was slender, clean-shaven and rakishly handsome, with hair the color of wheat. While Fen favored grime-darkened buckskins, guy wore tan breeches tucked into riding boots, a white linen shirt and cravat and a blue woolen cloak. He might have passed muster as a dandy on a city street, but when it came to a fight there was no one as quick and deadly and he was every bit as skilled in woodcraft as Cutter.

"Well if you lads are hankering for adventure," said Cutter, seeing his chance, "I have a notion."

Their heads swiveled, and their eyes locked on him.

Cutter made a gesture meant to encompass the whole stockade. "These walls, this noise, it's closing in on me. I long for the wild, free life we used to live. That we were *born* to live. The Reach is strong enough to thrive without us. I hanker for one more wander."

"Where to?" asked Fen.

Cutter shrugged. He hadn't given that much thought. "South and west. Down the Ohio perhaps. There is so much of this new land still to see. We'll trap and trade like we did in the old days."

The other two exchanged looks of surprise. "But what about your children, Abel?" asked Guy. "You'll be going further away from them."

The excitement faded from Cutter's face, replaced by melancholy. "My children have their own lives now. They have no need of me and haven't for a long time."

Fen and Guy glanced at one another and then at Cutter, and they nodded in unison. The Acadian reached out and clasped Cutter's hand in his. Fen clamped a big dirty paw on top of this.

"You're not going anywhere without us, Abel," said Guy.

"Aye!" exclaimed Fen. "This be a day to remember! For once this dandified fence rail and I agree."

Cutter was about to tell them that he thought to take Matty Armstrong with him, if she would go, but a horn blared as he opened his mouth to speak, sounding a warning. The three men turned as one in the direction of the stockade's main gate. It took but a moment to reach it. A sentry called down from the rampart.

"Two men afoot coming from the south, Captain!" The man brought a spyglass to eye and a moment later added, "Can't say as I know either one of 'em."

Cutter climbed a ladder to the rampart and took the spyglass offered by the lookout. Studying the two men in the distance, walking side by side across the fields laying fallow, he noted that one was lanky and short, while the other was one of the tallest men he had ever seen, taller even that Fen. Both were clad in buckskins. He could tell by their gait that they were bone-weary, and surmised that since they weren't running that there was noone and nothing chasing them. In the past, more than a few people had come to the gate at a run, pursued by Indians or brigands.

He returned the spyglass to the sentry and called down to Fen and Guy, who by now had been joined by two dozen others drawn by the warning horn.

"I know one of them," he said. "It's Christopher Gist. Open the gate!"

CHAPTER 3

The fields of corn, beans and squash that fairly covered the open ground to the east and south of the stockade now lay fallow. Most were encompassed by split log fences, which not only marked the the ground claimed by various farmers but also served to slow down an attacking force, or at the very least funneled them into the single trace that passed in a fairly straight route from the gate east to the woods and beyond.

Along this road were more than dozen cabins, just as there were a handful along the bank of the river to the south. The stockade had become rather crowded in recent years, and newcomers had built their homes outside of but within sight of the walls. A few families had built in the woods nearby, those who preferred space and privacy to the extent that they were willing to sacrifice some security.

The stockade's main gate was comprised of tall portals made of squared timbers two fert wide and twelve feet high, held together by six-inch bands of thick, hammered iron. It was so heavy that it took at least two strong men to budge one of them. Cutter was the first one out, raising an arm to wave at the pair of visitors, advance notice that they were welcome to come closer without fear of being shot. Others emerged from the stockade as well, Fen and Guy among them. Some people had emerged from the cabins along the road, alerted that something was afoot by the warning horn. All were warily curious.

The two men who had emerged from the forest to the southwest had to clamber over one fence after another as they made for the settlement. It wasn't often that strangers visited Cutter's Reach, especially this time of year, and so as the pair drew closer the crowd in front of the gate quickly increased in size, as did the number of those who took to the walls to have a look.

Wedged between Lake Erie on the west and the "civilized" portion of the colony of New York, these wild woodlands were still marked on many maps as the Land of the Six Indian Nations, those tribes being the Mohawks, Cayuga, Onandaga, Oneida, Seneca and Tuscarora, otherwise known as the Iroquois Confederation. Well to the north was Fort Niagara, built eighty years ago by the French, and north of that was the city of Quebec, the heart New France. Southward was the Pennsylvania colony, with precious few settlements this far to the west. The remote nature of this bend in the river, as well as its defensibility, had been the deciding factor in Abel Cutter's decision to claim the ground, just as it had motivated most of those who had settled here—that and the fact that New York and Pennsylvania couldn't agree which colony owned it, and were't that inclined to stake too strong a claim anyway for fear of aggravating the Iroquois.

"That feller in the lead looks a mite familiar to me," murmured Fen, rubbing his bearded chin, brows furrowed as he tried to figure out how. Right then the subject of his comment returned Cutter's wave from a hundred strides away.

"He should," Cutter replied. "That's Christopher Gist."

Those within hearing began talking excitedly among themselves, while a few hurried back into the stockade to spread the news. It wasn't every day—or even every year—that the most famous frontiersman of all came calling.

With no idea what manner of news Gist and his companion might be bringing with them, Cutter turned to Fen and Guy and said, "I'll go meet 'em." He glanced at the dozens of people gathered in front of the gate and then back at his old friends, both of whom nodded in understanding. In case Gist was the bearer of bad news, Cutter wanted to hear of it before anyone else did. As Cutter turned and started off to meet the new arrivals, Guy turned to the others.

"Let's get back to whatever we were doing, shall we?" he suggested pleasantly. "One might think you had never before seen men coming out of those woods still wearing their scalps."

"I ain't never met the famous Christopher Gist with or without his hair," said one man, and a few of the others chuckled.

Guy smiled affably, but Fen was having none of this affable repartee.

"Blood and hounds! Go on! Go on now! Clear the gate!" He advanced on the spectators, scowling as they did not respond with the alacrity he expected, and began waving his arms like he was herding hogs to market. "Move along, move along I say!"

"I'm sure you will all get to meet our visitors soon enough," added Guy benignly.

As he drew near the two arrivals, Cutter grinned and extended a hand to the small, angular one clad in grimy buckskins.

"It's been a long time, Christopher! Glad to see you're not on a diet of worms just yet."

Christopher Gist was a surveyor, explorer, cartographer and scout best known for being the first white man to thoroughly explore and map the country of the Ohio River as far west as the Great Miami River. Cutter knew that Gist had done so at the behest of the Ohio Company, for the goodly sum of money. The Ohio Company, established by several wealthy Virginians and invested in by a handful of well-to-do Englishmen. They intended to purchase the land from the English king and then sell it to settlers moving westward. When he became aware of the venture, Cutter hadn't approved. He worried that it would antagonize the Indian tribes with homelands along the Ohio, but he didn't blame Gist for this.

As it turned out, Gist had been befriended by many of the tribes along the Ohio River, thereby undermining the hold of the French in the area. Later, Gist had traveled south through the land known as Kentucky, derived from *ken-tah-ten*, the Iroquois word meaning the land of tomorrow, before returning to his home on the banks of the Yadkin River in North Carolina. It was a feat that would be celebrated throughout the English colonies, particularly Virginia, which had designs on the frontier to its west.

Gist's angular, stubbled face was split by a toothy grin as he took Cutter's proffered hand and shook it vigorously. Despite his small frame and the fact that he was closing in on fifty years of age, his grip was like steel trap.

"Not yet, though I have come close a time or two of late. And how are you faring, my old friend?"

"Well enough. I'm still above snakes."

"We've both lived longer than anyone thought we would, I wager," said Gist, chuckling. He relinquished his friend's hand when he noticed Cutter's inquisitive look at the other man. "Abel, this is Major George Washington, a military adjutant and emissary of Governor Dinwiddie of Virginia. Major, this is Abel Cutter."

Cutter extended the hand. "Pleasure to make your acquaintance, Major." His tone was cordial but his smile had faded. He couldn't imagine that the arrival of a military man could in any way be conceived as good news for Cutter's Reach.

Washington's grip was firm. He had a broad, strong, muscular frame. Cutter was himself taller than most men at six feet, but he had to look up to meet the major's blue-gray gaze. A large hooked nose and a wide, thin-lipped mouth dominated the man's oval face. He wore canvas breeches and a faded blue cotton shirt beneath a rumpled linen waistcoat, topped by a long brown leather capote. All of his garments were soiled and torn to varying degrees. It was clear to Cutter that he had been in the forests for a long time. The only thing that didn't look the worse for wear was his hat, pinned up on both sides in the tricorn fashion.

"Mr. Cutter," said Washington, with a small nod and a faint smile that had no warmth in it. "I have heard much about you, some good things, some bad. I confess to having harbored misgivings about this moment as there has been considerable debate regarding whether your loyalties lay with the British or the French."

Gist glanced anxiously at Cutter, aware of his friend's mercurial Scottish temperament. "Abel doesn't lean much one way or the other, Major," he said. "He's not much for politics 'cept as they may affect The Reach."

The frontiersman was visibly relieved when Cutter smiled, a wry smile rather than a friendly one, but a smile nonetheless.

"You are a plain-speaking man, Major and I respect that. What brings you so far from home?"

Gist didn't wait for Washington to reply. "Been milkin' a pigeon, Abel, if you ask me."

Washington's brows furrowed. "I am not familiar with that turn of phrase," he told Gist, his tone mildly admonishing. Turning his piercing gaze on Cutter again, he said, "I was sent here as an emissary for the Governor of Virginia, charged with instructing the Governor-General of Canada to cease and desist in the construction of French forts on British soil."

"Instructing? Not asking?" murmured Cutter, his smile now turning cold as the winter day. He had little patience for arrogance, but for Gist's sake he didn't say what he wanted to. "Milking the pigeon means wasting one's time trying to do the impossible."

Gist sighed. Cutter sensed that his old friend had already assumed that he and Washington would not get along. "I know one thing that *is* possible," said the frontiersman. "That you have some rum handy, Abel."

"Forgive me, old friend. You both look gallied, that's certain. Come, we'll talk inside."

He led the way toward the gate. They had taken but a few steps before Washington made the disgruntled observation that he saw no flag flying over Cutter's Reach. Cutter stopped and turned before they came within earshot of the anyone near the gate or on the walls.

"Most of the people here are from England or Ireland, and some few of us from Scotland. But there are also some who call France their homeland. There is a German family, a Swiss man with his family, two Spaniard brothers and a Dutch family. This by way of saying no flag can represent us all. Their loyalty is to each other. Out here, this is how it has to be." Cutter gestured at the nearby forest. "These woods have eyes, Major. If we flew the flag of England it would not be long before the French, the *coureur des bois*, and every tribe around would know of it. And that we don't run that risk is the *only* reason you do not see a French flag flying here today."

Gist, in a valiant attempt to change the subject croaked, "The only thing I wish to see at the moment is a jug of rum."

Cutter draped an arm around his friend's shoulders and headed for the gate, leaving George Washington to trail along behind.

CHAPTER 4

They passed through the congregation of the curious kept corralled just inside at the gate by Fen and Guy. The size of the crowd had increased in size so that it seemed nearly half of the settlement was on hand. Gist greeted all the people like they were old friends while Washington gave them a perfunctory nod. Cutter led the way to the blockhouse and gestured for Guy and Fen to follow. Once they were inside Gist looked around like he had just passed through the Pearly Gates.

"A chair to sit in and a roaring fire! Blessed be the Lord!" he exclaimed as he shrugged out of his pack and placed it and his long rifle on the floor next to one of the chairs by the hearth with its crackling fire and then collapsed in it. Cutter fetched a half-full jug of rum from his desk, pulled the cork and delivered the jug to Gist, who moaned with delight as he drank from it.

"This here kill-devil is nectar from the gods," he declared, gasping as the rum produced a warm glow in his innards. He leaned forward to offer the jug to Washington, who had shed his capote, looked around for someone to hand it to, and seeing no one volunteering, draped it over the back of the chair in which he then settled himself. He waved the jug away.

"I do not indulge, thank you just the same." He looked at Cutter. "However, a cup of hot tea would be welcomed."

"Tea!" grunted Fen in disbelief. He was leaning against a wall near the door, burly arms folded. He clearly didn't think tea was a suitable drink for a man and shook his head as he glanced at Guy.

The Acadian was amused. His eyes sparkled with mischief. Rarely could he refrain from an opportunity to rib his old friend. "Aye. Tea. That's what gentlemen drink, you Scottish lout. But then how could you possibly know that?"

"I regret to say I have no tea here, nor even a kettle to brew it in," said Cutter as he settled into the third chair in front of the fireplace. "But Guy will fetch you a cup from the tavern." He looked over his shoulder at Guy with an "if you don't mind" expression.

"*Oui, mon plaisir*," said Guy. As he opened the door and passed over the threshold he added, "Though I do think you should have sent Fen. I suspect old Taney would spit out his false teeth if Fen asked him for tea!"

Washington waited until the door closed behind the Acadian before looking at Cutter with brows furrowed. "You have Frenchmen here."

"Guy is Acadian. I suggest you refrain from calling him a Frenchman to his face." With an inquisitive tilt to his head, he added, "You have something against the French, I take it."

"You do not? You should, sir, you should. Trouble has been brewing up and down the valley of the Ohio River for ten years if not more. I predict soon we will have war."

Cutter sat there and remained grimly silent for a long moment. He chose his words carefully out of respect for his friend Gist, who was watching him anxiously, expecting him to be his usual outspoken self.

"I know that British traders have been trying to establish themselves south and west of here, in country where the

French *voyageurs* have long been trading with the Indians. And the existence of the *coureur des bois* is proof that the French have been doing this for over a hundred years."

Washington glanced at Gist in such a way that the frontiersman elaborated. "Over the years a fair number of Frenchmen began living with the natives. These men learned the customs and languages of the tribes. As it has always been due to tribal wars there are more women than men in most camps, these Frenchmen often took Indian wives. They lived like Indians. We didn't see any in our journey but that's because most are found now in the more remote—and more hostile—tribes. While it's true that there aren't as many of them these days as there were in the past, they are a force to be reckoned with, Major. They can have a fair bit of influence in tribal decisions."

The major nodded. "Noted." He turned his attention on Cutter again. "Are you aware, sir, that six years ago the Iroquois signed a treaty which ceded all the land west of Virginia to the British Crown?"

"So I've heard. Treaty of Lancaster, wasn't it?" Cutter grimaced and shook his head. Seeing this, Gant leaned forward in his chair and offered the jug to his friend. Cutter took a long swig even though his head still ached thanks to the excessive amount of kill-devil he had imbibed the night before.

On the subject of the British desire to expand their empire, Cutter was pretty sure that Gist and he were of like mind. But for some reason the old scout was clearly worried because he was treating this militia officer with kid gloves. This made Cutter wonder what degree of influence Washington had with Governor Dinwiddie—and the Privy Council that conducted colonial affairs. He didn't want to bring trouble to the people of The Reach, so it was out of consideration for them that he held his tongue, which was not an easy thing for him.

"That treaty ceded all lands claimed by Virginia and Maryland to the colonies," lectured Washington. "The Virginia charter claims all the land from the Chesapeake Bay to the Pacific Ocean. That includes the Ohio River Valley, sir."

Fen snorted derisively. "Iroquois don't claim all that, never had. They sure don't claim the Ohio River country. That has long been Shawnee country and, further west belongs to the Miamis and a few other tribes."

"The Ohio River country does not belong to Indians," insisted Washington. "It belongs to Virginia and, therefore, the British Crown."

Cutter had spent all of the discretion at his disposal by then. "The tribes of the Iroquois Confederacy joined together against the Huron threat. The French eventually sided with the Huron, and there was a long and bloody war. But that happened north of where you are sitting right now, Major, not south. The Iroquois never cared about the land south of here, so I'm sure they were happy to take whatever you were offering in return for their ceding land to you that they have never set foot in or made a claim to. Like Fen says, that's Shawnee country. Your treaty isn't worth the paper it was written on."

Gist groaned and extended a hand for the jug of rum, which Cutter surrendered. The frontiersman took a healthy swig, wiped his mouth with the sleeve of his buckskin jerkin and murmured, "I think we could all agree that ownership of that country is in dispute."

Washington looked like a frustrated bull. His nostrils flared as he exhaled loudly, leaning forward in his chair. "You are not hearing me, sir. It doesn't matter what tribe claims the valley of the Ohio River. It belongs to the British Crown. The French under the Marquis de Duquesne have busied themselves constructing a string of fortifications in that area. Mark my word. That will not be tolerated."

Cutter stood up abruptly and went to his desk, his steel-gray eyes hooded as he began packing tobacco in a corncob pipe. Gist knew his friend well enough to suspect that his patience was already worn thin, and that made the old scout cast about for words that might defuse the situation. Before he could come up with any Cutter addressed him.

"How the hell did you get dragged into this, Christopher?"

"It would seem that good ol' King George, God bless him, has ordered the colonies to raise militias, erect forts, and remove the French and Indians from British territory," he drawled. "But Governor Dinwiddie couldn't talk the Virginia House of Burgesses to put up the money for a militia. So the governor made Major Washington his emissary and sent him out here with a letter for Duquesne. The major hired me as a guide and we headed to Logtown to talk to Half Chief."

The pipe packed and lighted, Cutter perched on the corner of the desk and puffed. "That must have been your idea. Half Chief doesn't care for the French being south of the lakes any more than your king does."

Gist grimaced, knowing full well that Cutter describing George as 'his' king was a not-so-subtle reminder that his friend had no love for the British Crown.

Guy arrived at that moment with a mug of steaming hot tea and handed it to Washington, who took it without thanks, sipped it, then looked at Cutter and said, "He is your king, too. I will be frank, Mr. Cutter. I get the distinct impression that you think of this land as your own little fiefdom. I remind you, you stand on British soil."

Fen and Guy exchanged glances, then looked anxiously at Cutter. Both of them expected an angry response. But when Cutter spoke his tone was surprisingly calm, though just about as chilly as the morning air outside.

"The men who sit on those thrones thousands of miles away can squabble all they wish over this land. But in truth it belongs to the people who work it, fight for it, and sometimes die for it. Their blood and sweat is in this land."

Washington gave Gist a disapproving look. "You neglected to inform me that I would find a nest of disloyalty here."

"If it weren't for independent sorts like the Abel Cutter," said Guy, "you wouldn't have any colonies."

Gist decided it was a good time to continue his narrative on how and why he had come to be here. "Along with Half Chief and a few other Shawnees, we traveled on to Venango, only to find that the French had run ol' John Fraser out of his place and were fortifying it. The Frenchies were friendly enough, but told us to talk to their commander at Fort le Beouef, a feller by the name of St. Pierre. And he was neighborly, too."

Washington interjected. "But Captain St. Pierre would not read the governor's letter, saying instead that he would forward it on to Duquesne. He also refused to accept a treaty belt from our Indian companions. Instead he plied them with food and enough strong spirits that they could scarcely remember why they had come with us."

"He invited us to stay until a reply was received," added Gist.

"It soon became apparent to me that the French were preparing to send a military excursion by boat eastward down the Ohio River," continued Washington. "St. Pierre was buying time and I believe he was waiting for word from

Duquesne as to our fate. I decided Governor Dinwiddie needed to be informed of these developments."

Gist took up the narrative. "So we left Fort Le Beuoef, parted company with our no longer trustworthy Indian escorts, and headed home. We fell in with a party of Mingos who promised they would see us safely away from the French forts. But the very next day we stumbled on a small party of Frenchies and a fight broke out. All the French were killed, one way or another." The grizzled scout grimaced. "I figured the news would get back to Le Beouef right quick, so we parted company with the Indians and struck out on our own again, heading north instead of east to Virginia. Figured it was safer to take the long way back. When we get to Trenton the major can send a messenger on to Governor Dinwiddie."

Washington had been gulping down the tea before it cooled. Now he rose and set the empty mug on a squared beam that formed the mantel of the stone hearth. "We are in need of supplies to continue our journey, which we will commence at first light tomorrow."

"There are beds in the room above the tavern," said Cutter. "Guy will introduce you to Josiah Taney, the tavern keeper."

"*Ce serait avec plaisir,*" said Guy, with a mischievous twinkle in his eye as he glanced at Cutter, who knew that the Acadian was speaking in his native tongue precisely because of Washington's apparent dislike for the French.

He sighed as he watched Washington stoop to go out the doorway into the cold December sunlight, realizing that the lives and livelihoods of the people of Cutter's Reach was of no concern to George Washington and men like him who sought empire and power—and the glory that came with seeking both.

CHAPTER 5

O nce the door had closed behind Guy and the major, Cutter turned to Gist, frowning.

"Why are you helping the British? You don't have a political bone in your body. And as far as I know, you have no axe to grind with the French."

Gist nodded. "All that is true. I did it because Washington was going west one way or the other. And I took him so that I could do all I could to get him back alive. His family is wealthy. His father is a justice of the peace and a prominent public figure. The Washingtons made their fortune in land speculation. And the major's patron is none other than William Fairfax, a political appointee of the Crown who was once chief justice and governor of the Bahamas, elected to the House of Burgesses, and President of the General Council. In other words, if the major went into the Ohio Valley and disappeared there would be hell to pay, Abel. Believe me, it was best for everyone concerned that I accompany him."

Cutter nodded. "I know of William Fairfax. His grandfather was the fourth Lord Fairfax of Cameron. He claimed to be Scottish but he was born in Yorkshire. Another English overlord."

Gist stood, took one last swig of rum and put the nearly empty jar on the desk. He took a moment to grimly consider his next words.

"There was another reason I went along. I'm on good terms with the Shawnees and the French tolerate me. As you can see, the major is something of a firebrand. He's not much for diplomacy. Governor Dim-Witted's letter was just an excuse to give Washington a chance to take stock of the French situation. You know as well as I do that it's like rabbit hunting with a dead ferret to politely ask the French, who've been in these parts a hell of a lot longer than the British, to just pack up and go away. The major doesn't speak French so I did the interpreting, and I was able to make him seem a lot more diplomatic than he is by nature."

"You're a sly dog, my friend."

Gist made a dismissive gesture. "Nah, I just look out for the people I care about. You, your people, the Shawnees, and a whole lot of families just looking for a new beginning in the colonies and who could not care less about building an empire. But, well, no matter what we do, there's gonna be a war, Abel. In truth, I've seen it coming for years. And the thing is, you and your people are going to be caught right smack in the middle of it."

Cutter glanced at Fen, who was listening with a fiercely grim expression on his face. "Aye. That's what some of us have been trying to get away from."

"Ever heard of the Ohio Company?"

"We don't get much news here." Cutter's tone made clear he wished that was still the case.

"Rich land speculators. I happen to know a lot about the company. They built a storehouse near my home at Wills Creek. King George granted them five hundred thousand acres in the Ohio River valley. Some of Major Washington's rich relatives are involved with it."

"Bloody British kings," snarled Cutter. "Always taking other people's lands."

"The Company is to settle a hundred families out there. They just have to drive the French away and then they profit from trade with the Indians. You know the Shawnee and the Mingos are for the most part friendly with the Iroquois, who long ago allied themselves with the British. The colonies have no quarrel with them but the French have to go. And you know as well as I that they will not go quietly."

"Is that why you dragged Washington all the way up here? To warn me? A little out of your way if you were taking him back to Virginia."

Gist grinned like a cat. "That man doesn't know north from east when he's in the woods. Y'know, he came close to drownin' when we crossed the Allegheny two days down-river. I confess for a moment I considered letting him." He shrugged and sighed mirthlessly. "Your daughter, Bella, is in Philadelphia still? A teacher, if I remember right."

Cutter nodded. "I got a letter from her last summer. She seems to have quite a few redcoated admirers." He didn't sound pleased.

"And your boy, Joshua. Still living with the Tuscarora?"

"Ever since his mother took him home to her people. He and his Tuscarora brothers trade with the French in Quebec, which I suspect many in the Six Tribes frown upon, if they know. But that's the Tuscarora for you."

Gist put a hand on Cutter's broad shoulder. "I am sorry that news I've brought you is unsettling. You are concerned for your children, of course. In times like these we tend to want to bring our brood under our wing to better pro-tect them. But The Reach will be in the eye of the storm that's coming." He studied Cutter's expression, and sighed. "Reckon I'll make for that grog shop you have here and see how many feathers the major has ruffled. Besides, I need to do a bit more, um, irrigatin', myself." He retrieved his pack and rifle and nodded affably at Fen on his way to the door, which he opened only to step aside as he came face to face with Guy. Crossing the threshold Gist paused to say, "Come join me, my friends. I'm buying!"

Once the door was closed, Guy looked at Fen and Cutter and remarked, "I'm guessing Gist thinks there's going to be war."

"You think that's true?" asked Fen.

"Bad news usually is, *mon ami*," replied the Acadian, a fatalist at heart.

"I reckon that means we're not headin' west after all," Fen bemoaned.

"What are we going to do, Captain?" asked Guy.

Cutter had moved over to the fire, bracing an arm against the mantel, staring into the flames licking mercilessly at the long lengths of wood in the fire. He was stunned by the turn of events. Only a few hours earlier he had felt useless and at loose ends. Now he realized that the livelihood—even the very lives—of many now depended on his actions.

Of all the people who crossed his mind in that moment, foremost were his son and daughter. If war broke out, the Six Nations of the Iroquois would be in the thick of it, and since his son lived among the Tuscaroras, that meant his son would be, too. The tribe had adopted him. He had lived among them for a decade and a half. The Tuscaroras were his people.

As for Rachel, he could dare to hope she would be safe, assuming the coming war was restricted to the frontier, most likely around the great lakes. The French did not have designs on Boston and Philadelphia. Their expansion southward into the Ohio River country was not for empire but rather for profit, to expand their trade with the Indians.

"Well," said Fen, "don't fret over it, Cap'n. We been through tough times before. Tough times don't last. But tough people do."

Cutter went to his desk and sat down, taking a sheet of vellum from a drawer, dipping a quill pen into an ink bottle, and began writing out a bill of sale. Curious, Fen and Guy exchanged glances but said nothing until Cutter had finished writing and stood, unlocked the door to the storeroom, went inside and emerged a moment later carrying a small strongbox, which he placed on the desk. He was deep in thought, brow furrowed, and only when he had the strongbox unlocked and was lifting the lid did he remember his two friends.

"I didn't have the chance to tell you earlier," he said, "but I am buying Matty Armstrong's contract from Josiah, and will free her from said contract."

They approached the desk as he withdrew a bulging pouch of coin and a roll of paper money. He counted the latter and then took a handful of pieces of eight from the pouch. These Spanish dollar 'bits' were pure silver and eight of them made one dollar. They had been introduced to the colonies through the lucrative colonial trade with the West Indies and had been the most stable form of currency in the world, due to the vast output of silver from Spain's New World colonies during the past two hundred years. It formed the basis for all colonial bills of credit.

"That's a lot of money!" exclaimed Fen.

Cutter nodded, looking into the strongbox, at the result of two decades of profitable trading engaged in by he and his associates, minus a lot of money he had spent for The Reach as a whole, and to help out some of its residents when they were in need. "This comes out of my share only."

"You didn't have to tell us that," said Fen, smiling as he issued the mild rebuke. "It's unlikely I will ever be struck by the urge to marry and have children and settle down." He grinned. "I'm not tired of living, just yet."

"You prefer other men's wives or Injun squaws anyway," said Fen, only half-joking. "As for me, Cap'n, all I need coin for is a jug of rum now and then."

"You mean every day," said Fen.

Cutter put the coin and folded paper money into a second pouch, then locked the strongbox and stowed it away in the storeroom. When he emerged Fen said, "Will you be marrying the *jeune femme*, then?"

"No," growled Cutter, scowling as he picked up the pouch and made for the door. Sometimes his old friends crossed the mark when it came to prying into his personal affairs.

Once the door closed, Guy leaned against the desk, arms folded and murmured. "That man has had wretched poor luck with wives. Whenever I think about marrying some winsome wench, I think about the Captain, and I come to my senses."

"There's a highland saying," replied Fen. "The third's a charm."

PART TWO

Spring 1754

CHAPTER 6

The instant Joshua Cutter woke up, his right hand moved to the long rifle that lay beside him. In the process his forearm brushed the antler-handled hunting knife in its belt sheath. Even when he was home in Onroka, the village of the Wolf Clan of the Tuscarora, a fortnight's trek away, these weapons were never far out of reach.

He heard voices. People laughing and talking nearby. Other sounds reached him from further away: the trundle of wagon wheels and the clip-clop of shod hooves on cobblestone. The ringing of a ship's bell. Men—soldiers no doubt, marching in lock step. This tumult stood in stark contrast to the tranquility of a morning among the Tuscaroras. He had spent all of his adult life in the forests, alone or with Indian companions who did not ordinarily speak loudly, much less shout, unless there was trouble brewing or already boiling over and who moved silent as thought. The sounds that assailed his ears now made him homesick. He missed waking up in the village, where the only loud noises were made by children at play.

Waking up alone was a rare occurrence. For as long as he could remember, he had slept on furs on the ground in a longhouse of the clan to which his mother belonged. Ordinarily, twenty to thirty men, women and children occupied a longhouse. He had little experience with privacy. He would have risen naked but for a loincloth from those furs and except when the weather turned cold that would be all he or any other adult would usually wear, be it man or woman, save for moccasins, unless they were venturing out of the village.

Above him was the low, raftered ceiling of a small room, approximately ten feet by twelve. He knew now where he was. His momentary confusion wasn't entirely due to the ale he had imbibed the evening before. But he had dreamed of home and, more specifically, of a beautiful Tuscarora maiden named Genessee, a vivid dream during which they had strolled together through the woods, bathed in a crystal-clear mountain stream, and made slow, passionate love in the flower-sprinkled tall grass of a forest meadow.

Drawing a long, deep breath, he detected the acrid aroma of wood embers and old, musty timbers. His keen sense of smell picked up much more than that, however— the pervasive and pungent effluvium produced by many people—and his nose crinkled. That was to be expected, since he was in Montreal, along with about four thousand other souls. He profoundly wished he was back home in Onroka.

Propping himself up on his elbows, Joshua surveyed the room. He lay on the straw mattress of a narrow bed. There was a single small window in one wall. Golden morning light filtered through worn muslin curtains. Opposite the window was a stout, beamed door. Draped over a ladder-back chair in a corner was his beaded, buckskin long coat. A glance over the side of the bed confirmed that his knee-high moccasins were on the puncheon floor.

Yesterday morning, he and his uncle, Queheg, had entered the city. They had come with a goodly supply of pelts: bear, wolf, fox, deer, and mink. All this they had traded for knives, metal utensils, steel traps, brightly hued cloth and ready-made trade clothes, shot and powder and even a couple of Charlesville smoothbore muskets—items that were highly prized by the tribe that had accepted him as one of their own.

Joshua had been to Montreal before to engage in trade, and Queheg had even more experience than he in that respect. They knew with whom to barter. In general, the French traders were tough but fair. As he surveyed all the goods that now lay on or under a table near the chair, he concluded that he and his uncle had done well.

His aching body, throbbing head, uneasy stomach and terrible thirst informed him that he had indulged his weakness for strong spirits by imbibing far too much cider and ale the night before. For that reason he lay back down and closed his eyes, praying that these unpleasant consequences of that indulgence would soon subside—and that the next time he looked at the room it wouldn't be slightly tilting and slowly spinning.

Joshua disliked Montreal. It was too big, too noisy, and too smelly. Though he had been born at Cutter's Reach, he had grown up in the Tuscarora village east of the St. Lawrence River and north of the Falls of Niagara, a woodland idyll. He had been wholly accepted by his mother's people. He spoke the Iroquoian language better than his native tongue. Every moment away from the Onroka made him homesick. And while he had no quarrel with the French, he wanted as little as possible to do with them or their towns.

His uncle did not share these sentiments. Yesterday, after the trading had concluded, Queheg had set out to see the sights, while Joshua sought a tavern with rooms to let. Queheg had been to Montreal many times but he always wanted to explore it all over again. The buildings fascinated him. The clothing the people wore were of interest to him. So was the presence of representatives from many tribes. Patient and tireless, he roamed far and wide and missed nothing. Ordinarily a taciturn man, he would wax eloquent on all that he had seen once he returned home, regaling the many in his tribe who had never been to Montreal with tales about the immense French "village".

The growing presence of the French and British was of grave concern to some in his tribe, partly due to the fact that the Indian allies of the French, namely the Hurons and the Abenaki, were enemies of the Six Nations of the Iroquois. But Queheg was a fatalist. He did not concern himself with what the future might bring. Geopolitical gamesmanship between the world's two most powerful nations were beyond his control, so why worry? He lived for the day, and relished even the smallest things, the song of a bird, the whisper of the wind, the majesty of a tall tree, and the sign of the woodland wildlife.

Montreal had it's beginning as a trading post, established a century and a half ago by the famous explorer, Samuel de Champlain. A quarter-century later, a handful of French colonists built a settlement called Ville Marie on the island. The Iroquois had considered the island theirs, and had very nearly driven the French away. But Ville Marie survived and eventually came to be known as Montreal. Now it was a sprawling city on the larger islands of the dozens that marked the confluence of the Ottawa and St. Lawrence rivers, and it was second only in size and importance to Quebec, two hundred and fifty miles further up the St. Lawrence.

Joshua didn't worry about Queheg when it came to his uncle's wanderings in the French city and the reaction to him by the locals. The sole reason that the vast majority of Frenchmen were in this country was to trade with the

Indian tribes and the *coureur des bois*, the French-Canadian hunters, trappers and traders. It was in the best interests of the French to maintain good relations with as many tribes as possible, not an easy task when taking into account the long-lived animosities that existed between the tribes. Ottawas, Wyandots, Missisauga, Hurons and the six tribes of the Iroquois Confederacy—the Mohawks, Onandaga, Oneida, Cayuga, Seneca and Tuscaroras—all converged on Montreal to barter, and this was where the danger lurked, as there were some who had once or still were enemies of his tribe. Even so, Joshua had survived a fair share of perils while in Queheg's company, and knew from experience that his uncle was quite capable of taking care of himself.

The volume of sounds coming from the tavern below and the street outside—the Tue Saint Sulpice—had rapidly increased as the city awakened. With a perturbed groan, Joshua threw the covers aside and got up, bracing himself against a wall while the room did a slow and somewhat nauseating roll around him. Twenty years of age, he was tall, an inch short of six feet. His body was whipcord lean, broad in the shoulders, narrow at the flanks, chiseled by a life spent on the frontier. These attributes, along with his ruddy complexion, had been inherited from his father. His black hair was shoulder length and he had the limpid hazel-brown eyes of his mother, Ahuwasi Blount.

Thanks to his mother's genes, Joshua was devoid of facial and body hair. His black hair was cropped in a narrow, upright brush style, kept short at the back of his skull while increasing in length until it stood high and thick over his forehead. This was to make it harder for a foe from grabbing him by the hair and holding him fast while striking with knife, tomahawk or war club. He did not paint his body except during tribal ceremonies. Both arms, above the biceps, had been tattooed, connected circles that resembled chains.

He was naked from the waist up, as he did not normally wear a jerkin when it wasn't cold. A blue breechclout, secured by a leather belt, hung almost to his knees front and back. His fringed deerskin leggings were unsewn a few inches at the bottom so that they draped over the cuffed, beaded moccasins he seldom removed while away from home. But for the color of his skin, which while sun-dark was not the deep shade of brown of native Tuscarorans, he could have been mistaken for an Indian—and often was by those who did not look past his hair, eyes and clothing.

Long ago the Tuscaroras had left their northern homeland to seek new lands in the Carolinas, fleeing the encroachment of the French. But soon they were invaded by colonists again, Swiss and British settlers who lusted after their land. Ahuwasi's father was Tom Blount, the chief who had negotiated with the government of North Carolina in an attempt to make peace during the bloody Tuscarora War which had erupted because of the relentless appropriation of tribal lands by the quickly-growing population of colonists. Despite Blount's efforts, many Tuscaroras had been forced to migrate north, back to their ancestral lands near Great Lakes, where they had been accepted as the sixth nation in the Confederation of the Iroquois.

Moving to the window, Joshua peered out through dirt-grimed panes of glass. Straight ahead was the expansive Seminary gardens. To the right of this was the parish church of Notre Dame, and to the left a row of buildings that lined the waterfront. In that direction was the market plaza where his fur trading negotiations had been conducted.

It was there that he had parted company with Queheg, in the dying light of the previous day, their bartering concluded and all the furs they had brought with them traded away. They had come to the tavern, which Joshua remembered from his previous visit, but Queheg left all the goods they had acquired in Joshua's keeping and quickly took his leave. He would sleep in some quiet dark corner, if he slept at all, after a long time spent exploring the city, and then would return in the morning. Once he showed up, they would embark on the long trek home. Joshua hoped that would happen soon.

Many were the things that fascinated Queheg. Joshua had known him to stop and study a tree in a forest for no reason that Josh could discern. He would stand on the bank of a river and watch it go by with childish delight, as though he had never seen a river before. In his half-century of living, Queheg had accumulated a wealth of knowledge and experience but he still derived great pleasure in observing the simple joys of the world: the song of a bird, the way limbs danced in a strong wind, the profound serenity of a forest at a new day's dawning.

And so it was that his uncle's fascination with Montreal and all the goings-on within its walls never faded, and he had been coming here to trade for longer than Joshua had lived. It was Queheg who had convinced his mother to let him take her young son to the city the first time, two winters ago. Ahusawi was very protective, as Joshua was her only progeny. Many were the Tuscarora warriors who had volunteered to give her more children, but she had rejected the advances of them all. Many in the village thought it odd that she did not wish to have more children—especially a full-blooded Tuscarora child. Joshua wasn't sure why this was so. He wondered if it was because she still loved his father, a man he could scarcely remember.

He had been fully accepted by all the adults in the tribe, save one. But some of the children were not so open-minded when it came to the half-breed boy, even one who wanted nothing more than to be just like them. Only when he grew older, when he could read sign with the best of them, could outrun almost all of them, and could outshoot every one of them—only then did the other boys accept him.

At the same time, many of the girls in the village began to see him in a new light as he grew up. With bright eyes and brighter smiles, they flirted shamelessly with him, gazed at him with rapt desire whenever he walked by, or whispered and giggled behind their hands when they snuck after him on the occasions he went down to the creek to bathe. This was something from which his mother was powerless to shield him. And the fact that he was a little different from all the other boys was, in this case, to his advantage. He was exotic. Even though he pretended that he was unaffected by all the admiration, he could not hide from his mother that he was flattered. The attention he received, and the effect it had on him, were things from which Ahuwasi was powerless to shield him. All she could do was sadly smile.

And then Genesee had come into his life, and his mother's sadness deepened.

It was during his first journey to Montreal with his uncle that Queheg had tried to explain this to him.

"You are your mother's only child, Wonash." It was the name Awuhasi had given him, his Tuscarora name. The Wind, because he was so fleet of foot that he almost never lost the foot races which the young men of the Wolf Clan often engaged in to test each other's mettle. "She lives to care for you. You have been her life since the night you were born. She is happy to see you grow up strong and quick, but also she is sad because soon Genesee will be the woman who will care for you. Then Ahuwasi will be lost... until you have a child of your own." He smiled. "When that happens, she will have purpose again, and Genesee will share in the caring of that child with her. Do not worry, Wonash. You will see your mother filled with happiness again."

Joshua didn't share Queheg's confidence that he and Genesee would one day be man and wife. After all, she was the most beautiful girl in Onroka. She always resided in his thoughts. His heart always fluttered when he saw her, and he always forgot to breathe when she smiled at him. He had seen how the other young men looked at her as she went about her chores clad only in a loincloth, as most young women did when there wasn't snow on the ground. He knew what was in the minds of those other braves. He knew how they felt when they looked at her.

Genesee could have any one of them. But she seemed especially fond of him. Or was he fooling himself? Furthermore, her father was related to John Blount, who was the village sachem. Both of them had come north harboring bitter resentment against the English colonists who had driven them out of their Carolina home, and neither of them could forget that Joshua was the son of a man they mistook for an Englishman. Joshua suspected that at least a few of the village elders were not convinced of his loyalty to the tribe.

He looked again at the trade goods, tightly packed into two large buckskin knapsacks, save for the steel traps, which were securely tied to the packs. Straps allowed him to put one of the packs on his back. The other he would carry until he was reunited with Queheg. They were bulky and heavy—he estimated about forty pounds each—but his lean body was sinewy and he could bear the load. His shot pouch, which also carried flint and patches went over his right shoulder. He had tied lengths of rope to the Charlesville muskets, makeshift straps, so that he could sling them over a shoulder. Lastly he picked up his long rifle and left the room. Thoughts of Genesee motivated him to shrug off the ill effects of the strong spirits he had imbibed the night before. He felt a sudden urgency to return to Onroka, to see her again. To stake his claim, to lead her by the hand into the woods where they would consummate their desire for one another—and secure their future.

CHAPTER 7

The tavern was not as crowded or as rowdy as it had been the night before but there were a dozen people present, most of them eating breakfast, and all of them giving Joshua a long look as he descended the stairs. They were the same type of stares he had received on arrival the previous evening. His look and the way he moved caused most to assume he was full-blooded Indian—unless they noted his gray-blue eyes—and while Indians were fairly commonplace in Montreal they were seldom seen inside a tavern. Having paid his way the night before, spending all of the rather small amount of coin he had to his name, Joshua merely nodded at a stout, ruddy-faced and pleasant woman who was the sole proprietor and then walked out, making sure he met the gaze of every other person in the place, his features inscrutable.

Once outside, he paused to study the sky. The sun had not yet cleared the rooftops and there was a brisk nip in the air, but he noted the high clouds scudding in a northeasterly direction and decided it was going to be a fairly warm day, without rain.

"*Vous! Où sont tes manières? Éloignez-vous de la porte et laissez-nous aller à l'intérieur!*"

Joshua looked to his left. Three men stood there, apparently intent on entering the tavern, and one of them was letting him know that he blocked the way. They weren't gentlemen, nor soldiers, nor trappers, nor working men. This he could tell in a glance. They wore threadbare clothing. They didn't have the bearing of the upper class or the posture of military men. Their hands were without calluses and they were too pale to have spent their lives in the out-of-doors. He knew them for what they were—idlers. There were plenty of them in a city the size of Montreal, both male and female, usually of poor circumstances who had no trade and few skills and could not—or didn't care to—find honest work. Some of the women sold their bodies. Some of the men resorted to muggery. Joshua turned to face them, prepared for trouble.

"Peut-être qu'il ne parle pas français," said the largest of the three. He was thick in the body but not entirely due to grit or muscle. Like those of the others, his shoes were scuffed. His frock coat, breeches and stockings had long gone unwashed and were in need of mending. Unlike his companions, who wore tricorns, he had a bandana on his head, tied at the back.

"Je parle français," replied Josh, with a faint smile.

The big one scowled. "Then get out of our way. I have my mind set on a big bowl of steaming hot porridge. I'm cold and my belt buckle will soon be scraping my spine if I don't get something to eat."

"Enough talk," grumbled one of the others. He was skinny and tall, with a pale complexion and unruly curls of carrot-colored hair tied in a pigtail. Impatiently stepping forward, he made to shoulder Joshua aside. As he raised an arm and turned slightly, Josh glimpsed the butt of a coach pistol stuck under his belt on the left hip. Expecting Josh to step aside or be knocked back, he was startled when the collision didn't budge Joshua an inch. As Joshua took hold of him, the man stared at the hand, with its long slender fingers locked tight around his forearm.

"No need for that," said Joshua quietly, in fluent French. "I'll step aside."

The one who had tried to push Joshua out of the doorway didn't like being manhandled, either. A surly frown on his face, he began to reach for the pistol in his belt. "You damned well will," he growled.

Joshua stopped smiling then. His eyes darkened in the slanting morning light. "Don't do that," he said. It didn't sound like an order, or even a warning, but rather like advice.

It was calm, quiet advice that the red-haired man was wise enough to heed. When Josh saw that the pistol would remain tucked under the other's belt, he stepped aside. He realized that the other man would likely feel compelled to save face in front of his friends as the latter produced a sneering smile and said, "Good for you. Most Indians don't have any manners."

"He's not full Indian," said the third man. His attire was in better repair than that of his companions, consisting of a fawn-colored frock and matching waistcoat, dark blue breeches and a tricorn hat. His face was pale and angular. His lip-less mouth was like a knife scar. His nose was long and hooked, appearing to have been broken at least once. And his muddy brown eyes missed nothing. He spoke softly, without inflection. "He looks like one and acts like one and for certain lives with Indians but I'm thinking he is a half breed."

"Is that so," said the large man, and grinned as he rubbed his square jaw. "What happened?" he asked Joshua. "Your *pere* stick his pego in some red maiden's pitcher while she put up a fight?" He guffawed at his comment.

"Stow that, Louis," advised the third man.

Joshua put down the pack he carried and shrugged out of the one on his back, tilting the two Charlesville muskets and his own long rifle against them. The big man was momentarily perplexed, having expected Joshua to explode in a rage or tuck his tail and hurry off. He glanced at the soft-spoken man in the middle, who was watching Joshua warily.

"Look at this!" exclaimed the big man. "He doesn't dispute it, so it must be true!"

Joshua's first seemed to come out of nowhere to land squarely on his jaw. His head snapped back and he stumbled off-balance. Before he could regain his footing, Joshua was behind him, an arm locked tightly around his neck, the tip of a hunting knife's long, sharp blade against his jowly cheek, pressed just hard enough to cause a drop of blood to bead.

"I reckon my father is capable of many things," rasped Joshua. "But not that."

The red-headed one had taken a step back, putting more distance between himself and Joshua. He tugged the pistol from his belt, but the quiet one grabbed the weapon's barrel and pushed it down, whispering something in his comrade's ear before turning to face Joshua, arms held out to the side, hands open with palms turned up.

"*Pardonnez-nous, S'il-vous-plaît, m'sieu.* My fat and foulmouthed friend is a fool. He may deserve being cut—or even killed—for having said such a thing. But I beg you to remember that he is a French citizen in a French city. What do you think would happen to you if you indulge your justified wrath?"

Joshua dragged a deep breath into his lungs and let it out slowly. The soft-spoken one was also well-spoken. His words pierced the fog of anger. He loosened the strangle-hold on the big man's neck and lowered the hunting knife. "Apology accepted," he said, sheathing the blade as he released the man and gave him a shove before turning to retrieve his belongings.

"Knock him down, Louis!"

Startled, Joshua spun around—right into the lunge of the big man. The impact of a body twice as heavy as his sent him sprawling over the packs. Louis landed on top of him, knocking the wind out of his lungs. He realized that the sharp command had come from the one who had fooled him into thinking the confrontation was over. Then the back of his head bounced off the cobblestones of the street and for a few seconds the spinning world turned dark. His vision cleared just in time to see a meaty fist descending, and then the blow bounced his head of the pavement again. He felt himself slipping into a black oblivion. Another blow landed. Then another. He could hear the other man's snarl of rage, a distorted sound that echoed as from a deep well. The bile of fear and panic rose up within Joshua as he real-ized he might be beaten to death. That gave him a jolt of strength when he most needed it. His groping hand found the bone handle of his hunting knife. Without hesitation he plunged the eight-inch blade to the hilt into the big man's side, right below the ribcage. Louis produced a long wheez-ing exhalation as he fell to one side.

Joshua rolled over onto hands and knees, bringing the bloodied blade with him. He tried to focus on the blood-splattered cobblestones, and realized belatedly that it was his own blood that he was seeing, as it drooled from his mouth and splattered like thin crimson paint onto the worn pavement. He heard shouts of alarm and then another sound, a sound more animal than human, and turned his head slowly to focus on Louis. The big man was laying on his side in the street, making those chilling sounds of pure, terrified agony as he twitched and writhed like a damned sinner in the flesh-melting flames of perdition.

Men were gathering around. Joshua saw their feet, their stockinged legs. But there was something he didn't see—the packs, the Charlesville muskets, his own long rifle. A jolt of sickening alarm gave him the strength to get to his feet. The world began to spin and he teetered into someone who pushed him away and into someone else. He caught glimpses of faces etched with shock and alarm, the babble of a half-dozen excited Frenchmen. They looked afraid, and were backing away from him. He looked down and saw the bloody knife in his grasp, but he wasn't as worried about that as he was about his belongings, a sickening feeling residing in the pit of his stomach. Everything was *gone*. The other two idlers had made off with his rifle and everything else.

"Get back...out of my way...let me through..." he mumbled as he tried to push one man aside only to be shoved into another, who grabbed hold of him. He caught a glimpse of the two thieves, each carrying a pack and a musket. They were running as fast as they could down the street.

Joshua wrenched free of the grasping hands so violently that he lost his balance. Getting his feet under him, he realized all eyes were focused on him and not on the thieves making their escape. All but one set of eyes. He lurched forward, shouldered someone aside, and saw his long rifle in the hands of a plump, well-dressed man—one of the men he had spotted in the tavern this morning. He grabbed the weapon and wrenched it violently out of the other's hand.

"That's mine, damn you," he growled.

"Je sais, m'sieu!" gasped the man, holding his trembling hands up as though to ward off an attack, taking two steps back and then whirling to plunge quickly through the pack of onlookers and then out of sight. A moment later the throng suddenly parted and Joshua caught sight of a gray justaucorps with white serge lining over a long blue waistcoat—the uniform of a French soldier. He looked up into a young, wide-eyed face beneath a black tricorn trimmed with cheap silver lace.

"Laisse tomber le couteau!" shouted the soldier.

Joshua looked down at the knife. He had forgotten it was in his hand.

"Drop the knife, I say!" The command was edged with fear.

He looked up—just in time to see the brass butt of the soldier's musket a split second before it slammed into his face. Then the world disappeared.

CHAPTER 8

The first thing that Joshua was aware of was distant, muffled voices. The second was the tight bandaging around his skull. He reached up and touched it, and then gingerly brushed fingers over his face, which was swollen and hurt like the dickens. In fact, his entire body hurt. Prying his eyes open, he blinked his vision clear and found himself staring up at a gray stone ceiling. The voices became louder, clarified.

"...afraid that won't be possible, my friend. You see, he killed a man, and whether it was self-defense or murder is a determination that is up to a magistrate to make."

It all came back in a breathtaking rush to Joshua then, and a sudden panic gripped him. He tried to sit up but his body howled in complaint and he groaned weakly as he fell back, turning his head to see Queheg standing on the other side of cell door fashioned of flat-iron bars, alongside a tall, slender man in the uniform of a French lieutenant. Joshua had met this man before, had gotten to know him, and yet for a moment he couldn't retrieve the officer's name out of his befuddled mind.

"He is conscious at last!" exclaimed the Frenchman, vastly relieved. "Lie still, *m'sieu*. Your head was nearly split open."

Queheg implored the lieutenant to let him in.

"I am sorry, but I cannot."

"Let me in and lock the door." Queheg spoke French fluently, better by a long shot than Joshua could.

The lieutenant regretfully shook his head. *"Je suis vraiment désolé. Ce n'est pas possible,* my friend."

Joshua tried to sit up again, and by dent of sheer willpower managed to swing his legs off the narrow iron cot upon which he lay. The effort cost him dearly. The cell in which he found himself began to tilt and whirl. Nauseated, he squeezed his eyes shut, leaning forward with face in hands, trying desperately not to puke.

"He's dead, isn't he," he said flatly. It wasn't a question.

"Oui. He bled out on the street," replied the French officer. "I am no physician but I have seen plenty of wounded men, and it is my opinion that you pierced his lung. I got there just a moment after the soldier knocked you down."

Joshua remembered him then, and everything that the officer had said about himself, his career, and his family. His name was Jean-Paul Menard. He was a slender man with aquiline features and hazel eyes. His uniform was impeccable. The memory was of an observant, intuitive and amiable individual who was a good soldier, committed to his job and the men under his command. They had met during Joshua's first visit to Montreal. He had paid for the lieutenant's supper and they had shared a tankard or three of ale. He also remembered that the officer could hold his liquor better than he.

Menard was the grandson of an officer of the Carignan-Salieres Regiment, which had been shipped to New France a century ago, at a time when the Iroquois had crushed their Huron enemies and began raiding French settlements up and down the St. Lawrence.

The regiment was called home to France after that threat was over, save for four hundred men who were enticed into staying to protect French interests by the offer of land and money bonuses. Menard's grandfather had become a wealthy seigneur who married one of the *filles du Roi*, young single French women shipped to America to become wives of the soldiers stationed there. The sons and grandsons of the soldiers who had been loyal to the older Menard held Jean-Paul in high regard and some of them served under him.

Joshua took in his surroundings: the grim gray stone walls, the rusting gray iron grates of the cell door, the very narrow window carved into the outer wall, like a vertical gun slot, too high for him to see out of and big enough to let in fresh air—very cold fresh air. It was uncommon for him to be susceptible to cold, but he was shivering, and he put it down to his weakened state. Pulling a thin woolen blanket around his hunched shoulders, he glanced remorsefully at Queheg.

"I lost everything, Uncle. Even my own rifle."

"Not entirely," said Menard. "No sooner did I hear the accounts of some of the eyewitnesses—that Louis Auclair had been in the company of two other men who were seen running away with your goods, I had a good idea who they were and where I might find them. And indeed I found one a few hours later, a scoundrel by the name of Thierry Guipil. I recovered your rifle. A very fine rifle it is, too, *mon ami*, and I say that even if it was most probably made by German gunsmiths living in the Pennsylvania colony and not a French gunsmith." He smiled, making clear that the last comment had been lighthearted.

"Thank God!" exclaimed Joshua. I am indebted to you, Jean-Paul. I hope one day I can repay you in kind."

Menard made a dismissive gesture. "No need! I also recovered some of your goods. I am sorry to say the rest had already been sold on the street. If it is any consolation, I also confiscated a bag of money from Guipil. I have given all of this to your uncle. I hope you can replace some of the things you lost with those ill-gotten gains. Your knife is in my keeping and must remain so until after you stand before the magistrate."

Joshua nodded bleakly. "Unless he finds me guilty of murder, and then I suppose I won't get it back any time soon."

"Now, now, Joshua. Do not worry yourself. I will stand as witness to your character and I have already secured the assurances of some of the witnesses that they will testify on your behalf."

Joshua gingerly touched the bandaging around his skull. "I suppose you had something to do with this, as well."

"We are not barbarians, *mon ami*. You needed care and the physician we call upon when a prisoner is ill or injured provided it. Unlike his predecessor, who was a butcher, this one is very dedicated to his trade. I am just happy that we didn't have to summon a priest to give you your last rites!"

Joshua looked solemnly at Queheg. His uncle's brown, oval face, deeply creased by a hard and long life, usually had eyes and mouth that were always smiling, even in times of peril and hardship. But today his demeanor was grim.

"You should go home, Uncle," said Joshua. "I think I may be here awhile."

Menard touched the Tuscarora brave's buckskin-clad arm. "He may be right. It will be a few days or perhaps as long as a fortnight before Joshua is brought to court."

Queheg shook his head. "I will not leave my kin behind," he said flatly.

"An admirable trait. However, by tonight the word will have spread throughout Montreal that a Frenchman has been slain by an Indian. It won't matter that the former was a known thief and the latter acted in self-defense." The lieutenant glanced apologetically at Joshua. "Nor will it matter that you are not a full-blood Indian. In truth, that you live with Indians will cause many to think less of you."

"I am aware of that," said Joshua flatly.

"If I return to Onroka without him there will be trouble," Queheg told Menard. He said it without anger. He wasn't making a threat, but simply stating the facts. "Do you know who his mother is?"

Menard shook his head. "No." He glanced at Joshua. "You never told me."

"She is Awuhasi, the daughter of Tom Blount."

The lieutenant's demeanor made clear that he knew who Tom Blount was. Furthermore, he knew that another of Tom Blount's relatives was currently the sachem, or chief, or the Wolf Clan Tuscaroras.

"My people honor all those who have Tom Blount's blood in their veins. The Tuscaroras will not be happy that you are holding his grandson in this stone cage. Of all the Six Nations, the Tuscaroras have never made war against the French. Do you think your chief would be happy if we turned against the you?"

Menard was silent a moment, glancing from Queheg to Joshua and back again. Then he nodded.

"I understand. I will speak to my commander, and my grandfather, as well. By law a magistrate cannot withdraw from prosecution once a charge has been presented to him. So it's the *juge d'instruction* we have to convince. If we can persuade him that the killing was justified, he might make no charge. If he feels he must, then perhaps it will be a lesser charge, one to which the magistrate can make a quick and favorable ruling and order Joshua set free. I will leave you two alone to speak privately. Call for the jailor when you wish to leave."

When Menard was gone, Joshua rose and came closer to the iron bars, the surprise evident on his face.

"I have never known you to lie, uncle. Our people would not go to war for me. They cannot go to war without the rest of the Confederation."

Queheg shrugged. He was smiling again. "Worry not, Womash. I think your friend knows the truth. But he needed a good reason to set you free, and now he has one that he can use to convince those who have the power to let you go." He reached through the bars and clamped a reassuring hand on Joshua' shoulder. "Rest. If the French are wise, we will soon be on our way home, and you must carry your share of the goods. I will go now and use the money to replace what was lost."

Joshua was sorry to see his uncle go, but remained inscrutable as Queheg called for the jailor to open the cellblock door. Alone, he bleakly studied the cold, gray cell which confined him, then lay down on the cot and closed his eyes, resisting the claustrophobic pressure of the walls closing in on him, distracting himself with thoughts of Genessee. He could see her clearly, standing in the middle of Onroka, slender and naked but for a loincloth, perfect in every way, the eyes of all the young bucks on her, while her big hazel eyes were locked on him, a soft and inviting smile on her lips ...

CHAPTER 9

It seemed to Joshua that he had been cooped up in his cold, gray, stone box for weeks, when in truth it had been but three days when Menard came to get him.

The French lieutenant unlocked the cell door and stepped back, holding up the shackles he carried and looking earnestly at his friend.

"I wish it was not required, but I must put these on you."

Joshua nodded and managed a wan smile. "Well, I am accused of being a murderer, am I not? And worse, an Indian murderer." He held out his arms, wrists close together.

As he applied the shackles, Menard said, his voice lowered so that the guard beyond the cellblock door could not hear him, "I must be honest with you, *mon ami*. I did manage to persuade the court to hear your case quickly. But neither I nor my grandfather could persuade the *juge d'instruction* to listen to reason and drop the charge entirely." He glanced at the cellblock door, and leaned in a bit closer to whisper, "I have no proof of it, but my feeling is there are other forces at work here."

"Other forces?"

Menard pitched his voice lower still. "I will explain later."

With that he took Joshua out of the cell and a moment later they were emerging onto a narrow cobblestoned street where a carriage was waiting. Menard put him inside, then looked up at the driver on the bench and nodded before climbing aboard himself. Once the carriage was moving, the lieutenant breathed a sigh of relief.

"I think you have become a pawn in a dangerous game, my friend. A man named Philip St. Vrain has taken an interest in your case."

"Who is he?"

"A man as powerful as the Baron de Longuiel."

"The Governor of Montreal?"

Menard nodded. "St. Vrain owns the most important, the most influential, and the most profitable fur company in all of New France. He inherited it from his father. You probably sold many of your furs to one or more of his agents. Like his father, St. Vrain has many friends in high places. He either buys their compliance with coin, or through threats and blackmail. The Shawnee, the Abenaki, the Huron—these and other tribes depend on good relations with him

"Why would he find my case of interest?"

The lieutenant leaned forward. Joshua could not remember him being so solemn and serious.

"You live an idyllic and sheltered life in some respects, *mon ami*. You are probably unaware that when it comes to war with England the French are of two minds. Some of us wish for peace and accommodation. Others thirst for war. I am of the first group. While it is true that we may well be able to defeat the British forces currently stationed in the colonies, not just the regular troops but also the colonial militia, it would only lead to a larger, more prolonged conflict that, in the end, could go badly for us. Even so, there are some who believe we can defeat them so decisively that the British King George will be forced to come to terms that will secure New France through new treaties."

Joshua listened intently, but then shook his head.

"I don't understand how that can have anything to do with me, or my stopping a thief from making off with my property."

"Neither your father or mother ever spoke of St. Vrain?"

"My mother took me to Onroka when i was a very young child. I hardly remember my father. And I do not recall that she ever uttered that name. She sought to put the ways and wars of the white man behind us, out of sight and mind. That is a point of view she shares with many Tuscaronas, who just want to live in peace."

"Of course, because of what happened in the Carolinas, no doubt." Menard paused and pushed aside a curtain just enough to peer outside of the carriage as it rolled on, then studied his boots a moment with furrowed brow, rubbing his hands nervously. "How should I put this to you. From what I know of your father—whom I have never met—he is a man who has always wanted to live in peace, to engage in his business affairs and without conflict. I imagine that like many of us he wishes the situation to remain as it has been." He looked up at Joshua, grimly. "But I fear that is no longer possible. Any military man worth his salt would recognize the strategic value of Cutter's Reach. It is obvious to anyone who knows the terrain and understands the complexities of waging war in a wilderness that the valleys of the Allegheny and Monongahela are the gateways between the British colonies and New France. They are the most direct route between Quebec and Montreal on one side and Virginia and Pennsylvania on the other. Yes, there is the Ohio River valley if one were to engage in a flanking movement, but to do so successfully would require a much larger army than either side can presently muster." Reading Joshua's expression, he smiled apologetically. "I see you have no education or experience when it comes to the subject of martial strategies. Let me just put it simply. Your father—and every man, woman and child who live at Cutter's Reach—will be in the middle of a bloody and brutal conflict."

For a moment, Joshua was glumly silent, then shook his head. "But what does this have to do with me? I don't really know my father. I scarcely recall anything about the settlement in which I was brought into this world."

"In terms of you, personally, St. Vrain heard that Joshua Cutter was being held over for trial. I do not know if he wants you dead or held as a bargaining chip, but I believe he sees you as a pawn in a dark and perilous game of empire and revenge."

"Revenge??"

"*Oui.* Your father killed St. Vrain's father. From what I know, it was a quarrel over the right to trade with an Indian village. The story is that St. Vrain fired a pistol at your father, who had only a hunting knife. Your father was struck in the shoulder, but that didn't stop him. The blade of his knife found its way into St. Vrain's heart, thrust with such force that it broke through his ribcage."

It became clear to Joshua at that moment, and after a grim and thoughtful moment he said, "So it was a matter of self-defense. And now Philip St. Vrain wants me dead."

Before Menard could respond, the coachman checked the team of four horses pulling the conveyance and Menard peeked out of a window again, then threw open the door, stepped out, and took a long look up and down a narrow side street before turning to gesture at Joshua to follow. Stepping down, Joshua took one look at his surroundings and then turned a puzzled frown on the lieutenant.

"What are you up to, Jean-Paul?"

"Around the corner is the River Gate. Once through you will proceed to the Merriman house. Queheg is there, with your trade goods, and a canoe that will carry you both across the river."

Joshua stared at his friend for a moment, then put a hand on Menard's shoulder.

"What risk do you take by this act?"

"Don't worry about me. There are men in positions of authority who have commanded me to make sure you leave Montreal alive."

"But what about the charge against me?"

Menard shrugged, a very Gallic gesture of fatalism. "Given time, memories will fade. Documents may even be misplaced. Besides, there are events of much greater import happening now, or about to happen. Nonetheless, I would advise you never to return to Montreal my friend." He extended a hand. "It may well be that we won't meet again. But I would rather that than to see you put in the grave." He moved to the rear of the coach and extracted Joshua's long rifle, shot pouch and powderhorn from the boot. These he handed to Joshua and then clutched his friend's arm. "Come. There is no time to waste. By now our absence from the court will have become obvious."

They walked up the side street, through an alley and into a broader avenue. To the right was the open gate through which a few people were passing in or out, watched by a pair of sentries. Menard threw an arm around Joshua' broad shoulders and set their pace with long strides toward the gate. As they drew near the sentries Menard spoke loudly to Joshua.

"Before you leave, my friend, I must tell you a humorous tale I overheard in Madame Bisset's house of pleasures the other night. There was a noblewoman seeking a new young man for her ... retinue. Speaking to one eager applicant, she said, 'You do not have the look of a man who could well please his mistress, for your beard is nothing more than the kind of fuzz that ladies have in certain places, and it is easy to tell from the state of the hay whether the pitchfork is any good.' To which the young man boldly asked, 'Milady, answer me without deceit. Is there hair between your legs?' 'None at all,' she replied, to which he commented, 'Indeed, I believe you, for grass does not grow on a path well-beaten!'"

He burst into hearty laughter, and acknowledged the sentries in a way that made clear he was sharing the bawdy joke with them. Joshua couldn't be sure if they laughed because they thought it was funny or because Menard was an officer, but laugh they did. For himself, Joshua managed to smile.

Beyond the gate was a wide dirt path gently sloping down to the edge of the distant St. Lawrence River. There were several cabins along the way, and cattle grazed in the fields bereft of trees on either side. Joshua gazed longingly at the woods that seemed to stretch into eternity on the far side of the river, a thick carpet of green on rolling hills that seemed to stretch into forever. He turned his face up and into the morning sun, relishing the warmth of it after the three longest days of his life, spent locked in a cold stone cell.

When they neared the riverside Joshua spotted Mary Merriman sitting in a rocking chair on the porch of a somewhat rundown cabin, shoveling porridge from a wooden bowl into her mouth, wiggling the toes of the gout-swollen left foot that was propped up on a three-legged stool. The shack had not withstood the ravages of time very well and neither had Mary. Beside the shack, a grizzled old man was repairing a canoe balanced upside-down on stout wooden sawhorses. A bit further along, Queheg was sitting on his heels near a canoe loaded with trade packs, puffing on a hemp pipe.

As they neared the cabin, Mary lifted her left leg up and slowly put her bad foot on the weathered planking of the porch, then pushed herself out of the rocker and stood at the top of the porch steps, bracing herself against an upright. She was a large woman with a jowly face and carrot-colored hair that was wild and windswept. Much time had passed since it had last been subjected to a brush.

Joshua had met Mary before. She was one of the living legends of Montreal, an indefatigable, self-indulgent, foul-mouthed Englishwoman who had wed a French *voyaguer* whose scalp probably still dangled from an Indian lodge-pole. She had survived thieves, epidemics and one or two Indian raids, and in the process had killed a half-dozen men in self defense. Mary didn't look very healthy or very dangerous but she had earned her reputation as a woman not to be messed with.

Many visitors to Montreal arrived by barge or canoe, but some came overland, and Mary provided transportation across the broad St. Lawrence. Her hirelings waited on both the east and west banks, providing canoes to those who wished to cross to the city, often doing the rowing them-selves, as few knew the strong and quirky currents of the river better than they. Of course, they did not provide this service for nothing.

When they arrived at the cabin, Menard produced a small pouch and, sweeping the tricorn off his head, pre-sented himself to Mary with a respectful bow—before plac-ing the pouch in the woman's hand. She tested the weight of it and a smile dimpled her fat cheeks and didn't even raise an eyebrow as the lieutenant unlocked the shackles on Joshua's wrists. She glanced up the road at the distant city gate, then fastened beady eyes half buried in folds of fat on Joshua as he shook Menard's hand and gave profuse thanks.

"I hope no trouble comes to you for your act of kindness, my friend," said Joshua.

"I am not the one at risk here. You had best get across the river, *très vite!*"

Joshua nodded and turned to Mary. "Thank you, Mrs. Merriman."

She bounced the pouch in her hand and they all could hear the clink-clank of hard money.

"This is all the thanks I need. Get along with ye."

Joshua walked down to the river. Queheg was standing now, watching him approach, a grin spreading his creased cheeks. They clasped hands without a word said, then Joshua glanced at the trade goods in the canoe. Joshua wanted to ask if his uncle had recouped all that he had lost to the thief, but decided against it. He was sure that Queheg had done all he could.

Without a word said they climbed into the canoe, picked up the oars and began the long crossing. Once on the other side they wasted no time shouldering the packs and the muskets and bent their steps for the woods.

Reaching the trees, Joshua paused a moment to look back, half-expecting to see men running down the path from the city, the beginning of a pursuit from the city to which he would never return. But he saw nothing out of the ordinary.

Even so, as he followed Queheg into the dark green shade of the forest, he couldn't help but feel that his troubles were only just beginning. War was coming, and he worried that his dreams of an idyllic life with Genessee was now at risk.

CHAPTER 10

Charles le Moine, the Governor of Montreal, was not at all pleased to give an audience to Philip St. Vrain, but you couldn't tell it by the effusively warm greeting with which he met his guest.

It wasn't as though he had a choice, however. He was quite certain that the trader hadn't even paused in the anteroom, or had the courtesy of requesting that one of the governor's aides announce his arrival. No, St. Vrain. had simply marched immediately into the inner sanctum of Montreal's head of government.

St. Vrain was a singularly tall and slender man, with long, unruly hair the color of the granite cliffs of the region. Le Moine knew him to be in his late thirties, but St. Vrain didn't move like he was a man on the brink of middle age. His long strides brought him up to the governor's ornate, mahogany pedestal desk before Le Moine could come around the furniture to meet him.

"To what do I owe the pleasure of your visit?" asked the governor.

St. Vrain had a scowl on his face, and le Moine could not recall ever having seen the trading mogul smile. Today the scowl was more ferocious than usual, as the man dropped a rolled map onto the desk and then unrolled it, using the governor's silver snuff box to hold down the top left corner, and a heavy, green ledger bound in old leather on the bottom right corner. Then he stabbed a place on the map with a long middle finger.

"Cutter's Reach," he said, his voice a rumbling bass growl. "You must march on it at once, Le Moine."

The governor bristled at the way St. Vrain addressed him, as though he, the most important and powerful man in New France, was nothing more than a hired hand. It was Le Moine's steadfast conviction that he deserved respect. His father, Charles le Moine de Longueiul, had been Chief Administrator of New France. He himself had served as the Commandant of Fort Niagara. He had journeyed south to assist the governor of Louisiana in a successful effort to sub-due rebelling Indians. A few years ago, King Louis XV had named him Montreal's governor and, later, the Administrator of New France, the position his father had once held.

The governor was nothing if not a gentleman. He forced a smile upon his long oval face and moved to a sidetable even more ornate than, upon which were crystal stem glasses and a large silver tray bearing decanters. "Would you care for a glass of wine, my friend?" St. Vrain was by no stretch of the imagination his friend. In fact, le Moine was not aware of anyone in polite society that could legitimately qualify for the dubious honor of being his uninvited guest's friend. No, St. Vrain had no friends, not among the rough and tumble band of ruthless voyageurs who did his bidding, or even the numerous Indian tribes with whom he engaged in trade. He didn't need friends. He was one of the wealthiest men in New France, and one of the most influential. People did his bidding out of fear or, in the case of the Hurons, because of his generosity when it came to trade.

St. Vrain wore a condescending smirk on his cadaver-ous face. "This is not a social call, Governor. I have come to inform you that the time has come, at long last."

Le Moine had no real interest in a glass of port either, but he poured himself one anyway, taking his time. It wasn't until he had glass in hand, had sipped the contents, and then returned to sit behind his desk, that he responded.

"The time for what, *m'sieu?*"

"The time for war! The time to secure the future of New France. To show the *Anglais* that they will not wrest this continent from our grasp, and that if they hold onto their colonies it will be because we are not the thieving, land-hungry lot that they are." His voice dripped with contempt.

Le Moine gazed at St. Vrain a moment, then cast his eyes on the large, detailed map that lay on the desk between them. After a moment spent picking his words carefully, he said, "I wonder, is Abel Cutter still alive?"

"This is not about Abel Cutter," rasped St. Vrain, his eyes like steel blades flashing in sunlight. "It is about the future of New France. By now the British know about the forts France has constructed west of the Allegheny Mountains. One can safely presume that they will soon march to secure the valley east of those mountains. If you allow this, they will be poised to strike at your fortifications, as they most surely would. But take Cutter's Reach now and you will go far in securing the eastern flank of New France."

Le Moine did St. Vrain the courtesy of carefully studying the map for a moment. The he settled back in his well-upholstered chair and sipped his port.

"You are no doubt aware, sir, that the British have an entire regiment stationed in their colonies, and that in addition several of the larger colonies have plans to—or already have—formed sizeable militias. France cannot afford to field a standing army here. And even if our king were so inclined to send a force of regular soldiers to aid us, he would have to send them down the St. Lawrence, an exceedingly difficult and time-consuming operation in any season. No, we have learned how to fight in this country. What we call '*le petite guerre*'—engaging in guerrilla warfare, hitting the enemy with surprise and then fading into the forest, a strategy we have adopted from our Indian allies. It is the best way to fight superior forces, to whittle down their numbers, to slow them down and bleed them until they are forced to turn around and go home."

St. Vrain stood ramrod-straight on the other side of the desk, arms folded, a scowl on his gaunt features, waiting impatiently for the governor to finish his lecture on the successful way to carry out a conflict in the thick and seemingly endless forests, the craggy and inhospitable mountains, and the narrow twisting valleys down which deep, fast-running rivers rarely lent themselves to a safe crossing for wagons, or in some places, even mounts and men. When Le Moine was done and sipping from his glass again, the trader spoke.

"You do not require a force of regulars, or even cannon, to take a place like Cutter's Reach. But I would present you with a proposition." Suddenly he was pacing back and forth in front of the desk, bony fingers laced behind his back. "Give me license to do it myself, as the agent of your government. I can muster fifty of my voyageurs, and over a hundred, perhaps even two hundred, Huron braves. With a force of that size I assure you, I would see Cutter's Reach in French hands. Its walls and its people will fall in a storm of fire and steel. Then I will hold the location until you can dispatch your famous engineers to take custody of the place and to build the maze of fortifications you soldiers seem so fond of all around it. And should I fail you will have lost nothing, not a single one of your precious soldiers. But I will not fail."

This time, when Le Moine sat forward, he turned the map around for a longer look. St. Vrain ceased his pacing and leaned over the desk, fists planted wide upon it, and with his height looming over not just the map but the governor himself. The governor spent quite a long time gazing at the map, not because he was having trouble envisioning the strategic importance of Cutter's Reach, but rather because he did, even while he wondered if he could pull together a large enough force of soldiers to effectively carry out a successful siege of the location. And to, while the Indian allies of the French were usually eager for the glory of war, they hadn't the stomach to engage in a protracted siege.

Less than half of the army in New France were trained to the extent that, at least in Le Moine's opinion, they deserved the appellation of "soldier." The ranks had been filled by conscripts rushed through training so that they could be deployed to the numerous defensive forts along the frontier of New France. There was no denying that his troops were stretched thin, and there was absolutely no chance that France could adequately reinforce him. The Treaty of Utrecht in 1713 had held the two chief European powers at peace—relevant to one another at least—for a quarter of a century. It had been apparent to some Frenchmen, Le Moine among them, that this peace bought England the time it required to hasten the building of what would become a network of colonies, ably maintained and defended by the greatest navy the world had yet seen, in short a colonial and commercial worldwide empire. Meanwhile, King Louis XV and his chief advisor, Cardinal de Fleury, were more concerned with the military and political convulsions in Europe First had come The War of Austrian Succession, as the French and Prussians challenged the right of Maria Theresa to succeed her father, Emperor Charles V, to the Austrian throne, based on Salic Law, which did not allow women a royal inheritance. The war that ensued had put France and Britain at odds again, even long after Maria Theresa ascended the throne, in the War of Jenkin's Ear, the Jacobite Rebellion in Scotland, and the First and Second Silesian Wars. Britain depended on its superior navy to support and defend its far-flung interests. France had to counter with spreading its army much too thinly around the world.

Le Moine sighed and finally lifted his gaze from the map to meet St. Vrain's hawkish, unblinking stare.

"I am of course aware of your animosity for Abel Cutter, *m'sieu,* so forgive me if I wonder if you propose this service out of a desire to serve the crown, the foremost duty of a loyal Frenchman. Perhaps it is a business decision. Or perhaps you wish to remove one of your competitors. Or could it simply be vengeance that you seek?"

St. Vrain's eyes became hooded, and a faint smile again pulled on his thin, bloodless lips. Le Moine thought the smile exceedingly arrogant and even somewhat condescending, but his responsibility to king and country required him to swallow a rising ire.

"Why can't it be all of those reasons?" asked the trader. "Cutter has no love for England, nor England for him. There will be no great uproar should he happen to perish in the fall of The Reach. And when your men come to occupy it, mine will happily depart. Then, as I presume the British and their colonial militia intend to fortify at the forks of the Allegheny and Monongahela they will see themselves cut off to both the west and the north by your strongholds, and to the south by the Shawnee, who have no love for British scarlet."

Le Moine nodded, and topped off his glass with more wine. "You forget the Six Nations, *m'sieu.*"

St. Vrain made a dismissive gesture. "The Iroquois Confederacy has no taste for war. Before they joined together in their confederation, the five nations very nearly destroyed each other. The confederation was the means by which they intended to stop this practice. Now, two hundred years later, they are so passive that when the Mohawks arrived, instead of driving them away, the Iroquois welcomed them into their confederacy."

"I do not agree. The six nations of the Iroquois Confederacy are sleeping lions." He looked at St. Vrain a moment more in grim silence, then sat down, took a clean sheaf of vellum from an engraved rosewood box on his desk, dipped the tip of his quill pen into an inkwell, and began writing. "This letter authorizes your endeavor. However, I do not wish it to be common knowledge. Use it as a last resort, should you run afoul of the commandante of one of our fortifications in that country. You are not under any circumstances to use this to appropriate assistance, intelligence, supplies, or troops, from our forts. I am also requiring that you allow the people at Cutter's Reach to leave there with their lives. We are not savages." He affixed his signature, read what he had written while waiting for the ink to dry, then folded and sealed it. Rising, he presented the document with a flourish, and added, "Though I do not expect that they do that."

St. Vrain took the letter, and gave the governor a wry smile, well aware that Le Moine was protecting himself—and New France—should there be a hue and cry from the colonials and the British government following a massacre at Cutter's Reach. The trader performed a cursory bow, and without another word began to march out of the governor's office, his expression one of fierce elation. But at the door he stopped abruptly, and turned.

"Were you aware that Abel Cutter's half-breed son was to be put on trial today for murder?"

Le Moine was startled. "I was not. I leave civil justice to the magistrates. Was to be? Why was he not?"

"There are some in your ranks who still cling to the foolish notion that New France can be held without war, so they go to great lengths to avoid conflict. The younger Cutter killed a man in this city, and yet was able to escape justice, through the machinations of one or more of your subordinates. By the time I learned of Cutter's presence the deed had been done and he was free."

"I will look into it," said Le Moine.

Once St. Vrain had departed, the governor slumped into his chair, rubbing his forehead and sighing deeply. As much as he hated to admit it, the trader was right. There would certainly be war which, if nothing else, would open old wounds between many tribes. There would be blood and misery aplenty in the days to come.

St. Vrain didn't live in Montreal, although he could have afforded to reside in one of the most stately and sumptuous manors within the city's walls. Instead, he had a large log and stone house deep in the woods on the southern end of the main island, atop a rocky embankment overlooking the water and, not far to the south, Isle Perrot. There were a couple of reasons why he preferred being outside the city's towering walls. For one, he did business with many types of people, some of them brigands and other characters not welcome in the city. He was also visited by many Indians—on a nearly daily basis during the spring and summer—and he preferred to have his clientele as isolated from his competitors as possible.

When he arrived at his front porch, which ran the full length of the house and provided a panoramic view of the lake and islands to the south, seen through the trunks of towering pines, he was pleasantly surprised to find seven Huron braves there, watched over by a giant of a man named Victor. The Indians were scattered across the porch, most of them sitting, one of them lying flat on his back and another standing. St. Vrain noted that they were passing around two brown jugs of rum, which he had ordered Victor to give them. Scattered around the porch were the trade goods St. Vrain had given them in exchange for a goodly number of quality pelts.

He knew them all, and they greeted him affably and, in a few cases, with drunken exuberance. They had come that morning, bringing him the furs to trade for black powder and shot, knives and hatchets, a cooking kettle and clothing, along with a large portion of colored beads, which Indian women were quite fond of, and with which they decorated all manner of things.

Their leader was one called Charloe. He was taller than most Hurons, slender but broad of shoulder, his body scarred from many wounds and painted and tattooed with many symbols that heralded him as a great warrior. He was the one whom St. Vrain introduced into the house. Charloe was surprised. He had been here many times, and always treated with great courtesy and generosity, but he had never been allowed inside the house. Once inside, he glanced at the high-ceilinged great hall, with its dark wall panels and high book cases but St. Vrain gave him no time to do more. He grabbed the Huron's hand and dropped a leather pouch into his palm. The weight of its contents and the sound of coin clinking together as it came into his hand made Charloe to look with surprise at the trader.

"Two Tuscaroras left Montreal this morning, carrying trade goods across the river and then north for home. I want you and your brothers to stop them. You can keep the trade goods and I will give you another pouch of gold if you bring me their scalps."

Charloe thought it over for a moment, rubbing his chin, looking past St. Vrain rather than directly at the trader because there was suspicion glimmering in his eyes. In the past the Frenchman had at times called on him to lead a war party against other traders, or even other Indians, but never had he been employed to kill just two men, especially two men of the Iroquois Six Nations.

St. Vrain did not take umbrage at Charloe's hesitance, nor did he show his impatience, understanding that an Indian took the time to think about every possible result of an action—or inaction—before committing to it. Charloe did not ask for further details. He and the trader had been business partners for a long time, and the Huron knew that St. Vrain would tell him all the details that he would get, so asking for more was pointless. All that he was required to do was say yes or no. Removing hand from chin, he opened his mouth to speak when the trader interrupted him.

"I will tell you this. Both men are related to the Tuscarora sachem, John Blount, through his sister. Their deaths may take us one step closer to the war that is coming. The war with the British and their allies, the Six Nations."

Charloe was indifferent. His shrug and blank stare were disingenuous, disguising the fact that taking the lives of two men with that bloodline would bring him much respect from his people. "We will go at once."

St. Vrain caught him by an arm as he turned away. "When the deed is done, send those who follow you as runners to your villages, to inform your chiefs that I will be coming to visit with them soon, on matters of great import."

Charloe nodded, and moments later he and his followers were departing, some of them quite drunk and loquacious, or loudly effusive in their gratitude to a generous host. St. Vrain watched them until they were obscured by the woods, then turned and entered his home, to sink behind the desk in his well-stocked library, where he proceeded to indulge himself in quite satisfying imaginings of how and when Abel Cutter would receive word that his son was dead.

CHAPTER 11

Joshua and Queheg made good time that first day. The former was in a hurry to get home, to see his mother and the maiden he adored. They were both constantly in his thoughts. He liked to think that every stride that brought him closer to Onroka removed him further from the impending doom of which Menard had spoken, the war that would spread like a wildfire through the forest, that would consume fortifications and settlements alike in a maelstrom of blood and death.

Thoughts of his father also intruded. Seldom had he given much thought to Abel Cutter, having been separated from him as a child so many years past. His mother seldom spoke of him. He wasn't sure why, but suspected it was not due to any resentment or anger on her part but rather because thinking about his father was too painful for her to bear. He wondered if that was still true today, or if time had healed Anuwashi's emotional wounds.

She had never even told him why they had left Cutter's Reach in the first place. Only once did he ask. Her response had discouraged him from ever doing so again. He had wondered if somehow his father had wronged her. Perhaps it had been another woman. But now he had cause to think it could possibly be because of the blood feud involving Philip St. Vrain.

That night they made camp in a hollow, surrounded by thick brush and towering trees, so that the light from the small but hot fire they built would not be noticed from afar, a precaution that was second nature to them both. They dined on a white-tailed deer that Queheg had slain a mile or two earlier. They ate their fill and then Joshua and his uncle cut the rest of the meat into strips and impaled them on long sticks sharpened to a point on one end, and which were propped up over the fire by resting the tips in the fork of a sturdy branch. The meat they cooked that night would last them for much of the trip home.

As they sat around the fire, their bellies full, their thirst slaked from a nearby run, watching the crackling fire sear the meat, listening to the sizzling of grease that dripped into the flames, and the smoke wafting up into the thick and verdant canopy above, Jeremy made up his mind to ask Qeuheg a few questions, hoping his uncle had knowledge that could answer some of the questions that had been plaguing him all through the day. He broke a long silence during which they had relished the peace and contentment woodland dwellers experienced in the majestic forests that they called home.

"Uncle, have you heard of a man named St. Vrain?"

Queheg looked surprised. The smile that lived ever on his lips seemed to tighten just a bit. "I know the one you speak of."

"What do you know about him?"

He is known by some as the White Fox. He and his men trade with many tribes and have done so for many years, as did his father before him."

"My friend Jean-Paul says my father killed the father."

The creases on Qeuheg's bronzed brow deepened. He seldom looked away from one to whom he spoke, but this time his eyes were drawn to the dancing flames.

"I need to know the truth, uncle."

Queheg sighed. "I know it is because of the White Fox that your friend helped you, to escape, that the White Fox wanted vengeance I did not see it with my eyes what happened between his father and yours, but I believe it is true that Abel took the life of the older St. Vrain, yes."

"Was my mother at Cutter's Reach when this happened?"

Queheg was silent a moment, delving deeply into the past, then nodded.

Joshua thought about this information for a long moment. "Could it be that my father sent us away to protect us? That he feared retribution for the death of St. Vrain? If my French friend is correct, and I have no reason to think he is not, then the White Fox seeks vengeance to this day. Do you know that I never went before the magistrate? It was possible that I would have been sent to prison for who knows how long, or perhaps even executed, if St. Vrain could have used his influence to make it so. He must know by now that I have escaped his vengeance. What do you think he will do now?" He sighed. "A man such as that has a long reach. Perhaps I should not go home. Perhaps to do so would put the Wolf Clan at risk. Perhaps death walks in my footsteps. What would the sachem do if I brought death to Onroka?"

For once Queheg was no longer smiling. "Hear me well, Womash. You belong with the Wolf Clan. We are your people. We are your family. We will stand with you no matter what comes."

Joshua nodded, forced a smile, and then lay down in his blanket, his back to the fire—and to Queheg, so that his uncle could not see that his eyes remained open, and that he was far from being able to sleep. He could not help but fear that every step he took that brought him closer to Onroka put his mother, Genessee, and all his clanmates at greater risk. And he could not help but resent the father he could scarcely remember. If Menard was right, Abel Cutter had killed a man for furs, and in so doing had put his son, and all his son held dear, in danger.

It was pitch black when Joshua woke with a start, sitting up sharply as he realized someone was looming over him. He could barely make out Queheg in the deep shadow of the tree-sheltered hollow. His uncle's hand rested on his shoulder. He saw Queheg put a finger to his lips and then point to the south before making a walking sign with his fore and middle fingers. Joshua glanced at the firepit, from which smoke billowed and assumed Queheg had just doused the embers with water from his resin-coated water pouch.

Sitting up, Joshua looked in the direction his uncle was pointing, then up through the tree canopy to see that the night sky was a deep violet-blue. Dawn was coming. He sat quite still a moment, listening, but heard little in the pre-dawn quiet save for the soughing of a breeze in the tree canopy and the distant trickle of water in a rocky run which he knew to be a stone's throw to the east of their camp. But he didn't doubt that Queheg had heard more than that. Despite the fact that he had spent most of his years learning woodcraft, he was not as attuned to the forest as was the old Tuscarora. And he knew what Queheg was telling him. He held up a forefinger and Queheg shook his head.

More than one person was moving in their direction through the woodlands from the south.

Queheg pointed at him, and then at himself, and then to the north, indicating that they needed to move rather than wait in place. Joshua didn't question this advice. He rose, draped a trade pack onto his shoulder, slung one of the Charleville muskets over his other shoulder, then gathered up his long rifle, shot pouch, and powderhorn. Queheg had already done these things and in seconds they were on the move, with Joshua letting his uncle take the lead.

He was quite familiar with the way Queheg moved in the forest, zigging and zagging in order to avoid limbs, vines and dead wood that might make a sound to betray his passage, and Joshua was skilled in doing likewise. Despite not moving in a straight line they made good time. Now and then Queheg would signal a stop, and they would crouch down and breath tidally, straining their ears to hear the slightest of sounds.

In this way they traveled a couple of miles. By then the sun was rising. The first birds were chirping, accompanied by the staccato pecking of a woodpecker. When next they stopped they listened for a few more minutes and then Queheg pointed east, before again leading the way. A few hundred yards further on, Joshua heard the gurgling of a stream over rocks, and moments later they arrived at a small run tumbling down a slight decline. It was narrow enough that one could jump over it with a running start, but instead Queheg began walking in the stream, heading not north by northeast, which was the general direction of Onroka, but rather south by southwest. A quarter of a mile along, he turned west into deep woods. About five hundred yards from the run the woods thinned around a mound of earth on top of which younger growth formed a thicket of sorts. It was there that Queheg stopped and dropped his pack.

"They are too quiet for white men," he told Joshua, keeping his voice to a whisper, "and since they are not white men they will not stop until they find us."

Joshua nodded, shedding his trade pack. It was for this reason that his uncle had found a place to make a stand rather than to continue northward. And, too, he understood why his uncle had walked in the stream. The Indians following them would more than likely split up, some going north by northeast, the rest south by southwest, scanning the riverbanks for sign of where their prey left the water. He harbored no hope that, as careful as they had been, the warriors who were on their trail would lose their sign. And there was very little doubt in his mind that Philip St. Vrain had something to do with the peril that was now visited upon them.

They didn't have long to wait. The cry of a warbler broke the serene quiet of the early morning, a sound that was loud in Joshua's ears—loud enough so that the Indians who had ventured north along the stream looking for their sign would hear it in the hush of a woodland morning and turn around to retrace their steps.

Joshua crawled ten feet away from his uncle, taking not only his long rifle but the Charlesville musket as well. His long rifle used a .54 caliber round or minie ball. The Charleville was a .69 caliber, but it would shoot a smaller-bored round ball and could still be fairly effective at close range. He focused on loading the latter, even though his heart was pounding in his chest, all the while trying to slow his pulse with long deep breaths.

Once this was done he took a slow and thorough look in every direction. It seemed to him that this area had been cleared long ago—there were no old-growth trees within twenty yards in either direction. He wondered if the high ground upon which Queheg had decided they would make their stand was an old burial mound, and as the morning light strengthened he thought he saw another brush-filled clearing fifty or so yards further east—perhaps the location of another mound. It seemed likely that once upon a time a tribe had lived near here. He wondered what had happened to them, as there was little doubt they were long gone, else the burial mounds would not be overgrown with saplings and brush. Perhaps they had been driven off by another tribe. Or maybe a catastrophic disease had struck. His Indian upbringing had him thinking that maybe the land was cursed, or haunted. One thing was pretty certain now—that there would be more death here, more spirits to haunt the land, before too much longer.

In that very moment he saw them, and knew them instantly as Hurons, otherwise known as Wyandots. That name came from the old Algonquin word for "serpent"— *wendot*. The French preferred to call them the Huron, or "savage-haired", as the warriors wore their hair long, swept back from the forehead and hanging thick and coarse to the shoulders. The warlike tribe had a long history of friendship with the French; they had fought together in a savage, sixty-year conflict known as the Beaver Wars, out of which the tribe had become the most feared west of the great lakes. They were excellent traders and roamed far and wide, thanks in part to their expertise with the birchbark canoe and their fearless disregard for the territory and furs that other, lesser tribes laid claim to.

The three that suddenly appeared, silent as ghosts, from the forest to the east wore leggings and breechclouts. Two of them wore darkened, beaded buckskin shirts. The third was bare-chested. They were painted for war.

Joshua glanced at Queheg, who pointed fore and middle finger at his own eyes and then held the forefinger up and made a circular motion. Joshua nodded and took a slow, careful look around the brush-covered clearing. Queheg thought that there were more than three Hurons, and so did he. But he saw no sign of any others. When he glanced at Queheg again, his uncle pointed forked fore and middle fingers at the three moving slowly, quietly, through the brush toward the burial mound. Again Joshua nodded. His long rifle was already loaded. He poured gunpowder into the pan and pressed it down lightly with his thumb. He was somewhat surprised at the calmness that overcame him. He had killed his first man just days ago in Montreal. Now he was prepared to kill again. Only these would not be running away.

Out of the corner of his eye he saw Queheg, pressing the stock of his rifle snugly to his shoulder to take aim at the Huron on the right. Joshua eased the long barrel of his rifle slowly through the brush and sighted on the brave to the left, at a distance of about sixty yards. It would be like shooting fish in a barrel. He couldn't believe it would be this easy.

And it wasn't. Suddenly the one in the middle, the shirtless one, made a curt gesture and threw himself to the ground. The other two followed suit. Suddenly they had disappeared into the brush. Once again Joshua glanced at his uncle. He was surprised, but if Queheg was, he didn't show it. Lowering his rifle, Qeuheg began to crawl backward. An instant later a bloodcurdling war cry rang out. Joshua thought it came from the spot where the shirtless Huron concealed himself in the tall grass. The cry was answered a heartbeat later by more cries for blood coming from the other direction. Joshua was about to rise and turn when Queheg motioned for him to stay down, while he himself turned and crawled through the reeds to see how many were coming from the west. More cries rendered the quiet of the forest, coming from in front of Joshua. He saw all three of the warriors rising up from the brush and firing almost as one. He heard the shots ripping through the brush, one of them very close to his head, but didn't flinch, at least not much. Drawing a bead on the left-most Huron he squeezed the trigger. The warrior was thrown backward, sprawling into the brush again. Joshua was fairly certain he had hit his mark, dead-center.

Rolling over on his side, tilting the long rifle's barrel up a bit, he poured gunpowder down the barrel, then pulled a ball from his pouch, covered it with a cloth patch and used the rod to ram it home. The clearing was suddenly ringing with gunfire and savage cries for blood. The Huronss were swift as deer. He had just primed the long rifle when the shirtless warrior came crashing through the reeds right at him, his face twisted into a rictus of bloodlust, rifle in his left hand and a tomahawk in his right, the tomahawk sweeping downward. Joshua didn't have time to fire. He rolled away, the tomahawk's sharpened edge slicing through the sleeve of his jerkin, a lancing pain shooting through him as it ripped open his skin. He kept rolling, coming up on one knee, throwing the long rifle up to block the next mighty blow, which nearly knocked the weapon from his grasp. The forward impetus of his Huron assailant pushed against him and he let it, rolling onto his back, bringing his right foot up into the warrior's midsection, knee bent, and then straightening the leg as his foe's impetus carried him forward. In so doing. Joshua lifted the brave off his feet and threw him head over heels and behind him.

As soon as the weight of the warrior's body was off his leg he rolled to the right, planting one knee to the ground and bringing the long rifle to bear, hoping that after the blow it had taken it would still shoot true. He brought stock to shoulder and squeezed the trigger. The Huron was scrambling to his feet with the lithe and deadly grace of a lion. To Joshua's great relief, the long rifle spoke, spouting flame through a puff of smoke. The ball struck the warrior squarely in the chest, knocking him off his feet. He was dead before he sprawled on his back, the tomahawk, its edge red with Joshua's blood, spinning off into the brush.

Joshua threw a look over his shoulder, in time to see the third Huron who had come toward the mound from the east launching himself at Queheg, who was proceeding to reload his rifle when he heard his enemy's approach and began to turn. Joshua drew his hunting knife and threw it with unerring accuracy. In that instant he was grateful for the countless times he and the other boys in the Wolf Clan had practiced throwing their knives at targets painted onto logs or tree trunks. His target was moving fast from left to right and in a crouch but Joshua hit his mark nonetheless. The razor-sharp, twelve-inch knife blade buried itself in the warrior's neck up to half its length, and the warrior was dying before his limp body hurtled into Queheg. The corpse struck Joshua's uncle with such force that it knocked him backward and he rolled down the far slope of the mound, while the Huron lay face-down, writhing in his death throes.

The bloodcurdling cries of the Hurons had Joshua thinking there were at least three more. He dropped to one knee and reloaded his long rifle, faster than he had ever done before, prompted more than anything by concern for his uncle. The warriors were coming up the very slope that Queheg had been thrown down. One of these appeared right in front of Joshua as the latter was tamping down ball and patch. Still on one knee, he left the ramrod in the barrel, primed the rifle and fired it from the hip with his target only a few feet away. The impact of the .54 caliber ball threw the Huron backward, his chest pierced by the ramrod as well as the ball itself. Before he hit the ground, Joshua was on his feet. Wrenching the ramrod out of his victim's corpse, he began running down the slope after Queheg, the thick brush whipping and tugging at him.

To his left, and halfway up the slope was one warrior. The other was closer, and to his right. The latter had just finished reloading and, seeing Joshua, half-turned, bringing his musket to bear. Faster than thought, Joshua hurled himself to the ground. As he did so Queheg came surging up the slope and out of the brush, tomahawk raised, throwing himself at the Huron with a hoarse cry that made even Joshua' blood run cold in his veins. The Huron was startled, and for a fateful instant took his eye off Joshua. Then Queheg's body slammed into his and they went rolling down the slope, in a tangle of arms and legs.

Joshua's first impulse was to make sure his uncle was all right, but there was at least one other Huron foe still standing. Before even looking around in an attempt to locate the brave's position, he rolled out of his kneeling position, a move that delivered him to the dying brave with Joshua's blade in his neck. He heard the loud and deadly click of a hammer being pulled back. The warrior still standing had emerged from the brush with his musket to shoulder, tracking Joshua' movement. Joshua threw himself to the ground, grabbing the dying brave and pulling him up onto his side as a shield with his left hand. Even while he was dying the brave flailed against Joshua whose free hand closed around the handle of his hunting knife. He yanked the blade out of the Huron's neck and then plunged it with all his might into the man's heart, turning the knife so that the blade passed between the ribs. He stabbed again, and once more, until he felt the other's life leave his body. Then he dared raise his head, aware that the last Huron had not yet fired his rifle.

But that brave had vanished.

In that moment the Huron human shield breathed his last desperate breath. Joshua pushed the corpse away and managed to get to his feet and turned to confront Queheg, who was passing through the reeds and into view again after his second tumble down the western slope of the burial mound. The Tuscarora's shirt was knife-torn and blood-stained. Alarmed, Joshua reached for him, but Queheg dropped to his knees after latching onto Joshua to pull him down as well.

Joshua held up one finger and then pointed in the direction of the Huron who had been a hair away from shooting him. His uncle shook his head and held up two fingers, then extended his arm while his hand seemed to move twice over invisible swells, informing Joshua that there were two remaining foes—and they were moving away. Having never known Queheg to be wrong, Joshua began to relax. In the process, his hands began to shake, and when he looked at them, he saw the blood on one of them. At that exact moment he felt the throbbing pain shooting down his injured arm. The fear he had forgotten, that had been submerged beneath a rush of pure primeval survival, was taking its turn and had him marveling at the incredible fact that he and his uncle had survived against so many Huron warriors. He couldn't even begin to decide if it had been courage, skill, luck or fate.

Queheg acted swiftly. He took a trade shirt out of one of the packs, cut it into strips with his blade, and applied a tight dressing on Joshua's wound. For once, that familiar half-smile of his was nowhere to be seen. Grimly, he loaded his rifle and then Joshua's, after which he moved among the dead and took scalps. He didn't bother asking Joshua if he wanted to participate, knowing that the answer would be no.

"I know one of them," he told Joshua. "You killed Charloe. The Hurons are bad. He was one of the worst. You killed him. It will bring great honor. Our people will sing your praises."

Joshua just shook his head, trying to deal with the pain throbbing through him. In his opinion, killing the notorious Huron had been necessary, not praiseworthy.

The bloody topknots tied to his belt, Queheg picked up both packs and with a grunt informed his nephew that it was time to move on, pointing northward with his chin. Joshua opened his mouth to object to his uncle carrying all the trade goods, to say that he was capable of taking one, but Queheg looked at him with a curt shake of his head, pointing to the Charlesville muskets instead. Joshua slung them over his shoulder, took his long rifle in hand, and followed his uncle off the burial mound, aware that when they made night camp he would be subjected to fresh agony, for only then would Queheg use gunpowder and a fire-heated knife blade to cauterize his wound.

Now and again they would stop, hunker down, and listen. When they were on the move. Joshua continually checked their backtrail. His mind was racing. Who or what was behind the Huron attack? Had the Indians seen them leaving Montreal, laden with trade goods, and followed? Or had someone sent them. Someone named St. Vrain.

CHAPTER 12

O nroka had been the home of the Tuscaroras for centuries, dating back to the days when the Six Nations had been tribes who were not allied together. In fact, they had long warred one against another, so severely that the tribes built strong palisades around their villages. The first white men to see these fortifications called them "castles." Many Tuscaroras migrated south to the Carolinas for the express purpose of escaping the conflict among the tribes in the region, but many of the Wolf Clan remained. This had been before the white colonists arrived in the Carolinas. When they did, trouble broke out, and the southern Tuscaroras waged war against these trespassers. Outnumbered, they could not win. Eventually the colonials organized, beat them back, and eventually went on the offensive. Their towns raided, their women and children dragged off into slavery or worse, some of the Tuscaroras, led by Tom Blount, made peace. Others headed north again, back to their traditional homeland, as by then the tribes of the Iroquois had made peace among themselves.

Joshua had never been happier to be home. Ever since the Huron attack at the burial grounds he had been on edge, expecting more to come for him and his uncle. The journey back had seemed to take a lifetime, when in fact, less than a fortnight had passed.

The gates swung open as they drew near and they were greeted like returning heroes, mobbed by children and adults, males and females alike. Even the camp dogs were excited to see them, a cacophony of barking and howling overlaying the very animated chatter of the people, the women asking what they had brought back from their trading of pelts, the men asking what they had seen and what talk they had overheard.

Joshua searched the sea of faces for the two people he longed so much to see—his mother and Genessee. He spotted Anuwashi first, and threw his arms around his mother as though he had been denied her company for a year rather than just a month. Since his departure from Onroku there had been times when he feared he would never lay eyes on her again.

Anuwashi was in her mid-forties but she had the supple and slender figure of one half of her age. Though there were lines now around her eyes and mouth she was still quite pretty. As it was late spring and the days were warm, she, like nearly all the others in the village, male or female, young or old, wore very little, in her case, on this day, a beaded ankle-length deerskin skirt and moccasins adorned with little bells that chimed softly when she walked. There was a necklace made of polished and painted stone and shell in various shapes and sizes, from which depended an arrow-head-shaped stone adorned with colored glass and beads in the design of an orb that was half white and half black, representing the sun and the moon joined as one. As far back as he could remember, Joshua had almost never seen his mother without that pendant that now rested between her bare and still firm breasts.

Joshua reluctantly left his mother's embrace and turned to help Queheg with the trade goods. Some of Onruka's citizens had given them pelts to trade for specific things, and now it was time to distribute those trade goods. But Queheg leaned close and murmured to Joshua beneath the excited voices of the crowd that had gathered.

"I will do this. Go tell your mother what happened. She should hear it from you."

Joshua nodded and returned to Anuwashi, who took him by the hand and led him out of the press of people. When they were far enough away that they could speak normally above the excited hubbub, he took a deep breath and spoke.

"I have important news, mother."

"I assumed as much. Does it have anything to do with you wound?"

Joshua blinked in surprise, and shot a telltale glance at his arm. Both he and his uncle had agreed to conceal from their people that they had both been wounded, at least on the occasion of their homecoming. He had sewn the tear in his jerkin in the hope that his mother wouldn't notice but Queheg had decided he should wear one of the calico shirts acquired in trade. They did not want to alarm the tribe as a whole, or dampen Anuwashi's joy upon the return of her son.

"How did …?"

She smiled pensively. "I have been watching over you your entire life, Wonash. I know when you do not move as you usually do." She did not relinquish his hand, nor did she stop walking, until they had reached one of the entrances to the longhouse of their family. The interior was empty—all of its residents were at the gate. Anuwashi tugged once on his shirt and he removed it, moving gingerly when he had to use the injured arm. She studied the crude dressing that

Queheg had applied to the deep gash on Joshua's arm, then gently removed it.

"How is Genessee?" asked Joshua. "I did not see her at the gate."

Her fingers stilled. She looked at him. Then shook her head. "I do not know." Exposing the wound, she grimaced as she looked at the red and angry skin around the wound clotted with scabbing and pus. "You did not keep the wound clean. Come with me."

He followed her to her place in the longhouse, and she opened a large basket near her bedding and knelt to search its contents. "Who did that to you?" she asked.

Joshua took a deep breath and told her what had happened at the burial mounds. It was a straightforward telling, absent any embellishments. While he spoke, she found a small wooden bowl with a lid. The bowl contained a brownish-green paste, which she applied to his infected wound.

"They must have followed you from Montreal," she surmised, maintaining a stoic expression.

"Yes. And something else happened there."

As he told her of his shooting of the thief, of his time in prison, and of the details of his escape, her expression changed. And when he mentioned Phillip St. Vrain he even glimpsed the fear that glimmered in her eyes. He could not remember ever seeing his mother afraid.

"I had hoped that man was dead," she said, finally.

"My friend, Jean-Paul Menard, told me that St. Vrain's father quarreled with mine over trading with some Indians and that St. Vrain shot him and then my father killed him with a knife. He said that Philip St. Vrain might want revenge. But I have no proof that he sent the Hurons to kill me and Queheg."

Anuwasi returned the bowl to her basket, then wiped her hand on her skirt. She murmured, "What your friend told you, that is truth. I wasn't with your father at the time. You were only a few years old, and while I had enjoyed traveling with him when he searched for trade, after you were born he insisted I stay by your side. But I tended his wound when he made it home. He was badly injured. But your father is very hard to kill. Most people accept their fate when death comes for them, especially when to fight for life is the greatest agony. Not him." Another pensive smile touched her lips.

She continued. "In those days there were not many settlers at The Reach, and two years after the killing of the elder St. Vrain, our settlement was continually harassed by Hurons and *coureur des bois*. They had to travel far to attack The Reach, so it was assumed someone was behind it. Finally, one of the *coureur de bois* was captured. He was quite willing to tell your father the identity of the man behind those attacks. He even said that St. Vrain knew of you and wanted you dead. In fact, he desired that your father would *watch* you die, or at least *know* that you had died, before he breathed his last."

Joshua listened to the noise of the camp for a moment, disparate thoughts colliding in his head, then glanced at his mother. "Do you still love my father?'

"Sometimes I hated him. I hated him for not hunting St. Vrain down and killing him, even though I know why he didn't. St. Vrain inherited much from his father. The respect of the French. A great fortune. And the loyalty of the Hurons. Our lives were not the only ones at stake. Had St. Vrain died at your father's hand, all the people at The Reach would probably have perished as well."

"Revenge."

"Of course. We all indulge in it. I spent many years while you were growing up hoping to get word of St. Vrain's death. But it never came, and you grew up and my greatest hope of your father seeing you as a child went away."

"Did he marry you?"

Anuwasi smiled pensively. "He wanted to. But your grandfather would not hear of it, so we could not be joined in the Tuscarora fashion. And there was no preacher at The Reach while I was there, and none within a hundred miles or more."

Queheg appeared in the nearest door of the longhouse. "T told John Blount of our fight with the Hurons. He has called the council. We are to be there, to tell them everything that happened."

Joshua nodded. It had been their duty to at least inform their sachem of the ambush. He looked back to Anuwashi, to see that she had turned to the big stone ring in the center of the longhouse to stir up the embers half buried in the mounds of ash from the morning's fire.

"Do you not wish to come?" he asked her. Women were welcome in the tribal council meetings, where they could say their piece if they so desired.

"No," she said softly, and there was a rare melancholy lurking in her tone. Joshua assumed she was thinking about Abel Cutter. The tragedy of her holding onto the love for all these years, doing it for him, was like a punch in Joshua's gut. It took his breath away as for the first time he was confronted by the full scope of his mother's sacrifice.

"Come back to see me when the council meeting is over. I will have a good meal for the both of you. I think it has been a long time since you have had one."

Joshua's stomach suddenly ached worse than it had been for the past week of travel through the woods.

Following his uncle out of the longhouse and into the bright sunshine of a beautiful spring day, he whispered, "Have you seen Genessee?"

Queheg just shook his head and led the way with long strides to the big council house located in the center of the town.

When they returned to the longhouse a couple of hours later, Joshua looked relieved while his uncle appeared troubled. A few other members of the extended family entered, nodded and smiled at Queheg and Joshua, whom they had earlier welcomed home, then went to the other end of the longhouse out of respect for Anuwashi, and to give her time alone with her son and brother. Anuwashi served them roasted venison with beans, corn and squash grown in Onroka's gardens.

The two men ate as though they had not eaten in months. Anuwashi waited with infinite patience, sitting across the lodge fire from them, smiling warmly. Finally Queheg realized what she wanted. He wiped venison grease off his chin with the buckskin sleeve of his shirt.

"We did not bring happy news," he told her. "John Blount in particular was very unhappy. He knows war is coming, but he doesn't want it."

"Of course not," she replied, and it was clear that she was very proud of her cousin, their sachem. "He had his fill of war in the Carolinas. He saw too many of his family die. He was hardly more than a boy then. But he was a Blount. That is why many listened to the advice that he and others gave—to return to our homeland. And no one and nothing was going to stop him not even his uncle, Chief Tom."

Queheg nodded. "He says he will send word to the Onondaga that there must be a meeting of the chiefs of all six nations. Whether the Indians we fought had anything to do with the French, if the Hurons are raiding on this side of the lakes, then all the tribes must be ready for a war with them. He wants me and Wonash to go with him."

Joshua couldn't stop thinking about Genessee—and, now, to worry about her. He realized he had not seen any member of her family either. He wasn't paying attention to his uncle's narrative, until Queheg spoke his name.

He knew the history of the Confederation as well as anyone in Onroka. It was said that hundreds of years ago a being descended from the sky and spoke to the Onandaga chief, Ayenwathaa, also known as Hiawatha, telling him the Iroquoian tribes had to stop fighting one another and form themselves in a league. Hiawatha had been the husband of a beautiful wife and father of several daughters, all of whom were slain in a conflict with another tribe. Instead of seeking vengeance in his grief, Hiawatha traveled the length and breadth of the northern woods, explaining the idea of a league to various tribes that lived along the Mohawk River, and persuading them that their survival depended on living together in peace. He spoke of visions of a wars that stretched far and wide, provoked by white men who spoke two different languages. If one tribe in the league was attacked, the rest would be obligated to rise up against the attacker, and soon peace would reign, as no one would want to fight all the Iroquois tribes at the same time.

Hiawatha had been accompanied a prophet named the Dekanawidah, a highly respected spiritual leader who suffered from a speech impediment. On the other hand, Hiawatha was a great orator. He was so persuasive and persistent, beating down the resistance to change by the tribes who had for generations been so fiercely independent—and sometimes mortal enemies. Soon the five tribes gave in and formed the government according to the advice of Hiawatha and the prophet. Later, the Tuscarora were accepted into the league, which then became known as the Six Nations. The Senecas and Cayogas were the guardians of the west. The Mohawks and Oneidas were responsible for protecting the eastern range of the Confederacy. In the center, the Onondagas were the keepers of the council fires and their town was the seat of confederation government.

Now Joshua and his uncle had to travel there so that all the council members could vote on war or peace.

Except he didn't want to go.

Anuwashi listened intently to her brother's words, then spoke. "You go, Queheg. I need Wonash to find his father."

Queheg was surprised. He looked at her, then at Joshua, his features inscrutable. It was impossible to know whether he approved of her decision or not. When it came to her offspring, though, whatever she wanted would stand. Not even the sachem would challenge her. When it came to family matters, the wishes of the female elders were almost always accepted as law.

Rising, Queheg nodded and grabbed a venison drumstick and left Joshua with his mother, drawn out of the longhouse by the sound of drums and laughter. An impromptu celebration had broken out to celebrate the arrival of sought-after trade goods and, of course, the safe return of two of their own.

Once her brother was gone, Amuwashi glanced over her shoulder at the kin at the other end of the longhouse, leaning forward to speak to her son in solemn muted tones.

"My son, Genessee is gone."

"Gone?" Joshua was pale. "You mean..."

"No. She lives. But she has left Onroka, with her family, which as you know has very old and very strong ties with the Oneida."

"So she will be back soon," said Joshua, feeling a rush of relief. He had begun to fear that something bad had happened to Genessee and that no one had the heart to tell him. He was aware of the situation with the Oneida; Genessee and her family had occasionally gone to see their relatives, staying a few weeks or longer.

Anuwashi sighed and shook her head. "No. Word is she will marry the son of the Oneida sachem. I cannot be sure if she will even return before that happens."

Joshua was stunned. He stared at his mother in disbelief, then began shaking his head. It had to be that someone was misinformed. "No. No that can't be right. She loves me. She told me so, many times!" He opened his mouth to continue, then read the stricken expression on Anuwashi's face. "What is it, mother? What are you not telling me?"

"You are right, Wonash. She *does* love you. I could see it in her eyes, hear it in her voice. I know that measure of love. It was her father that stood in the way of you being with her. Her father was frightened by the depth of his daughter's love for you. That is why he took her away."

He was puzzled. "But... but what's wrong with me?"

She smiled pensively and took his hand in both of hers. Having never lied to him, she wasn't going to start now. "You are not full blood."

He stared at her, slack-jawed, as it took a moment for him to comprehend what she was telling him. It wasn't hard to believe that Genessee's father could be prejudiced against him. In years past, especially during his youth, others in the tribe had been. But he thought he had earned their trust, had done everything he could possibly do to earn it. So he was at a loss what else could have been done to exorcise the curse of the white man's blood in his veins.

Anuwashi seemed to know what he was thinking, and squeezed his hand. "Some things—and some people—you cannot change. It isn't fair to you or to her. My son, be aware, you may try to blame her, or even hate her. But you will always love her. Take solace in knowing that her love for you will never fade, either."

He drew a ragged breath into his aching lungs but that did nothing for the anguish in his heart. Through a tremendous effort of pure will he pulled himself together. "Why do you want me to go to The Reach," he said woodenly. "Is there a message you would have me carry to my father?"

She smiled softly. "You are my message." She embraced him tightly, and Joshua felt her slender body quivering as powerful emotions rushed through her. Finally she had composed herself sufficiently to break the fierce embrace and hold him at arm's length for a moment. "Both of you stay alive. I could not bear to lose either one of you."

He looked at her a moment, taken aback by a clear vision of what lay in store for him. His mother had not seen Abel Cutter for nearly twenty years, had almost never spoken of him during that time, and yet she was still in love with him. This, then, would also be his fate, where it came to Genessee. A lifetime of longing, the torment of being forever apart from the person he was meant to be with. He wondered how Anuwashi had endured her ordeal, but decided it wouldn't be fair to ask her. He would have to find his own way. So he remained silent and merely hugged her tightly, hoping to comfort her.

She luxuriated in her son's arms a few moments, then gently but firmly extricated herself and pushed him away. "I will give you some food and ..."

"No, mother. I can take care of that along the way. I will leave now." He realized that he was teetering on the brink of a deep pool of emotion and quickly gathered up his belongings, then hurried out of the longhouse, hoping that his mother understood why he had to go so abruptly.

He looked back only once, as he was passing out of the Tuscarora castle's main gate. His mother waved at him from the longhouse. He waved back then began loping toward the nearby woods. It was fortunate that he knew this ground like the back of his hand, because he could no longer keep hot tears from blinding him.

PART THREE

Spring 1754

CHAPTER 13

"**O**h, dear God! I can't breathe!" panted Bella Cutter, wincing as Mrs. Mollett tugged even harder on the laces of the whalebone stay, with such vigor in fact that Bella staggered, pulled off-balance.

"Pfft! Ye should have been introduced to stays as a young lass," opined the housekeeper. "Now be still! Plant your feet and keep hold of that bedpost!"

Bella tried to take a deep breath and couldn't, which only contributed to a rising panic as she began to think she might actually pass out. "I'm trying!" she groaned petulantly, knuckles whitening as her slender fingers closed tighter still round the curved and polished mahogany of the bedpost she had been clinging to since the torture had commenced.

"Try harder, girl. You want to have the tiniest waist of all the ladies at the ball, don't ye?" Mrs. Mollett was a short and elderly woman with pale skin that looked like old parchment and gray hair pulled back in a severe bun. But she had surprising strength in a body that at first glance looked rather frail. And Bella had long suspected that the housekeeper also had a sadistic streak—and that it was on full display now. She felt sure that Mrs. Mollett was grinning maliciously behind that stern and stoic mask she wore.

When she had the stay laced to her satisfaction, Mrs. Mollett brandished a strip of notched brown paper and put it around Bella's waist. "Hmm. Seventeen inches." She nodded approvingly. Still clinging to the bedpost for dear life, as now she was fairly sure that she *would* pass out, Bella would have breathed a sigh of relief that the torture was over—had she been able to breathe. "Your waist 'twas nineteen inches, girl."

Bella rolled her eyes—but only after Mrs. Mollett had turned away, putting the measuring paper on the bed and picking up the panier. "Two inches was not worth the ordeal. There is nothing wrong with my figure. I am not fat!"

"True enough," begrudged Mrs. Mollet. "In fact, ye're on the skinny side, if you ask me. A bit taller than most young ladies, too. All the more reason for a tight corset."

The housekeeper bent over and held the pannier as Bella relinquished her grip on the bedpost to turn and place a hand on the older woman's bony shoulder before stepping into the basket hoop. She already wore a cotton chemise, and had put her shoes on, along with stockings and silk ribbon garters. As Mrs. Mollett tied the pannier to her now-seventeen-inch waist, Bella sighed. Tall and skinny. The housekeeper was as dour and stern as a Scot could be, and in that moment Bella felt quite sure that if she had ever had anything nice to say about anyone she had most likely managed to refrain from doing so.

Once the pannier had been lashed around her, three petticoats were pulled on over her head. Finally came the French gown with its ruffled bodice and sleeves, fashioned from cream-colored velvet trimmed with white lace and scarlet embroidery, secured around Bella's waspish waist and flaring out over the hoops of the pannier beneath layers of petticoats. Mrs. Mollett stood back with arms folded and grimly surveyed the finished product.

"How do I look?" asked Bella as she turned to face her torturer. A mirror stood in the corner, so she could have seen for herself, but she wanted to coerce a compliment from the housekeeper.

"Well, all I can say is that it's about time ye looked like a proper young lady," said Mrs. Mollett. "If ye ask me, your aunt is far too lenient with ye. She ought to have made ye attend a ball last year, if not the year before. Next year ye be twenty years of age, and ye should be betrothed by now, if not wed. Ye don't wish to live out your life as an old maid, do ye?"

"You are a mean old witch, I hope you know," said Bella tartly, and went over to the mirror, turning this way and that as she gave her attire a critical eye. The gown's 'jacket' was designed to make her upper torso appear like a V, while the pannier spanned almost five feet at the hips, giving her an hourglass shape. The cut of the jacket and the stay had pushed her pert young breasts into prominence thanks to the scooped neck of the gown. She had but two dresses that she wore regularly, both quite plain, one of linen for the summer, the other wool for the winter. Her Aunt Martha had bought her some fancier attire, but Bella refused to wear them as they required at least some of the torture devices Mrs. Mollett liked to put on her.

Growing up as a girl on the frontier she had never imagined she would ever be dressed like this. In fact, it had been difficult to keep her in clothes. Her father had called her a free spirit—an excuse, she supposed, to explain her running around The Reach bare-ass naked or nearly so. As she grew into a precocious child, she had loved to spend time in the fields and the forest, learning all she could about the flora and fauna, and inevitably getting dirty to warrant a daily bath. Hating baths, she had learned to swim so she would be allowed to wash herself in the shallows of the Allegheny.

Mrs. Mollett was not offended by the comment, which perturbed Bella. The old witch would not even give her the pleasure of being mildly annoyed.

"Someone beneath this roof needs to be. Now mark me words, girl. There will be young ladies of high standing at the regimental ball. Observe them closely. Emulate them the best ye can. Do *not* sit down under any circumstances! If ye must eat, eat like a bird, not like a hog. Never participate in discussions of politics or business. That is man talk. And for heaven's sake don't look too long into a man's eyes like some brazen hussy!"

"Yes, yes," said Bella absently. She was busy studying herself in the mirror with a critical eye. Seeing herself in a ball gown for the first time made her feel out of place. It was certainly a beautiful gown, and for once she was grateful to Aunt Martha for buying it. She could hardly have afforded such a splendid garment on a school mistress's salary. Her long, lustrous red hair was tied up in a braided bun, which highlighted a face that, with its high cheekbones and rather long nose and somewhat squared jaw, was average at best. She was quite sure that there would be many far more beautiful women than she at the ball. Her eyes were her saving grace, big cornflower-blue eyes under thick arching brows.

Then there was her figure. In her eyes she was too tall and too gangly and even the torture of the stay could not give her an appealing shape. She considered her shoulders to be too wide, her breasts too small, and her feet too large. Not for the first time she marveled at her good fortune to have Lieutenant Jeremy Hull of the 45th Regiment of Foot persist in inviting her to the ball. Yes, there had been a few city gentlemen who had expressed an interest, and one or two more officers of the 45th, which had been stationed in Philadelphia for going on two years. But it had been clear to her that all of them were most interested in getting her in their beds, perhaps thinking she would be an easy mark, so desperate for attention that she would gladly spread her legs for them, as was true of a good many young ladies in the city, attracted to the thrill of being desired by a scarlet-uniformed soldier.

Bella couldn't deny that she had considered accepting an offer a time or two. As Mrs. Mollett had so cruelly pointed out, she was on the verge of her twentieth year—and still a virgin. Many thought her a very industrious and devoted teacher, quite prim and proper, but the truth was that she threw herself into her work to keep errant thoughts from distracting—and depressing—her. At night, though, she often couldn't ignore her almost desperate desire to be touched in that special way by a man, and sometimes she touched herself.

Jeremy Hull seemed cut from a different cloth than her handful of other suitors. He was a perfect gentleman. He looked at her in a different way from the others. She allowed herself to believe that he was very fond of her for reasons that went beyond sex. He was charming, and one of the most handsome men she had ever seen. In addition, he came from a well-to-do family. For all those reasons he obviously could have had any woman in Philadelphia for the asking. But he seemed to have eyes only for her. Bella couldn't quite comprehend why this was so, but she wasn't about to look a gift horse in the mouth.

"Well, girl, we've done all we can," sighed Mrs. Mollett, a statement which further pricked Bella's self-confidence. The dyspeptic housekeeper was never effusive in her praise even when it was warranted.

"Don't you mean you can't put a bonnet on a sow and call it a princess?" asked Bella, with a fierce petulance.

For once, Mrs. Mollett appeared shaken. Her stern visage softened. She opened her mouth to say something, but couldn't seem to find the right words. With a little shake of her head, she turned to the door of Bella's bedroom and held it open.

"Go on down now and see what yer aunt has to say. I daresay she has been more excited about this day than ye seem to be."

Bella gave a little shrug, trying to conceal her satisfaction. It seemed she had effectively concealed her enthusiasm for attending the ball, which was so high that it had kept her awake the past two nights. She was halfway across the threshold when she stopped, turned, and smiled softly. "Thank you." This time she was sincere, feeling rather guilty for the her attitude, even though the housekeeper deserved it.

She carefully made her way down the mahogany staircase in the central hall of the Gallatin House, which had stood for more than a quarter of a century at 620 Chestnut Street. As she neared the bottom, Mrs. Mollett in tow, the front door opened and the valet, Loney, entered the home, having lighted the exterior lamps that flanked the entrance to repel the gathering gloom of day's end. In that same moment a tall case clock made by the famous German clockmaker Christopher Sauer, began to melodiously chime the hour. It was six o' clock. Bella's heart was already racing, but now picked up the pace.

Loney, a tall and lanky black man with graying hair, looked up and smiled broadly. His awed expression, which Bella found rather flattering, was that of someone who had just laid eyes on a beautiful work of art.

"Why, Miss Bella, I thought you was an angel come down from heaven!"

Martha Gallatin emerged from the dining room with a rustle of silk petticoats, smiling brighter than any lamp could as she gazed at Bella and exclaimed, "Oh but she *is* an angel, Loney. Yes she is! Our angel." She hurried across to Bella, holding out her hands. Bella took them. "I hope this beau of yours knows how very fortunate he is. You are radiant, my dear, simply radiant." Martha glanced past Bella at Mrs. Mollett. "Don't you think so, Annie?"

It was clear to Bella that her Aunt Martha was having some fun at Mrs. Mollet's expense, putting the housekeeper on the spot.

"She looks better than she ever has, ma'am."

Aunt Martha gave her a scolding but affectionate look. Bella laughed, knowing how faint was the praise that passed the crabby Mrs. Mollett's lips.

"All thanks to you, Aunt Martha," she said in her soft and self-effacing manner.

Martha was a short, plump, gray-haired lady with a pretty oval face and gentle, doe-like eyes. She squeezed Bella's hands. "It was nothing, my dear child. You deserve only the very best. I just wish you had been raised in a more... civilized place than The Reach. I am grateful that your father saw fit to send you here to me after the death of your mother, God rest her soul." She sighed, struck by a sudden melancholy, but then shook her head and fiercely banished those morbid memories. "But you're here now, finally, and I am blessed with this opportunity to spoil you as you deserve to be spoiled." Then she clapped her hands to her cheeks and exclaimed, Oh! I very nearly forgot!"

Turning, she opened the drawer of a nearby side table and took a small leather-bound book from it. This she presented to Bella. Inside the book was a pencil, powdered graphite and clay bound in a wooden cylinder.

"Your ball book, my dear. Every lady who attends a ball simply must have one! In it you write the names of all the gentlemen who wish to dance with you. If you don't then you might promise the same dance to two men, and that is simply *not* good form!"

"You mean I have to dance with others besides Jeremy?" asked Bella.

"Well, no, you don't *have* to, dear." Martha chuckled softly. "In fact you cannot dance with any man to whom you have not been formally introduced. But, if you want to, you may." She leaned closer and melodramatically whispered like a conspirator. "And it doesn't usually hurt to make your beau a little jealous. In truth, you may find out just how much he cares for you."

"I am surprised that Abel Cutter let her come to Philadelphia," said Mrs. Mollett. "At least now, thanks to ye, mum, she has become a civilized young lady. When first she came, she was little more than a savage. She could shoot a gun, and knew an Iroquois from a Shawnee, but I remember that we had to teach her how to curtsey."

Bella glanced around at the housekeeper with eyes like daggers. "Iroquois is not a tribe, it's a language. I love my father and I will thank you not to denigrate him in my presence."

Mrs. Mollett was a bit taken aback. Martha smiled faintly. "She has that Cutter temper, doesn't she," she said, then quickly changed the subject. "You have caught the eye of such a dashing young officer, Bella! He comes from a very good family, you know."

Bella nodded. She was not much interested in Jeremy Hull's lineage, but she knew that in the British army an officer's commission cost a goodly sum and that Jeremy's family had plenty of money. It also had a long and illustrious genealogy full of lords and ladies of circumstance and influence, prominent politicians and highly successful businessmen. Martha had gleaned all of this and more from Jeremy a month earlier, when he had accepted an invitation to supper, which everyone involved understood was a prerequisite for getting permission from the matriarch to court her niece. In addition, she had surveyed some of her contacts in the city and was then convinced that the lieutenant was a suitable company for her only living kin. For her part, having grown up in a frontier settlement where very few people had money, Bella had no particular desire to have much of it since she knew it was quite possible to live happily without it.

"Oh! I do hope that's your new beau now!" exclaimed Martha, tilting her head as she heard the rattle and rumble of carriage wheels on the cobblestones of Chestnut Street. "A gentleman is always on time, you know."

Bella decided not to mention that, at least in her opinion, she had never had a beau. The distinct sound of a four-in-hand stopping in front of the house made her heart lurch. Now more than ever she found it nearly impossible to catch her breath.

CHAPTER 14

"**I** believe he *is* here now, ma'am," said Loney as he parted the lace curtains on one of the sidelights that framed the front door and peered out. He was smiling broadly as he turned and approached Bella with a burgundy wool cloak taken from the wooden rack in the great hall, which he draped over Rachel's shoulders. Being without a family of his own—he had lost his true love to dysentery twenty years before, as well as the unborn child the young woman carried—he heaped the affectionate caring on Bella that he would have bestowed upon his own child. He was smiling as proudly as a father while he secured the cloak's clasp. All the while, Bella's Adam's apple bobbed as she tried to swallow the lump in her throat.

Martha took note of this and the expression on her niece's face and smiled warmly. "My dear child, I do wish your mother was here to see you at this moment. She would be so very proud of you, and so very happy for you."

Breathing high and fast, Bella glanced wide-eyed at Martha. Mention of her mother made her think of her father. She wondered what he was doing now, and also whether he would be proud, too. She knew that he loved her, so much so that he had sent her to Philadelphia to "become a proper lady"—but also to get her out of the blockhouse which had become a cheerless, grief-shadowed place after the death of her mother, Abigail. She had known then that the decision to send her away had been difficult for him, but he had done so as it had been her mother's dying request. In so doing he had consigned himself to a life of loneliness. The older brother she had never met had not returned to The Reach during her time there, and she had concluded that he never would and that she would never know him. The anguish that was obvious on Abel Cutter's face when they had parted company had made her cry—and still could when she dwelled too long on that day.

"I wish my father was here," she murmured, and then looked startled. She had been thinking aloud, and regretted doing so when she glimpsed the disapproving frown on her aunt's face as she turned to face the door. Aunt Martha had always resented her father for taking Abigail so far away. With her it was always how proud Bella's mother would have been—or on occasion how disappointed—about this, that or the other, but seldom mentioned Abel Cutter.

The banging of the front door's brass knocker made Bella jump. Loney opened the door and stood aside, inviting Lieutenant Jeremy Hull inside with a sweep of an arm. Jeremy nodded, smiled and thanked the valet—and then looked at Bella and froze in his tracks, slack-jawed and enraptured, gazing at her as though she was Aphrodite risen from the foam.

Bella was staring, too. Jeremy Hull was a strikingly handsome man. His thick mane of hair, black as a raven's wing, was brushed straight back, save for a thick and unruly curl dangling from a widow's peak. Long sideburns framed a high-boned, square-jawed face that she found handsome beyond compare. His dress uniform—the scarlet coat with the deep-green lining, cuffs and collar of the 45th Regiment, the unblemished white muslin shirt beneath a red waistcoat with gold buttons, the spotless white gloves and the white breeches, the tall and highly polished black leather boots—showed off his broad-shoulder, lean flanked physique to good effect.

Martha looked from one to the other of them as they stared speechlessly into each other's eyes, then advanced on Hull, extending her hand, "Lieutenant, so pleased to see you again."

Jeremy managed to look away from Bella long enough to remove his tricorn and flash a bright smile at Martha. He took her proffered hand with a gallant bow and brought it to his lips. "Lady Gallatin," he murmured, and then brandished a paper-wrapped bouquet of asters and black-eyed susans from behind his back. "I beg you to accept these as a small token of my great regard."

Martha made it seem as though she had never before received a bouquet so remarkable, and bade Mrs. Mollett to fetch the ivory Japanese vase, during which Jeremy glanced at Bella with a rakish smile that triggered a shameful stirring of heat in her loins. Once Martha took back her hand to pay adoring attention to every blossom in the bouquet, Jeremy turned to face Bella, who remembered belatedly to offer a hand, which the lieutenant brought to his lips. A little shiver waltzed up and down her spine.

"This evening I marvel at my great good fortune, Miss Cutter, to be the lucky man who will have the belle of the regimental ball on his arm," he said.

Bella was rendered speechless and chided herself mercilessly for being so socially inept. Jeremy rescued her from embarrassment by proffering a hooked arm. "Shall we, Miss Cutter? I confess I can't wait to see how green with envy my fellow officers become when they see me with you."

Cheeks burning, she placed her arm on top of his, her hand resting atop his hand, and her fingers curling between his, a small intimacy that Aunt Martha missed. She rose on tiptoe to give Bella a kiss on the cheek then turned to Jeremy.

"Have her home by ten o'clock, lieutenant, if you please."

"You may rely on me, ma'am." Jeremy click his heels together and bowed slightly at the waist.

At that instant Mrs. Mollet arrived with the vase and moved the lighted lamp on the marble-topped table to one side, making room for the import that only came out of storage on special occasions, as it was one of Martha's most valued possessions, a tall green Qianlong vase decorated with stylized images of fish and seahorses, brought to her by her husband on his return from Shanghai, where he had established trade contacts that resulted in the long-term, profitable result of his enterprises—and made Martha one of the most well-to-do ladies in the colony. Martha handed the bouquet to the housekeeper and began placing the flowers one by one in the vase, arranging them just so, while Mrs. Mollett stood by with a resigned expression on her wrinkled face, as she knew the Martha could take a quarter of an hour to get the flowers just as she liked them.

"Have a grand ol' time, Miss Bella," said Loney as he opened the door. He looked at her fingers laced into Jeremy's, then glanced up at her with a cocked brow and a crooked smile.

The coachman in his livery opened the carriage door as Bella and Jeremy approached the four-in-hand. It was a chilly, foggy and overcast night, and Bella prayed it wouldn't rain. She glimpsed a man using a long candle holder to light the street lamps that lined Chesnut Street. These lamps were a new feature to be found on the more important streets in the city, the invention of Philadelphia's own Benjamin Franklin.

Jeremy gave Bella a patient hand up as she managed, with some difficulty, to get in and sit down with the hooped skirt. He followed her in and sat down facing her. Once the coachman had closed the door and climbed up to his bench, the lieutenant picked up a nosegay of white and red roses that had been lying on the cushioned seat beside him, the thorns clipped from the stems that had been wrapped in ribbons and shaped so that it was easy for a young lady to hold.

"I hope you will accept these as a token of my affection, Miss Cutter."

Bella forgot all about the discomfort of having to sit with her spine straight as a ramrod—sitting back just made it almost impossible to breath, so tightly was she bound in all her finery. "They're beautiful!" she exclaimed with pure delight. "Where ever did you find such perfect flowers this time of year?"

"A florist on Chancery Lane. He has quite the greenhouse. White and red you know, are symbolic of the union in the Kingdom, the red of St. George for England, the white representing the white salture of St. Andrew for Scotland."

Bella smiled so broadly that her cheeks dimpled. She knew full well that the joining of two kingdoms a century and a half ago was not the union to which Jeremy was really thinking about, or hoping for. Her eyes seemed to turn a deeper shade of blue as she gazed at him at bit longer perhaps that a proper lady should. She was no longer able or even willing to elude the desire that she harbored. It was a look that unveiled the lieutenant's own pent-up desires, and for a breathtaking moment, the expression on his face made Bella wonder if he was going to take her right then and there. But Jeremy composed himself. His expression made quite clear that it was an epic struggle to do so. He reached out the window and tapped loudly on the side of the coach.

"Drive on!" he called out to the coachman.

The coach lurched as the driver put the four horses in the conveyance's traces into motion, and they began to roll with a clatter of shod hooves and iron-rimmed wheels on cobblestone. The window shades were up, so Bella could look out at the fine homes that lined Chestnut Street. Now and then she gazed at the nosegay of red and white roses. The one thing she couldn't do at that moment was look directly at Jeremy. She was still struggling to tamp down the fever that had quickened her pulse and warmed her cheeks the moment their eyes had locked.

In the past few years, she'd had more than a few opportunities to throw caution and custom out the window, to lean against a wall and raise her skirt for a quick and passionate coupling with any one—or more—of the men who had courted her since her sixteenth birthday. She suspected that had she remained on the frontier she would have done just that, years ago, and by now would probably have a husband and children. The consequences of such an act, though, had given her the willpower to restrain her passions. Such things could not be kept a secret, and she hadn't wanted to disappoint Aunt Martha, who was so utterly committed to producing in her a proper young lady of high station—and high morals. And, too, she had never felt that fullness of heart that she experienced in Jeremy Hull's company when she had been with previous suitors. For one thing, she could tell that those other men hadn't felt true affection for her. All they had wanted was to poke her. For some men, being the one who took a young woman's virginity was a feather in their cap, not to mention the topic of a bawdy tavern tale guaranteed to make other rakes jealous.

Jeremy was silent for a few moments, at first glance seeming to appear to be inordinately interested in the passing scenery. But Bella sensed that he was agitated and deep in thought. A stab of anxiety prodded her into asking, "A penny for your thoughts?"

With an apologetic smile, Jeremy leaned forward and sighed. "I must confide in you, Bella."

She looked into his eyes, which again inflamed that nearly unbearable heat in her loins, and forgot about breathing as she expected him to put words to his desire for her, the mere prospect of which had her mind reeling. What was he going to say? How should she respond? She fidgeted anxiously.

"You must speak of this to no one," he said, as serious as she had ever seen him. "I would ask for your word on that."

"Of course," she murmured.

"You may hear this at the ball, so I feel I should be the one to tell you."

Now Bella was perplexed, and both relieved and disappointed at the same time. Clearly what he had to share with her did not involve the matter of a physical union.

"We will be going to war with France soon," he said, pitching his voice low, apparently unwilling to be overheard by the coachman.

"Oh, come now, Jeremy. That rumor has been afloat for years now."

"True enough. But this is no rumor. It's going to happen. Maybe not tomorrow, or next week, but it will happen soon. Very soon." He sighed and sat back, his chin resting on a thumb, a forefinger draped over his upper lips, a brooding pose. Seeing him like this quelled Bella's feverish desire somewhat. Clearly he was troubled, and that worried her.

"You have met Leftenant Woodward, I believe? He is General Warburton's aide-de-camp. From him I know that war is coming. Governor Dinwiddie of Virginia, with the approval of his Council, has raised a force of militia. As we speak, they are marching west to establish a fort where the Allegheny and Monongahela Rivers meet to form the Ohio. This they hope will stop further expansion southward by the French. The game is afoot, Bella."

Bella was silent for a moment, expecting more, but when nothing more seemed forthcoming, she shrugged. "But that's so far away, Jeremy. What could it possibly have to do with you and your regiment?"

He looked at her with such melancholy longing in his eyes that her heart skipped a beat. "Because the French won't stand for it. Because they and their Indian allies will make short work of the colonial militia, as poorly trained and poorly equipped and, I suspect, poorly led, as it must be. Elements of the 45th will march to prevent that from happening. We are duty bound to do so. The 45th is the only full regiment in the colonies. Besides, such an act could not be allowed to stand without consequence, else the French will be emboldened." He leaned forward again and captured her hand in both of his. "Then I will have to leave you."

Bella was stunned. "No, no you cannot be sure of that. It...it may not happen. It can't happen." She began shaking her head, unable to convince even herself, then slumped back on the bench, despondent, and winced as whalebone poked her in the stomach and forced her to sit up straight again. "War," she muttered bitterly. "I suppose that's what you want, isn't it? That's what every soldier wants, I suppose. A chance for glory on the field of battle, isn't it?"

"My father was a soldier, and his father and his father before him were, as well. It was..." he paused a moment, searching for the right word, "... not really a choice. It is expected of me." He glanced at her sharply. "That I tell you in the strictest confidence. Of course, I am more than willing to serve king and country. And, I confess, war hastens promotion. But what we speak of now is not about glory. It's about you, Bella."

She blinked, befuddled. "What does this war have to do with me?"

"Well, for one thing, I want you to be proud of me."

"Proud of you? I'm not your mother, Jeremy." She instantly regretted her words, words prompted by selfishness. The last thing she wanted was for Jeremy Hull to go to war, not just because war would put him in harm's way but because she would not see him for months. She chided herself for being selfishly petulant.

He smiled pensively. "No. But if my wishes come true, you will be my wife. And a man wants his wife to be proud of him."

CHAPTER 15

B ella sat there and stared at him in stunned silence.

"I realize you have only known me for a few months now," said Jeremy. "But I prefer to think that you are aware of how very fond I am of you." He shook his head and softly laughed at himself. "No, fond is not the word. I am very much in *love* with you, Bella Cutter. I think it happened the moment we first spoke. I would... I would live my life for you. I would try to give you everything your heart desires. You would want for nothing." He paused, earnestly searching her face for a sign that he had won her over. "I... like to think your aunt would approve of me, don't you? I mean, when I mentioned the regimental ball a fortnight ago, she even said I could take you unchaperoned. That is surely a sign that she trusts me with your honor, don't you think?" He waited and was met with more stunned silence. "I come from a good family, as you know, though I'm not sure that matters much to you. I have no vices to speak of. And... and you are the only woman I have ever felt this way about. I am certain you are my true love, Bella!" He paused again, in true torment now, his eyes beseeching her. "Please, my darling. Say something!"

Bella's befuddled mind was awhirl with so many diverse thoughts rushing into and out of the light of her comprehension that all she could do was just shake her head. This brought such consternation to Jeremy's expression that she was struck with remorse.

"Forgive me," she heard herself say. "I just...I just don't know what to say. This comes as such an unexpected surprise." She smiled wanly.

"I see." Jeremy was downcast. "When you think of me, if you do..."

"Of course I do. I think about you all the time."

"What do you imagine about us?"

Bella's cheeks burned, so madly was she blushing. She dragged as much air into her lungs as the stay allowed and exhaled slowly, buying herself a few precious seconds. From the day they had met she had thought of Jeremy Hull often. She wasn't sure why but he seemed different from all the other men who had shown an interest in her. She fantasized about being with him, but as a lover, not a wife. She didn't dare tell him this. And she realized that the fever that raged inside her every time he crossed her mind, and especially all day today, was nowhere to be found at the moment, oddly enough.

"I...I didn't dare think so far ahead," she replied at last. It occurred to her that Jeremy may have expected her to leap into his arms, overjoyed by his proposal, regardless of how round-about it had been. His disheartened demeanor caused her a stab of regret. To cheer him up—and to subdue her guilt—she smiled a soft and genuine smile, tilting her upper body forward despite the discomfort caused by doing so, and put her hand on his. "I am not saying no, Jeremy. I just...I just need time to think."

"But what does your heart tell you?"

What to say? That she knew she wanted to sleep with him but wasn't sure about bearing his children? No. That she wasn't even twenty years old, and young ladies almost never married before they were at least that old, and usually a few years later than that? No. That she wasn't sure if she loved him? Certainly not. She didn't want to drive him away. She didn't want to risk never seeing him again. She was at a loss what to say, but knew it was cruel to leave him hanging by the rope of her silence.

"Well, I know that I am ..." she began, hesitantly.

The coachman called out in his loud, gruff voice. "General's house just ahead, guvnah."

Bella saw her chance to change the subject and seized it. "I do hope I don't embarrass you tonight," she murmured, and this she meant from the bottom of her heart.

Jeremy smiled. "You couldn't possibly. To have you on my arm will make this the very best day of my life."

The coach pulled to a stop and a moment later the carriage door opened and the coachman gave Bella a hand down. Ahead of her was a short walkway to steps that led up to double doors framed by lamplights that cast away the night shadows. Both doors were open, and she caught a glimpse of a broad and brightly lighted foyer filled with men, most of them in uniform, and ladies, most of them young and slender and clad in splendid finery. From somewhere inside she could hear music. She looked up at the house itself. It made even her aunt's home pale in comparison.

Jeremy settled the fare with the coachman—there would be plenty of coaches lined up to take ball-goers home when the event was over—and then took Bella's arm in his. Noticing that she was somewhat taken aback by what confronted her, he leaned in and whispered, "If any lady has a right to be here, it is you, Bella."

She smiled gratefully as he led her up the steps and into the house.

There were two dozen people crowding the wide hall-way and what seemed like nearly a hundred more in the adjacent ballroom. The ballroom was unlike any room that Bella had ever seen, a magnificent space with fluted columns lighted by wax candles in four crystal chandeliers and silver candelabra. The oak paneling on the walls were adorned with tapestries and caryatids. All the lighting made the room quite warm.

The full orchestra—it consisted of all four groups, the woodwinds, brass, strings, and percussion—were playing a minuet from a platform opposite the archway through which the couple passed. About fifteen couples were engaged in this elegant dance that had dominated French and English ballrooms for a century, one couple performing at a time while the others watched. Still more couples occupied tables for two located here and there against the walls, as well as a couple of larger tables set up for games of whist. A large crowd stood around the long refreshment tables adorned with snowy white linen, silver and pewter platters and bowls, and ranks of crystal glasses.

Just inside the ballroom, Bella frantically reviewed all that she had learned about these occasions, the instruction coming from Aunt Martha during nightly sessions that had occurred ever since she had accepted Jeremy's invitation. There were an astonishing amount of strict rules which, if broken by a woman, could lead to public humiliation and censure, and if broken by a man, might even result in a duel. Balls such as this one were at the center of public life and entertainment. Some people attended them simply for amusement. Others saw the event as an opportunity to dis-cuss current events, politics or philosophy, to engage in busi-ness discussions, and to fall in and out of love. Unmarried women were required to wear white or pastel-toned gowns with a minimum of jewelry, while those who were wed could wear any color dress and all the adornments that they desired. Most of the gentlemen wore dress uniforms.

Jeremy led Bella to one of the refreshment tables, where a dizzying array of refreshments were available and kept stocked by obsequious, white-suited servants. There was shaved ham and thinly sliced beef, ice cream and sorbet, gingerbread cookies and pound cake. Lemonade, punch and tea in large bowls was accompanied by sparkling wine, brandy and port in bottles. Bella tried a gingerbread cookie and found it had a very rich flavor, molasses lightly spiced with cinnamon and ginger. She accepted a glass of lemonade with which to wash it down. She was then led to a group of two officers, both with young ladies on their arm, and Jeremy performed the introductions.

Bella didn't fail to note that Jeremy failed to formally introduce her, but she already knew one of the other officers. Lieutenant Geoffrey Bale was, like Jeremy, in the 45th's Grenadier company, and that was all she knew about him. But it was the other officer, Lieutenant Robert Lindon, with whom she was already acquainted. Meeting him again made her heart lurch in her chest. Jeremy could tell that the two knew each other, and commented on the fact.

"Yes indeed," said Lindon. "Miss Cutter and I met on Market Street." He was gazing at Bella with a rather anxious expression on his angular face.

"The covered area of Market Street," clarified Bella, since everyone knew that the eastern end, nearest the docks, was lined with notorious pubs and populated by prostitutes, both of which catered to seamen, while the roofed area further inland was visited by nearly everyone, as there were over a hundred vendors of meats and other groceries who proffered their wares in that area. Her cheeks were quite warm. She knew all too well that Lindon appeared slightly ill-at-ease because he had mistaken her for a prostitute. Or so he claimed after the fact, by way of an apology at the time for suggesting they slip into one of the nearly alleys for a quick fucking.

"I was shopping for fresh meats," she added, then her soft full lips quirked as she added, "and, if memory serves, so was the lieutenant."

Lindon looked a bit pale and quickly tried to change the subject. "So, Jeremy, the rumors are flying here tonight about our deployment westward, though General Warburton has yet to confirm it." He gestured at Bale. "Geoffrey and I have been debating which companies will be involved, as surely the general will not lead the entire regiment into the woods, considering that the 45th is the only full regiment in the colonies. I would hear your opinion on the matter."

With a smile and regretful shake of the head, Jeremy replied, "Perhaps later, my friend. Right now, I want to dance with this fetching young lady. Surely you understand. If you will excuse us."

Bella breathed an audible sigh of relief, relief that was short-lived as soon as it registered that she was going to have to dance. Fortunately, the minuet had come to an end and the master of ceremonies was calling for a reel, which Bella considered the simplest of the most common dances of the day. Thanks to Aunt Martha, she had been given dance instructions a year ago on a regular basis by a foppish young man. She and Jeremy teamed up with another couple, making one of seven quartets that responded to the call.

Each dancer performed show-off steps for two phrases, and then reeled, passing their partner right shoulder to right shoulder, reversing direction, turning right to re-enter the figure and then pass right again. Bella performed the 'beaten' step, which consisted of hopping four times on one foot, the other extended to the side before bringing it to the calf, then to the side again, and then to the calf again. She ended up facing the other man in the quartet and began the process all over again before being reunited with Jeremy, who proved to be quite an accomplished dancer. Bella kept her eyes averted and focused entirely on her steps.

What seemed to her to be a lifetime later the dance was over, and as the spectators applauded and the master of ceremony called for a country dance, Jeremy escorted Bella back to the refreshment table. He poured two glasses of sparkling wine and proposed a toast.

"To the most beautiful young lady at the regimental ball," he said.

They entwined arms and sipped from the glasses, gazing at one another, and as they sipped Bella saw right through to the lieutenant's soul and knew, in that instant, that he truly *was* immersed in her. It was a confirmation that took her breath away—a moment she knew, somehow, that she would always remember.

Jeremy escorted her to an unoccupied table and when they sat in the comfortably upholstered Queen Anne chairs, he placed an arm on the intimate table between them, palm up and open. Bella put her hand in his and was rewarded by a broad smile on his impossibly handsome face.

"Forgive me for not introducing you to Leftenants Bale and Lindon," he said.

"I noticed. But it's quite all right."

"It isn't that I am not proud to have you on my arm, Bella. The truth be known, I have to be the happiest man in this hall. It's just that…well, I didn't want to see you dance with another."

"I'm grateful, if only because obviously I am not a very accomplished dancer."

"You dance like an angel."

Bella noticed Geoffrey Bale approaching them, and without a young lady on his arm. Her eyes widened, as she feared that he might break with custom and ask her for a dance without benefit of introduction. But when he arrived, Bale gave her a cordial bow and then turned to Jeremy, with a grim expression on his face.

"The Captain wants to see all of his officers, Jeremy. At once."

He pointed across the ballroom at a stout, gray-haired officer standing alone at one of the tall, curtained windows that overlooked the street, an arm extended to push one of the draperies aside so that he could look out at the evening, the other arm bent behind his back.

"I'll sit right here and wait for you," Bella told Jeremy.

"With respect, Miss, the Captain would like to meet you," said Bale.

"Me? Why?"

"You *are* the daughter of Abel Cutter?"

Surprised, Bella glanced at Jeremy, who shrugged and said, "I suppose he must have looked at the guest list."

"I am," she told Bale, and took a deep, shuddering breath. "Has something happened to my father?"

"I am afraid I do not know, miss."

She rose and took Jeremy's proffered arm, finding it difficult to breath as they followed Lieutenant Bale across the ballroom, and this time it wasn't because of the constricting elements of her gown.

CHAPTER 16

When they arrived before Captain Warren, Jeremy clicked his heels and bowed slightly.

"Sir! I have both the honor and the pleasure to introduce Miss Bella Cutter. Bella, Captain Edward Warren, commander of the Grenadiers, 45th Regiment of Foot."

Bella curtsied and the Captain bowed, a faint smile on his creased and square-jawed face. His voice gruff and gravelly, he said, "Miss Cutter, a pleasure. Forgive me for interrupting your evening, but I have important news to impart to these officers." He clasped hands behind his back as he looked at one lieutenant and then the other. "I have just received word from General Warburton. The Grenadiers company, with two Battalion companies, will march west by southwest to rendezvous with a force of militia under the command of a Major George Washington, who has been charged with the task of constructing fortifications in the valley north of the convergence of the Allegheny and Monongahela Rivers. This is to secure one of the few viable river crossings in that region. As you may know, the Monongahela River valley is squeezed between two steep mountain ranges, and the crossing of which I speak is one of the rare places with accessible banks."

"May I ask to what end, sir?" asked Bale.

"The French are known to have constructed three forts the on the western side of the Allegheny Mountains. Last year they built Fort LaBouef on French Creek and Fort Presqu'ile on the shore Lake Erie. Then, not long ago, they built Fort Duquesne in the area where the Allegheny and Monongahela Rivers feed into the Ohio River. In addition, rumors have it that they may be preparing to build yet *another* fort even further east, on the Allegheny River near French Creek. These forts not only create a barrier to further westward expansion by the British Crown but would also amply serve as supply depots for a French invading army."

Jeremy and Bale exchanged wide-eyed looks.

"What would the French want to invade?" asked Bella.

Captain Warren was taken aback and clearly somewhat annoyed by the question, since it was posed by a young lady who in his opinion had no business inserting herself into a discussion of military matters.

"Those four French forts are like a dagger aimed at the guts of the colonies. An army could quickly march on Philadelphia, even New York, sundering the colonies in half. If that should happen, England's foothold in the Americas would be dealt a possibly fatal blow. Holding that river crossing on the Monongahela is vital, too vital to trust to mere militia."

Bella looked at Jeremy, eyes widening, as she realized the potential danger to him.

"Those forts, they may exist simply because the French wish to protect their interests," she said, and realized she was trying to convince herself as well as the captain, that the risk of a French offensive eastward was not real, which would mean that Jeremy would not be in the path of an invasion with what would amount to about one hundred other British soldiers.

Captain Warren's eyes narrowed. "You are related to Abel Cutter, are you not?"

"He is my father."

"Hmph," snorted Warren. "The consensus is that Abel Cutter sympathizes with the French. I see the apple has not fallen far from the tree."

Bella's chin lifted to a defiant angle. "My father believes it is best to live and let live. He doesn't take sides."

"Well that's the problem, isn't it, Miss Cutter? Your father just happened to establish his settlement in one of the most strategically important locations between here and the lakes. He is right in the middle of two nations that have been at odds for seven centuries, ever since the Normans led by William the Conqueror won the Battle of Hastings." He wagged a finger at Bella. "Mark my words, young lady. Your father had best pick his side, and it had best be England, as it is England which will win the war. And believe you me, war *is* coming."

Bella looked at him, tight-lipped and frowning, then turned to Jeremy. "I need some air," she said bluntly, and then to the captain and Lieutenant Bale, "If you will excuse me, gentlemen." She didn't wait for them to excuse her, though, turning and making for the exit.

She was outside on the stoop only a moment before Jeremy arrived.

"I am so sorry," he said, contritely. "I didn't know the subject of your father would come up."

"My father can take care of himself. When do you think you will march?"

"A few days, if not sooner."

"I would like to go home, Jeremy."

He nodded, unable to conceal his disappointment, and left her for a moment to acquire a coach. A moment later he was helping her into one. They rode a few moments in silence. Bella was staring out a window, obviously deep in thought, and Jeremy did not intrude.

Then she looked at him and solemnly said, "I would come with you."

He stared at her, not comprehending. "You don't want to go home?" he asked.

"Yes, I do. I mean I want to come with you when you march."

Jeremy stared at her in disbelief. "Bella! It's not safe where we're going."

"I know where you're going," she replied sternly. "I was born in the forests and mountains you are going to. I have been away from them for some years now but I daresay I know the country better than you."

"Well, yes. Yes, of course. But we may be marching into war!"

"The frontier is always at war, in one form or another. While I was growing up at The Reach we were attacked twice by Indians. I learned how to shoot a rifle before I was ten years old. I can read sign. I can hunt, skin and butcher out a deer."

Jeremy was at a loss for words. He gestured, shaking his head, began to speak once, then again, and both times thinking the better of it.

"I also know that civilians follow soldiers into war all the time," she said. "Artisans, traders... and harlots."

"Bella!"

She smirked. "I've even seen a copy of *Harris' List of Covent Garden Ladies*."

He could only stare at her, stunned into slack-jawed silence. The volume she spoke of had been compiled by a notorious Covent's Garden pimp who had a black book which listed hundreds of women of loose morals. The *List* sold quite well and more than a few gentlemen, both married and single, owned a copy. Prostitution was and had been commonplace for centuries in English cities and was believed by some to be a necessary evil, or even a public service, since it saved countless decent women from becoming the target of the tremendous sexual appetites of the male of the species, or being lured into wedlock for the wrong reasons.

"I–I don't know what to say," Jeremy confessed. He slumped back on his cushioned bench, looking glum and rather devastated. Bella took pity on him. It was true that camp followers were a given when there were soldiers on the march, civilians who provided additional supplies and services such as blacksmithing, sewing, cooking, sutlery and in some instances sexual favors for coin, but she realized he might have mistaken her reason for bringing it up.

"I'm not suggesting that I sign on as a harlot," she said, with a gentle smile, suffering the discomfort accompanying her leaning forward to reach out and lay a hand on his. She tried to lighten the mood with humor. "Although I like to think I would be a quite popular one."

"Indubitably," groaned Jeremy.

"I have two reasons for going, and I *must* go. I really have no choice. The first is to return to The Reach and joined my father in this time of peril. If I stayed here, I would live in a perpetual torment. So, once we reach your destination I will travel north to Cutter's Reach."

He stared at her again, this time with alarm. "That's at least a week's journey over rough country. Indian country."

"If it makes you feel better, I will persuade Captain Warren to send me under escort. I can tell him I intend to speak to my father about placing his loyalty where it belongs."

"Would you? Speak to your father, I mean."

Bella sighed. "Well, honestly, no. If there is a war, he will have to choose a side, since he happened to pick a site for

his settlement that both the French and the British covet."
She didn't mention that her father might not even listen to
her if she offered a suggestion as to which side he should
choose. She remembered her father as someone who was
not easily swayed—a trait, she realized, that she had inherited. "Perhaps, once your captain establishes a hold on The
Fork—as those of us born to that country have called the
place where the Allegheny and Monangahela meet—you
could be my escort. Especially if I'm your wife."

Jeremy stared at her, as one would do who was certain
he had misheard or misunderstood someone's comment.

"You do want to marry me, don't you, Jeremy?" she asked
with a soft smile.

He sat up straight, grabbing her hands in his and impulsively leaning forward to give her a kiss on the cheek. But
before his lips could arrive at their destination, she had
draped her arms around his neck and turned her head
slightly and planted a kiss on his lips, a kiss that swiftly
became a hot, hungry, impassioned one, her soft lips rolling hungrily over his. When the lingering kiss was done he
loomed over her, the burning desire in his eyes ablaze in
hers as well. Then she smiled—a smile as wanton as any of
Mr. Harris's black book trollops had ever smiled, and she
began to writhe and contort in a desperate attempt to at
least loosen the stay and remove the pannier. Bracing himself with one hand against the coach wall behind her, Jeremy
watched, chest heaving as passion seized him. There was
something erotic about the way Bella writhed and moaned
in frustration as she had trouble achieving any of her goals
when it came to undressing.

Jeremy quickly curtained the windows. He pounded on
the roof of the coach and growled a shout meant for the
coachman. "Keep driving until I say otherwise!"

Bella continued in her efforts to at least loosen the stay—until she realized Jeremy was unbuttoning his breeches. She stopped struggling and leaned back, simply lifting her gown and spreading her long legs, kicking off her slippers and planting her heels on the edge of the bench upon which she sat, her eyes begging him to take her.

He paused, his breeches down around his knees, and asked, "Are you sure you don't wish to be married first?"

She stared at a man's privates for the first time in her life, and murmured, "Make me yours…now…*please!*" Her voice was soft and husky with desire. "Later you can make an honest woman out of me."

He grinned and descended on her, his weight pinning her down, her arms closing round him, and her breathless squeal muffled by his plundering mouth as they became one.

Once their passions were spent, they remained entwined, arms and legs entangled, quiet for a moment until Jeremy murmured, "You're aware that the coachman must be aware of what just transpired. I mean, we weren't exactly quiet as church mouses, and the coach did yaw a bit for a spell."

She smiled wantonly and shrugged. "As long as he is not acquainted with my aunt."

Bella touched his cheek as she breathed an audible sigh of contentment—and relief. The desire pent up inside her, manifested by so many sleepless nights populated with such wild fantasies that she blushed even now to think of them, were a thing of the past. She was no longer a virgin, and it had been much, much more exhilarating—and fulfilling—than she had ever imagined that it would be.

"Speaking of which, I should get you home. And, I suppose, we should inform your aunt in the next day or two. We don't have much time, Bella. Soon we will march." He began to button himself up, and then paused with the job half-done, with a sidelong glance at her. "Unless you wish to go again," and accompanied that with a rascal's crooked smile that she was thrilled to see.

"I would love to," she said, a throaty whisper. "But I think we should be wed first, don't you?"

"But... but we have so little time."

"A regimental chaplain would do."

Jeremy was suddenly quite solemn. He couldn't forget her reaction when he had earlier broached the subject of marriage, albeit in a very roundabout way. She had at the very least seemed taken aback, as though the notion had never occurred to her. She had certainly not seemed at all amenable to the idea.

Had she changed her mind so suddenly? Was it due to her physical desires? Or could Captain Warren's comments about the coming conflict had something to do with her change of heart? Could it be that she wished to be his bride primarily to have just cause for following him west, so that she could be reunited with her father? Was it possible that Bella Cutter was using him in pursuit, not of wedded bliss but rather the furthering of her own ends?

"Is something wrong, Jeremy?" she asked.

He smiled and shook his head. "I do love you, Bella, more than life itself. I think I knew you were the only woman for me the moment I laid eyes on you. I—I don't have the words to express how you make me feel. I just hope..." He shook his head. "I just hope you know how much you mean to me."

Bella leaned over and kissed him, a long, slow kiss on the mouth, filled more with promise than the wild passion her kisses had conveyed a few moments before.

"I love you, too, Jeremy."

"My darling!" He kissed her, a kiss that became ever more impassioned, and a moment later they were joined again, in a feverish, almost violent, coupling.

A half hour later they arrived at the Gallatin House. As the coachman gave her a hand in descending from the carriage, Bella caught a whiff of strong spirits emanating from the man. It wasn't surprising that a coachman would take a nip or three from a flask. She also noticed the smirking expression on the man's face. Her brow raised, her lip curled in a rather saucy smile. She was rather surprised that she didn't feel the least bit embarrassed or self-conscious. There was no way she could conceal her disheveled hair and clothing. As Jeremy emerged from the coach, Bella ascended the stoop, only to turn when she heard the coachman speak.

"Thank you, sir. I hope you enjoyed your tour of Philadelphia." The coachman grinned and winked, then tilted his head in Bella's direction. "She's a pretty one, I give you that. I prefer me women with a bit more meat on 'em but I venture to say she must have a tight little honeypot, eh?"

Jeremy grabbed the man by the neck and shoved him hard against the carriage's flank, banging the other's head against it.

"She is my future wife, sir," rasped Jeremy. "I would beat you like the cur you are but there is a lady present. If you value your health, have a care with your words in the future. Now wait for me while I escort the lady to the door."

The contrite coachman mumbled something and clambered back up to his bench.

As they arrived at the front door, Bella murmured, "You can't really blame him. I mean we did couple like animals, didn't we. He can be forgiven for assuming I'm a hussy." She gave him a sultry little half smile then leaned closer and whispered in his ear. "I am *your* hussy now, Lieutenant."

Jeremy growled deep and low in his throat as he pressed into her. "I'm of half a mind to take you again right here on your aunt's..."

The door opened. They jumped apart even before they recognized the tall, cadaverous Loney. The valet looked Bella over from head to toe. Utterly forgetting to breathe, she watched his expression. It didn't change one whit, even though a man would have to be blind, or blind drunk, not to notice her disheveled condition.

"Welcome home, Miss Bella," drawled the old black man, then turned rheumy eyes on Jeremy. "Welcome, Lieutenant. Please, come in." He stepped to one side, opening the door further.

"Oh, well, he can't stay," said Bella, crossing the threshold, only to be turned around by the hold Jeremy maintained on her hand. He raised it to his lips as he executed an immaculate bow.

"My thanks, miss, for making this evening an unforgettable one." He released her hand and turned a smile on Loney. "She was the belle of the ball."

"I will be sure to pass that happy news on the Missus Gallatin. She wasn't feeling too well this evenin'. Drank a tonic and turned in early."

"I hope she feels better in the morning. Please convey to her that I would drop by tomorrow in the afternoon. Say two o'clock? It is a matter of the utmost importance."

Loney gave Bella's gown a look from top to bottom, a rare smile tugging at the corners of his mouth. "Indeed. Good night, suh."

Jeremy caught one last glimpse of Bella hurrying up the staircase as Loney closed the door.

Part Four

Late Spring, 1754

CHAPTER 17

Having lived for decades on a wild and dangerous frontier, Cutter usually awakened quickly, unless he had been drinking, and then it depended on the quantity of buttered rum he had consumed the night before, or how long and passionately he and Matty had made love. These days, since Matty slept with him, he liked to linger in bed after walomg, under the covers, his body touching hers, a devilishly alluring experience that it seemed he would never grow tired of. Nor was it one he would ever take for granted. Despite the fact that he'd had two wives he had spent most of his nights alone, as circumstances had compelled him to send the first one away and death had taken the second. So he knew from experience that nothing could be taken for granted.

But this morning he woke with a start, breathing high and fast, his skin crawling. Jumping out of bed, he moved swiftly to one of the gun loops, removing the wooden flap so he could peer outside. From what he could see, there was nothing happening out of the ordinary in or around the stockade. He drew a long breath and leaned his back against the wall, using the heels of his palms to roughly rub his eyes. A chill began to spread through his bones, one that wasn't due entirely to the morning's coolness.

He realized now that he had been dreaming, a dream rent by the bloodcurdling cries of Indians on the warpath, the shouts of male settlers, the screams and cries of women and children, all of this underscored by the angry roar and crackle of flames. With a grimace, he silently chided himself for letting his apprehensions get the best of him.

He heard the blockhouse door downstairs, creaking open on its old, thick leather hinges. He stepped out of his bedroom into the narrow upstairs hallway and looked down the steep steps that would take him to the structure's main room. As he did, Guy Rimbaud appeared down below and looked up.

"There is someone here to see you," said the Arcadian. "He has some news you should hear."

Cutter nodded and went back into his bedroom. As he got dressed, he glanced at Matty, still sound asleep. All he could see was the side of her face and her tousled red hair, the rest of her covered by the quilts. He was quiet, not wishing to wake her. She would get up in her own good time, and dutifully perform her chores, cleaning and cooking. She was a free woman now. After buying her indenture from Taney he had freed her from the contract. She had the papers to prove it.

There were some in The Reach who had thought he would marry her, but that was something he hadn't seriously considered. He and Matty had never talked about it. She seemed quite content with the arrangement as it stood, and accepted the cold shoulder that some of the married women gave her, not to mention the gossip. The general consensus was that Matilda Armstrong was biding her time cohabitating with Abel Cutter, waiting for a younger man— or a richer one.

For himself, Cutter had settled for her company and expected nothing more. He had accepted the likelihood that the conventional wisdom regarding Matty's long-term fate was probably closer to the truth than that she would stay with him forever. He was reconciled to the fact that nothing lasted forever, especially his love affairs. He also didn't give a rat's ass what the inhabitants of The Reach thought about his situation, or about him. Though most of the people looked up to him, and occasionally depended on him—when times were more difficult and dangerous than usual—their opinion of him had never much factored into his decision making.

Clad in his buckskins, Cutter went down into the common room, and his solemn expression brightened as he laid eyes on the man who stood with Guy near the fireplace.

"Ongahelas!" he exclaimed and lengthened his stride to reach the old Indian, grinning from ear to ear as they clasped hands as though they were about to arm wrestle.

A broad grin deepened the creases on the other's face. "Cutter! Cutter! My heart is gladdened." He was a tall, slender man, clad in breechclout, leggings and moccasins, with a scarlet robe draped over one shoulder, and a mantle made with turkey feathers and some of the finest stitching to be found. Despite his age he stood straight, was strong and agile. Ongahelas was Lenni Lenape, the tribe also known as the Delaware because when discovered they had lived along the river by that name. The Delawares were known far and wide for their friendliness, handsomeness, dress, wood carvings and, most of all, their woodland prowess. As colonists expanded westward, they relentlessly forced the Lenni Lanape people off their ancestral lands. In just a few decades, their number decimated by foul play and diseases imported by the colonists, the tribe was but a shadow of its former self, with small groups scattered hither and yon. The group to which Ongahelas belonged had for years lived a few days march to the west of The Reach. Cutter and others in the settlement had engaged in dealings with them, and a good relationship had long been established.

Cutter implored his friend to sit in one of the chairs by the hearth, where Guy was busy poking and prodding the burnt logs from last night's fire to expose the still-glowing hearts of heat, before using a bellows to incite these into flame. With Ongahelas seated, Cutter sprawled into a chair facing his guest.

"Tell me, how are your people. How did you fare over the winter? No trouble from the French?"

"We are well. They have been busy building forts near us but they do not bother us. I have parlayed with their leader, a man named Villiers. He has been more than fair with us. He has promised that his people will not bother us. And he has traded with us fairly. He has made it plain to his Abenaki allies that we are his friends and he expects them to respect that. Most of the time they do."

"Well," said Cutter, relieved, "This news makes me happy. I have worried about my friends, the Lanape." He was always careful not to use the name the colonists had given Ongahelas' people.

Ongahelas nodded, acknowledging Cutter' sentiment. Then he leaned forward, with a serious expression replacing the broad smile that had been inhabiting his face. "I am worried for your and your people, Cutter," he said solemnly. "Villiers has made promises to the Abenaki. He has given them many gifts. It is from a few of the Abenaki that I have learned that colonials have come to the forks of the Ohio, and there has been a fight. Frenchmen have died, and Villiers is preparing to exact revenge. He may already be on the march, and hundreds of Abenaki warriors eager for scalps travel with him. I have not seen it but heard that the colonials have built a fort at Great Meadow."

Cutter's smile was gone now, too. He glanced at Guy, who tilted his head curiously and asked the Lenape, "From which direction did the colonials come?" he asked Ongahelas.

"From the south."

"Virginians, then. I wonder…" murmured Guy, with a wry smile.

Cutter finished it for him. "If Washington leads them."

Ongahelas rose from the chair. "I must go home. I fear that the war that is coming will be the end of my people, if we stay where we are."

"You can bring your people here," said Cutter.

The old warrior put a hand on Cutter's shoulder. "You have been a good friend of the Lenni Lanape. But this place is coveted by both the French and the English. I think the soil will be drenched with blood. My people will head south and west." His smile was pensive. "We will find a new place to live, but I think not for long. There are not enough of us anymore to be anything other than wanderers, and soon we will be no more."

Cutter could not mask his sadness, as he realized this was probably the last time he would see his friend. There was nothing he could say to persuade Ongahelas to stay. The Lanape was not the only tribe of peaceful Indians who were doomed by the changing times and the clash of empires.

He walked with Ongahelas to the main gate, and there they embraced. Cutter watched him break into a ground-eating lope as he headed for the distant line of trees, then returned to the blockhouse. Guy was still there, staring gloomily into the small fire he had earlier provoked. When Cutter entered, he fixed his usual devil-may-care smile back onto his angular face.

"The first time I laid eyes on that man, Washington, I knew he was trouble," said the Arcadian, as Cutter went to his desk, shuffled through the maps there and found the one he sought.

Guy joined him, and Cutter stabbed the map with a forefinger. "Great Meadow." He moved the finger across the map. "Fort Duquesne. Villiers is probably already on the march. There is no time to lose."

"What are you saying, *mon ami?*"

"I am going to try to make Washington see reason."

"*Mon dieu!*" exclaimed the other. "I regret to inform you that you waste your time—and risk your life—in such an endeavor." He studied Cutter's grim visage a moment, and sighed, well aware that once Abel Cutter made up his mind there was little chance of dissuading him. "Let me come with you, at least."

"No, I need you here. You will begin preparations for a possible siege. Place *cheavaux de frise* all the way around. As for the river, collect all the chain you can. Hopefully it will be enough to be pulled tight across from one bank to the other and prevent canoes from reaching our walls."

Guy nodded. The Allegheny ran too deep and fast here for anyone to reach the stockade from directly across the river by boat, which meant attackers would have to come down the river in canoes. A stout chain from one side of the Allegheny to the other directly upstream from the stockade could foil such an effort.

"What do you want me to tell everyone?" he asked.

"I'll tell them. Find Fen. The two of you spread the word that I have news, one hour, in front of The Axe'n'Ale."

As Fen left the blockhouse, a brooding Cutter went around the desk and sprawled in the chair behind it, picking up the map to study it in the flickering orange light cast by the hearth fire. Guy was right. It was a fool's errand to try to stop a war that was, and probably always had been, inevitable. But then, he *was* a fool, to think that he could make a home in a place so remote that kings on faraway thrones would not desire it. Once before he had lost a home to men with unbridled greed and avarice, drunk with power and yet hungering for more.

He decided then that it wouldn't happen again.

The brush of bare feet across wood brought his head around, and he saw Matty descending the stairs. She had on her worn elderberry-dress. As she crossed the room she smiled sleepily, running fingers through her tousled golden curls. Seeing that the fire had already been stirred into life, she changed course and came around the desk to sit in his lap, wrapping her arms languorously around his neck. Reading the concern on his face, she tilted her head querulously.

"Someone was just here. I heard voices. A bearer of bad tidings?"

"Aye. War is coming to the valley."

Matty's smile disintegrated. "Coming here? To The Reach?"

"Probably. I am going to let everyone here know. I will tell them everything I know, and have heard. Some may decide to leave, to go back east where it should be safe. If so, you might want to consider going with them."

Now her her brow furrowed. "You don't wish me to stay?"

He grabbed her by her narrow waist, lifting her effortlessly as he rose from the chair, kicking it back away from his legs and planting her derriere on the edge of his desk.

"There are less than sixty able-bodied men here, Matty. The odds of our holding The Reach are slim. You don't want to be here if we're overrun. Could just be Indians. Even if it's the French, there will be Indians with them. Trust me, you don't want to fall into their hands. I'll wager that just about every white woman taken by Indians would rather have died."

She looked at him for a solemn moment of silence. "You want me to go?"

Cutter huffed and circled the desk to stand by the hearth. It was a question he had anticipated, while hoping that Matty wouldn't resort to what he saw as a feminine ploy. "I want you to stay...alive."

She remained on the desk, her back to him, looking down at her dangling feet, silent for a long moment. "Where would I go?" she asked softly.

Cutter drew a long breath. The question seemed to confirm what he had suspected for some time now—that Matty was with him because of a lack of options. And even though he *had* suspected this, he felt a rush of emptiness with a stab of resentment hot on its heels. He shook his head, chiding himself while feeling sorry for her. He walked back to the desk, reaching out to touch her hair. She didn't pull her head away.

"I have some coin left." Buying her from Taney had taken most of his savings, but not all. "You can have it. It's enough to tide you over until you find...something. Or someone."

She shook her head, sliding off the desk, which put some distance between them. Looking at him earnestly, she murmured, "I won't take the last of your money, Abel. You've already spent enough on my account."

He cursed himself silently for the way he had presented his offer. In hindsight he realized it would have been better not to suggest that he was low on funds. "If it wasn't for the troubles that are coming, I would want you to stay. I hope you know this."

"I believe you. You've never lied to me."

The door opened and Guy entered. He flashed a broad smile in Matty's direction. "Good morning, lovely! You sure know how to brighten up a room."

Matty smirked. "I happen to know you say that to all the girls."

Guy chuckled. "I can't deny it, but in your case I mean it." He looked at Cutter. "Fen and I spread the word. Folks are already gathering."

Cutter just nodded.

Guy saw something on both their faces and cleared his throat. "Well, I think I'll go join Fen in the tavern," he said and beat a hasty retreat.

"I'd best get over there, too," Cutter said and went to the door. He took his long coat from the peg by the door and put it on. As he reached for the door, she spoke his name and he looked back.

"I'm not going anywhere," she said. "I don't want to. If we die here, so be it. The Reach is my home now. You can't make me leave. But if you don't want me with you, I will find another place to say. I could always go back to working at the Axe'n'Ale, for wages this time."

Cutter swung around and with a few long strides had reached her, wrapping an arm around her waist and pulling her into him with such fervor that it almost knocked the wind out of her.

"The hell you are. If you won't leave The Reach then you're staying right here with me. I don't know if you love me, or if I love you. But maybe that doesn't matter anymore. I do love waking up beside you."

She draped her arms round his neck and rose up on tiptoe to plant a long, lingering kiss on his lips. When the kiss was over, she murmured, "I'll make some stew for tonight."

"You're a good cook. I'm sure it will be a fine stew. But I won't be here. There may be a slim chance of keeping the war out of this valley. I don't hold out much hope, but I have to try."

He turned and opened the door and as he was crossing the threshold, Matty said, "You *better* come back, Abel Cutter. If we're to die, I want to die with you."

That stopped him in his tracks again. He looked back at her and wondered if that his doubts about her had been unfounded. She stood there, barefoot, red hair mussed, hands on hips, and a breathless, just-kissed look on her face—an image that he knew right then would be seared forever in his memory. He smiled gratefully.

"That's one hell of a way to say I love you," he said and closed the door.

CHAPTER 18

The day had just broken when a sentry arrived at George Washington's tent and woke the colonel from a troubled sleep. Washington shot to his feet, groping in the semi-darkness for the sword and pistol atop a makeshift, map-draped trunk near at hand. His abrupt action startled the sentry who had stuck his head between the tent flaps, opening his mouth to speak, while Washington listened for the sounds of battle. When he heard nothing of the sort he remembered the breathe.

"What is it, sergeant?"

"Two men just arrived at our gate, colonel. One of them insists on speaking with you. He says his name is Abel Cutter."

Washington breathed an audible sigh of relief and took his hand away from the weapons on the table long enough to retrieve his coat, draped across a camp stool. It was a red British officer's uniform with lace cuffs that had been virgin white when he had marched out of Virginia months ago on the orders of Governor Robert Dinwiddie with a hundred and thirty men, charged with the task of building a fort at the forks of the Ohio River.

He had found this location, known as Great Meadows, an ideal place for a fortified base of operations. It was flat and open and crisscrossed by a pair of streams that provided plenty of drinking water. One of his officers had named it Fort Necessity.

But a string of events had him wondering now if he hadn't led his men into a trap.

First there had been the visit by the Mingo chief known as Half King, who informed him that a small party of Frenchmen were spying on his position. Half King and his band of Mingos led him and forty of his men to the French encampment, which they surrounded and fired upon. The French commander, Joseph Coulon de Villiers, the Sieur of Jumonville, quickly surrendered. While he was showing Washington his orders, which were to simply surveille and under no circumstances to engage, Half King had charged the officer, splitting Jumonville's skull open with a tomahawk and then scalping him. The other Mingos fell upon the rest of the French party, killing and scalping all but one soldier, who managed to escape into the forest, while Washington, stunned by the grisly massacre, stood by.

Little wonder, then, that this morning he wondered— and not for the first time—whether, in fact, the governor had sent him to his doom.

Donning the coat, Washington looked down at himself. The coat, along with his breeches and tunic, were soiled and dirty, as were the tall black boots he hadn't taken off in at least a week. Then he looked at the sentry and nodded.

"Bring them here."

Washington looked bleakly around the tent as he quickly fastened his sword around his waist, stuffed the flintlock pistol in the belt, and stooped low to negotiate his six-foot-two frame through the tent flap to scan the interior of Fort Necessity.

The stockade consisted of a circular wall of split timber with sharpened tips. In the center was a small storehouse, more timber covered with bark and animal skins, where the expedition's powder and supplies were kept relatively dry. But nothing was remotely dry. It had been raining on and off for days. The ground within the compound was a black mire. Water stood a half-foot deep in the rifle pits his men had excavated around the exterior of the little fort.

Coughing and moans of several men drew his attention to the field hospital—little more than a few tables under a couple of tarpaulins, with the sick and wounded—two dozen of them now—lay on a floor fashioned from more timber laid side by side. Fortunately, several of the men who had volunteered for the Virginia militia were doctors or knew something about medicine, and two of them were across the way now, caring as best they could for their patients, giving them water and comforting words, changing the dressings on their wounds if they had any. Some of them had been shot in the clash with a small force of French soldiers less than a week ago. Most of them were ill with a fever.

Washington was glumly contemplating the nature of his troops, recalling how they had looked departing Alexandria, Virginia on a warm April day, some of them clad in buckskins, others in a red regimental uniform with gray stockings and black tri-corner hat, but not a man among them with any military experience. Washington could not escape the fact that he didn't either, having learned all he knew about military principles and history from books.

One of the gates opened slightly and the sentry he had spoken to earlier entered with the two visitors in tow, another sentry bringing up the rear. Although it was still half-dark due to the low gray clouds blocking out the rising sun, Washington recognized both of the newcomers. Cutter was accompanied by the burly, bearded, buckskin-clad frontiersman named ... Washington searched his memory for a moment, and then the man with Cutter spoke as he cast a skeptical look around.

"This be a stowie steid," said Fen MacGregor. "I've seen nicer beaver lodges."

Cutter gave his friend a severe look but said nothing, instead walking toward Washington, closing the gap swiftly with long strides. He extended a hand and Washington took it. Cutter pulled him closer and whispered, "You have any idea what kind of trouble you're in, Major?"

Washington stiffened. "I am a colonel now, and I am well aware of my situation, sir."

Cutter looked at him for a moment, his rain-drenched mane clinging to square-jawed cheeks, then shook his head. "I am not sure that you do. Come, let's go inside." And before Washington could invite him in, he walked past and entered the tent.

Telling the sentries to return to their posts, Washington followed Cutter, and was in turn followed by Fen MacGregor. There was barely enough room inside the tent for the three of them. Cutter barely glanced at the maps on the table; he had a much more accurate map of the wilderness in his head.

"There is a large force of French and Canadians marching here, perhaps as many as six hundred, along with a few hundred of their Indian friends. My guess is they will be here by day's end. And there are some already here, in the deep woods on the ridges to either side of this position."

Washington strove to mask his alarm. He lifted his chin and looked down his long nose at Cutter. "And what are *you* doing here, sir?"

"The Indians we trade with at The Reach tell me things. There isn't a person within two hundred miles of this spot that doesn't know you're here. News travels on swift feet in the forest. When I was told that your Mingo allies murdered a French officer who was your prisoner, we came at once."

Washington glanced from him to Fen and back again. "To fight at our side?"

Cutter laughed, a derisive sound. "You need to turn around and go home, Colonel. That's the only way you and your men will survive."

"And what business is that of yours?"

Cutter fumed, clenching his teeth to stifle a profane retort. "I don't want a war. It's bad for business, not to mention for my people. And if you and your command die here, there will surely be a war. The British will have to send an army, officially to avenge your death, but in truth to save face. Too many good men perish for the reputation of nations."

"There are already British regulars on the march. I received a letter from Governor Dinwiddie a fortnight ago, informing me that three companies of the 45th Regiment set out from Philadelphia to support us. Four days ago a runner from Captain Warren, the commanding officer of that force, arrived with word that those men are but a few days away."

Cutter looked past Washington to Fen, who grimly muttered, "Bloody hell. We are in trouble now, Cap'n." Being a Scotsman, he could sink into black moods, and he had been warning his friend for days that they were likely going to their doom.

"Don't despair," said Washington. "Come with me. I wish to show you something."

He led them out of the tent and to a ladder that gave them access to a rampart from which they could peer over the sharpened tops of the stockade's logs. Near at hand was a swivel cannon.

"I received reinforcements of over a hundred men a fortnight ago. With them came nine of these cannon, capable of firing grapeshot up to two hundred yards. As you can see, they are all mounted on the walls. From here you can see the rifle pits that my men have made, including a trench that leads to the nearest stream. I assure you, sir, that we are well entrenched, and well able to withstand an attack."

Cutter took a long look around, taking note of the swivel guns and the diamond-shaped trenchworks. He noticed less than dozen cattle grazing between the rifle pits and the stockade walls. Then he gave Washington a long look, and nodded.

"You've done well, Colonel. The problem is that your enemy is not going to fight you according to your book-learned rules of combat. They aren't going to come marching out of the woods in nice neat rows. And I expect you are short of food."

Washington grimaced. "As you can see, we have a few head of cattle left, some bags of flour."

"And where are your Mingo allies?"

The Colonel's eyes narrowed. "How do you know I had any?"

"There ain't much happens in this valley that the Cap'n don't hear of," replied Fen. "All the tribes hereabouts know they can trust him to treat 'em fair. They tell him everything."

"I know the Mingo chief, Tanaghrisson, also called Half King," said Cutter. "He offered his help to you, didn't he, Colonel. His hate for the French burns hot, as he blames them for the deaths of some of his kin."

Washington nodded bleakly. "I see. That explains a lot. At any rate, Half King insisted that I abandon this ground and return home. I was not prepared to do that, and so he took his men and went home. Besides, a few days ago I received word from Captain Warren of the 45th Regiment."

Cutter stood there and studied the colonel a moment, arms folded, head tilted to one side. "No, I figured you wouldn't fancy a retreat. Your governor wouldn't be happy with you, would he? You're a brave man, Colonel. You've proved that time and time again, coming this way with Gist, and going west another time since then, if what I've heard is true. You're a proud man, too, and I understand pride. But I'm telling you right now, you will not be able to hold this position. Not even for three or four days. Mark my words, those British soldiers won't get here in time. I think you know that, too. Those Frenchmen out there, they won't be coming out of those trees lined up in nice, neat rows. They won't fight you like that. They know better. Your cannon are impressive. They are also useless, especially in this weather. And there's another thing to consider. If there is a big fight, and if the Indians who side with the French are involved and take losses, the French won't be able to stop them from wreaking their vengeance on your men. Request a parlez with the French commander now, Colonel. The French don't want your blood. They just want you gone. I suspect they'll deal, if you do it soon. I would be surprised if they didn't know about the redcoat relief column heading this way, and you won't last long enough for it to reach you. Do it, Colonel. Reach terms with the French, if not for your reputation's sake, then for the sake of your men."

Washington was silent for a moment, clearly struggling with the decision Cutter had presented to him as he surveyed the interior of Fort Necessity from his vantage point. He was cognizant of the peril he and his command faced and understood that the odds were against him. As for his reputation, his legacy, would it fare better if he were the first to surrender to the French, or if he stood his ground and perished with all his men in a fight against a superior force?

He took a deep breath and fastened his gaze on Abel Cutter.

"I thank you for coming, sir," he said. "I appreciate your concern and admire your courage. You say you came because you want to prevent a war. But this war is inevitable, and has been for quite some time. You are free to stay and fight, but I will not think ill of you should you choose to leave. If you decide on the latter course, I suggest you do so when night falls. Now, if you will excuse me, I have many matters to attend to."

While Cutter grimly watched Washington climb down from the ramparts and cross the fort, making for the makeshift field hospital where the sick and wounded were housed, Fen glanced over the ramparts to study the dark forest a hundred yards away, then sighed.

"Reckon we better slip out of here soon as its dark," he said, then glanced at Cutter. "We *are* leaving, aren't we, Cap'n?"

"I don't understand that man."

"The Colonel? What's to understand? He is here to make a name for himself, no matter how many good men give their lives for it. Back in the old country we met plenty like him, on both sides. T'be honest, I canna ken why we came all this way to try to talk sense into that man." He gestured down into the fort. "Look at 'em, wearing those red coats like they're real British soldiers. Just seeing the scarlet turns me blood cold. I remember what the scarlets done to our folk, Abel. Remember it like it was yesterday."

"I'll tell you why," replied Cutter. "Because this is a fight we can't avoid. No matter how much I wish we could. If Washington and his men are wiped out the war will on, for certain. Then you'll see real scarlets. A lot of them. Armies of them. Thousands will die for the ownership of this land. Maybe we will, too, and the people we care for." He clamped a hand on Fen's beefy shoulder. "Let's find a place to get some rest, and we'll head home when night comes."

They descended from the rampart and found a spot between a few empty wagons and the wall. Like Fen, Cutter lay down, using his pack for a pillow, long rifle beside him, his hand resting on it. Unlike Fen, it took him a while to drift off to sleep.

He woke with a start, to the crackling of muskets being fired, the shouts of men inside the fort and the war cries of Indian braves outside. A light rain was falling, and mere moments was a deluge. Leaping to his feet, he grabbed his pack and strode for the nearest ladder, Fen in his wake. They climbed up to the rampart, and on his way up was struck by the flailing arm of a man plummeting to the ground. Once at the top, he crouched low and moved away from the swivel gun which yet another of Washington's amateur soldiers was attempting to man, only to cry out and then slump forward, draped over the sharpened tips of the thick timbers lashed together to fashion the fort's walls. Another man huddled in terror beneath the cannon as musket balls pelted the battlements behind which he cowered or buzzed like a swarm of angry bees in the air overhead.

Cutter moved past this man, grabbed the one who had been hit by his scarlet coat and pulled him down onto the walkway. His hand closed around the fallen one's neck, noticing the slowly spreading stain of blood on the man's tunic, below the ribcage and to the right. Having felt a pulse, he handed his flintlock to Fen, slipped his other hand under the soldier's coat and around to the lower back. When he brought his hand out it was streaked with blood.

He glowered at the one who cowered nearby, frozen by fear, and reached out with his bloodied hand to grab the man's shoulder.

"He's alive," growled Cutter. "The ball went through him and hit nothing vital. Since you won't fight, tend to his wound, and save the life of one who will. Do you hear?"

The other nodded. "I will," he panted. "I will!"

Cutter took his rifle back from Fen and moved further along the rampart, away from the swivel gun. Only then did he chance a quick look between the sharpened ends of two logs. In a glance he could see the muzzle flash of dozens of long guns, resembling a swarm of fireflies, in the gloom of the forest's edge. The war cries came from the wooded gloom. Directly below him, some of Washington's men were returning fire from the rifle pits.

Having seen all he needed to, he sat with his back to the battlements and grabbed Fen when his old friend made to rise up and fire his rifle.

"Don't bother," said Cutter, seeing the fierce blaze in Fen's dark eyes. He smiled faintly. Fen MacGregor Scottish blood boiled with a fierce yearning to fight when the occasion arose, the odds of survival be damned.

"Not like you to step sideways when a fight's on," said Fen.

"They're not attacking, just counting guns."

Fen grunted and plopped down beside Cutter, clearly disconsolate. "And I reckon you're doing the same."

Cutter nodded, leaning his head back against one of the wall's stout logs, closing his eyes. Fen didn't fail to note that his friend's rain-drenched visage bore not a hint of concern. Mashing his coonskin cap down lower on his forehead, the burly Scotsman huddled there as the deluge intensified, wishing fervently that he was back at The Reach, nursing on a jug in The Axe 'n' Ale.

CHAPTER 19

The shooting continued for hours, sometimes sporadically, at other times with intensity. Washington's men returned fire from the top of the rampart and through gun slits carved into the palisades, but rarely saw more than fleeting shadows and muzzle flash. Cutter doubted that the French and their Indian allies were taking many casualties. For one thing the French soldiers wore uniforms of blue and green, which aided them in blending into the foliage. For another, he suspected they were wise enough to move after firing.

As the day wore on the rain intensified. The rifle pits began filling up with water. Ammunition and firelocks were drenched. Muskets were fouled by wet charges. When word spread that all of the cattle had been killed before anyone thought to retrieve them and bring them into the stockade, moral plummeted. Some of the men broke into the storehouse and grabbed the kegs of rum. Soon, much of Washington's command were both discouraged and drunk.

When at long last night approached, and a deep violet dusk descended on Great Meadow, a solitary Frenchman stepped out of the woods carrying a white flag and called out, "*Voulez-vous, parlez?*"

Cutter was roused into action. Descending from the battlements, he found Washington conferring with a couple of his officers in the storehouse. Two guards stood on either side of the door shattered by the rum-seeking looters earlier, and they barred his passage until Washington instructed them to stand aside. As Cutter entered the storeroom he heard the distant French query again. He didn't wait for Washington to acknowledge him.

"Why have you not answered?" he asked.

"We are debating whether it is a ruse," replied Washington stiffly, offended by the other's tone.

"It is a courtesy," snapped Cutter. "One that they do not need to offer. You cannot hold this place, Colonel. The French know it, your men know it, and surely you must know it."

One of the officers stepped forward, frowning. "I insist that you show the colonel the respect that is his due, sir." It was a more a warning than advice.

Cutter glared at the officer. "Don't pick another fight you can't win."

Washington gestured at the officer to stand down. "I am hesitant to trust the French, Mr. Cutter."

"Why? I wouldn't trust the Indians with them, nor the *coureur des bois,* who are more Indian than French. But, generally speaking, French officers are men of honor."

"Who is this insolent backwoodsman?" asked the officer who glowered angrily at Cutter.

"Go see to the men, both of you. And find whatever rum remains and appropriate it. I wish to speak to Mr. Cutter in private."

Once the officers were gone, Cutter said, "You *must* respond to the French, Colonel. If you refuse a parlay then on the morrow they will attack. Your men are hungry, tired and low on powder and ball, I suspect, having wasted so much today in firing into the trees. This fort will fall, and the French may not then be able to restrain their Indian allies. I realize that a surrender may not do much for your reputation. But to preside over the massacre of your command would do far worse."

Washington was silent a moment. Cutter could read the man quite well. The colonel was in anguish, stubborn pride and concern for his legacy warring against his common sense and concern for the men under his command. Finally, and with a profound sigh, Washington leaned heavily on a barrel of flour and contemplated his mud-caked riding boots.

"Very well," he said, his voice hollow. "My officers are hot-headed. Will you accompany me?"

"That's not the French commander, just an envoy. You should not be the one who goes out there to hear their terms."

Washington thought it over, then nodded. Cutter was right. There was a military tradition to observe. The French commander had sent an envoy forward to initiate the parlay, and it behooved him to send his own envoy to meet the other.

"Yes, of course. I am not familiar with the protocol of surrender. I confess, I may have underestimated you, Mr. Cutter, when we first met. And, knowing your fervent desire to remain removed from the current unpleasantness, I understand the chance you've taken by being present here, with me, on this day."

Leaving the storehouse, Cutter pulled Fen aside and informed his old friend of the task at hand. He wasn't surprised that Fen disapproved of getting any more involved in the situation. But Fen also knew that there was no point in trying to change Abel Cutter's mind. There was one thing Fen was adamant about—that he would accompany his old friend out of the stockade.

The lone French officer who awaited them cordially asked them to stand by for a moment. He turned to face the dark woods and waved the white flag over his head. Three more Frenchmen emerged from the woodland gloom. Cutter recognized one of them, Captain Louis Coulon de Villiers. Villiers recognized him, as well.

"*M'sieu* Cutter, may I say I am surprised and disappointed to find you here. My understanding has always been that you are no friend of the British."

Cutter nodded. Villiers had been the commandant at Fort Duquesne since its inception three years earlier. He had sent an envoy to The Reach to request assurances that the settlers there were not hostile to the proximity of a French stronghold. Cutter had responded with a letter giving not only assurances but a clear declaration that he had no fondness for the British, and why.

"That's still true," he told Villiers, a slender, dark-haired man with a smile that didn't fool him. This man had been born into a prominent French-Canadian family. His grandfather had been commandant of the French royal army, and Villiers had proven himself a talented soldier who had a knack for acquiring the trust of Indian leaders.

"Then what, may I ask, are you doing with these invaders?" He gestured at the nearby stockade.

"I came to try to persuade Washington to go home."

"That is what I wish for him to do, as well." Villiers extended a hand, palm up, to one of the two aides who had accompanied him to the parlay. The aide handed him a leathern packet which he proffered to Cutter.

"The documents this contains present my terms for Colonel Washington's surrender. He and his men will be free to leave this valley with all the belongings they can

carry—except for their muskets and cannon. They will be
granted full military honors."

Cutter opened the packet, unrolled the surrender documents, written in French, and read them from beginning
to end.

"This seems fair enough, except that you are requiring
them to travel several hundred miles through hostile forests
with but blades and a few pistols? What are their chances
once word of this spreads? Your Indian allies respect you,
Captain. They will do your bidding, but once they leave
your presence you know as well as I what they will do."

Villiers gave a little shrug. "Perhaps you are right, *m'sieu*.
I may be willing to allow Washington's men their muskets."
Reading Cutter's expression, he smiled grimly. "I think that
perhaps you are not aware that Washington is responsible
for the murder of my brother, Joseph, who commanded a
small scouting party of thirty men, charged with finding out
what the enemy was up to."

"No," said Cutter, his eyes darkening. "I was not told of
this."

"Only one of my brother's men escaped the butchery
of the Mingos allied with Washington. That is why I know
of the massacre. And that is why my superiors urged me to
avenge the dead and chastise those responsible for violating
the rules of engagement adhered to by civilized nations."
Villier's spoke with a fierce enmity. "It is a good thing, for
Washington, that his Mingo friends abandoned him. Were
they here, all of them would be put to the sword."

"Under the circumstances, your mercy does you credit,
Captain."

"Well, you see, *mon ami*, that while I ache for vengeance,
I know that to kill Washington and all his men would guar-
antee war—a war that could rival any in the history of man

in terms of blood and brutality, as both sides would have to rely heavily on their red allies. So we are alike in one respect, at least. We hope to avoid what I fear is unavoidable. To be true to ourselves, we must do all in our power to prevent the inevitable."

Cutter smiled sympathetically. "And I thought Scotsmen were fatalists."

"So, as you have read, Washington must sign this document which states that my objective in laying siege to yonder fort was to avenge the assassination of a French officer and the murder of French soldiers under his care and keeping. That will *not* be negotiable."

Cutter grimly shook his head. "I'm not sure he will sign it."

"Then he and his men will die here. And, sadly, so will you and your friend." Villiers spoke the words with regret. "Unless, of course, the two of you flee, which I doubt a man like you will do. If I am wrong, slip away tonight, because if I do not receive these documents signed by Washington by dawn tomorrow, this land will run red with blood."

Rolling up the documents, now wet with rain, Cutter returned them to the packet and nodded to Villiers. "Thank you. I will make sure he understands." He turned to go, then stopped and looked back. "There are British troops heading this way, I'm told. Reinforcements for Colonel Washington."

Villiers nodded. "I am aware. I have some very capable scouts." He gave a slight bow. "Thank you for informing me, nonetheless. When they arrive they will find nothing but a burnt ruin. My instructions were to send the Virginians home, not to engage the British army. If they wish to meet me on the field of battle they are welcome to visit Fort Duquesne."

"Maybe they'll turn back," said Cutter, realizing that was just wishful thinking on his part.

"Who can say. Only God knows. I am sorry, *m'sieu*, that this war is coming to your doorstep. I believe that all you want is for you and your people to be left alone to live in peace. But you settled in probably the most strategic place between the lakes and New York."

Cutter smiled ruefully. "Just my luck."

The following morning the sky was still overcast but the rain had stopped. Washington sent Cutter out at daybreak to meet with a young French officer and present to him the signed surrender documents. The officer accepted them with flawless politeness.

Two hours later Villier's force emerged from the forest to the martial rhythm of two drummers flanking an officer in charge of the French flag, three golden fleur-de-lis on a royal-blue field. They formed two columns in front of Fort Necessity's gate. Their Indian allies remained behind them, as did the buckskin – and homespun-clad Canadians. Cutter estimated there were at least five hundred French soldiers, nearly a hundred Canadians and a couple hundred Indians, most of whom were Abenaki, also known as the Wabanaki in the day when they had lived in the land now claimed by the Iroquois Confederacy. The conflict between the kingdoms of Britain and France for hegemony in the New World overshadowed a longer-lived animosity between the pro-British Iroquois and the pro-French Alqonquin tribes, of which the Abenaki were but one.

The bedraggled militia Washington led out of the stockade looked a sorry lot. With them came a few wagons, which had to be pulled by men, since all of the draught animals had been killed. All the sick and wounded who were able enough to walk did so, but there were enough of those who could not that they filled a wagon. Another wagon carried what was left of their supplies, without what was left of the rum, which Washington had insisted be left behind.

When the defenders of Fort Necessity emerged, the Indians allied with the French began to whoop and holler, brandishing their weapons. For a few tense moments Cutter wondered if they would attack. It depended on the hold that Villiers had over them, as the Abenaki cared nothing for traditions that adhered to surrender among the civilized nations.

Cutter and Fen stood apart from the rest, posting themselves near the now-opened gates of the fort. Though too far away to hear the exchange between Washington and Villiers, it appeared to be courteous. They were able to watch a number of French troops enter the stockade to destroy the swivel guns and what was left of the rum. Villiers was on top of things, making sure that the strong spirits did not fall into the hands of his unruly Indian allies and the French commander had no use for the cannon. Cutter was aware that Fort Duquesne was already very well-defended.

For his part, Fen MacGregor was impatient, and he wasn't one to keep his thoughts to himself.

"We should get while the gettin's good," he told Cutter. "Maybe we can slip away without anybody being the wiser. Truth is we should've skedaddled last night, like your friend, the Frenchy captain, said."

"I told you to go last night if you wished. You go on now. I'm thinkin' I'll head east a ways."

Fen was astonished. "What the Hell's bells for?"

"Washington said that three companies of British regulars were just days away, coming from Philadelphia. I'm pretty sure I know the route they'll take. I will tell them what transpired here. If their orders were to reinforce Washington, then there will be no reason for them to continue into this valley. On the other hand, if they come this far, and see whats left of this fort once Captain Villiers burns it to the ground, which he will do I'm sure, then God only knows what the redcoat commander will do."

Fen sighed and put a hand on his old friend's shoulder. "I admire what you're tryin' to do, Cap'n, but you're spittin' into the wind. Have ye asked yerself, why would the lobsterback commander believe ya?"

Cutter smiled. "I have an ace up my sleeve. I prevailed on Colonel Washington to write a letter to confirm the news that he has retreated."

"War's comin', Cap'n, and ain't a thing you can do to stop it. You need to be at The Reach when it arrives there. Ye ken the folks there depend on you?"

Cutter recalled how, not too long ago, he had been convinced that The Reach no longer had need of him, how he had impulsively planned to abandon the settlement and head westward into the great unknown. Now he could see more clearly. The people of The Reach depended on him, not when things were going well, but rather when a crisis arose, as it had so often in the early days.

"You and Guy get started on what needs be done. I won't be far behind you. With luck I will be home within a fortnight."

Fen sighed again. He knew there wasn't a chance in hell of changing Abel Cutter's mind once he had made a decision.

"Aye, I'll go. But I think I'll slip out the back way, so as not to have a passel of Abenakis on my tail all the way home."

Fearing that he would not see his oldest and dearest friend again, the burly Scotsman turned and walked away. Neither of them were the type to indulge in an emotional parting.

Cutter watched Fen re-enter Fort Necessity. There was no back door, but Fen was nothing if not resourceful, and would no doubt find a stout rope to aid him in going over the wall.

Even so, he kept an eye on Villiers' Indian allies. None of them seemed to pay any attention to Fen's return to the fort. Their focus was on Washington's beaten and bedraggled troops, and he wondered what were the odds that the Virginians would reach home, and if Colonel George Washington appreciated the irony that his life and the lives of his men depended on the brother of a man he had let his Mingo ally murder while he just stood by and watched. He had, of course, broached the subject with the colonel last night, and Washington had confessed that he was taken by surprise, and so shocked by the brutality of the Mingos who had been with him at the time that he had been too late in responding.

Later that day, as the sun began to break through the thinning cloud cover, and Washington led his ragged and weary militia out of Great Meadow, Cutter slipped away into the woodlands. He paused to look back once, and saw the French marching west while the Abenaki whooped and danced as Fort Necessity was consumed by fire. They had found the rum that the Virginians had left behind, and Cutter reckoned they would celebrate well into the night. After that, he expected them to part company with the French, and go off to engage in bloody mischief.

CHAPTER 20

When it came to the route by which the redcoat soldiers would travel from Philadelphia to the Allegheny country, Abel Cutter was pretty sure they would stick to the Susquehanna River, which had carved passes through the succession of mountain ranges on its way to the ocean—the Tuscarora, the Blue and the Trent to name a few. He intercepted them as they emerged from the passage through the Allegheny Mountains, several days after taking his leave of the doomed Fort Necessity.

For a time he stood atop the gray shoulder of a high ridge, a granite outcropping from which he had a clear view of the countryside for miles around. Down below he saw the column making its way west along the northern bank of the river, a scarlet snake followed by quite a few wagons. From his vantage point he could see them still two hours later, when they had stopped to make camp. Not until then did he descend from his vantage point and move closer, wishing to arrive before the night shadows arrived, as he didn't care to be shot by a nervous sentry.

He was escorted to Captain Warren's tent and was given a cool reception when he identified himself.

"Abel Cutter!" exclaimed Warren, surprised. "I have heard of you." It was abundantly clear he didn't approve of what he'd heard. "What brings you to me?"

Cutter produced a folded letter on fine vellum carried under his belt, a missive a bit worse for wear even though he had carried it rolled in parchment tied with braided hemp. "This, written in Colonel George Washington's hand, will introduce me."

Warren took the letter and read it, his lips moving as he did, now and then vocalizing parts of the missive. "... confronted by a vastly superior force of French regulars and Algonquin Indians... thirty men dead, over seventy wounded... perilously short on powder and shot... surrendered..." He looked up at Cutter, clearly exasperated, while speaking that word. "Was he not aware that we were coming? Did he not receive my message dated two weeks ago? Could he not have held his position for a few more days?"

"Yes," said Cutter. "Yes. And no."

Warren huffed, clearly aggravated. He turned to a young aide. "Go fetch my officers." The aide saluted briskly and hurried off. Warren turned back to Cutter and made a curt gesture. "Come with me."

He led the way into his tent. Cutter had to marvel at the interior, noting how starkly different the captain's accommodations were compared to Washington's at Fort Necessity. In the center was a map table. To one side was another table adorned with an assortment of decanters and a large platter piled high with sliced meats. On the other side was Warren's camp bed and several large trunks which he assumed contained the captain's wardrobe.

Warren moved to the map table and jabbed a blunt finger at it. "We are here. Tell me, where was Washington when last you saw him?"

Cutter walked up and took a quick but thorough look at the map, then indicated exactly where Great Meadow was located. "He erected a stockade and dug rifle pits. But the stockade is gone, burned to the ground by the French. By now I suspect he is somewhere around here." He pointed again. "Heading home for Virginia."

"And the enemy? How many did they number?"

"I'd say at least five hundred regulars, a hundred *coureur des bois*, and as many as two hundred Indians, mostly Abenakis. By now they are back across these mountains to the west There are three forts in this area here. I have seen one of them. The French are skilled in building fortifications, by the way."

Warren's eyes narrowed. "Why do I get the impression that you are trying to discourage me from proceeding?"

Cutter's stoic expression betrayed nothing. "Because I am."

"You favor the French."

"I've learned to get along with them. I had to, for the sake of the people at The Reach."

Warren looked at the map again. "Perhaps I should proceed to The Reach. It has considerable strategic value."

"So I've been told."

"Would you object?"

Cutter knew that the captain was baiting him, and decided to let it happen. He knew he was taking a risk, but in just a few moments he had developed a considerable disdain for Warren.

"I most certainly would. You are not welcome there."

"Typical Scotsman. Hot tempered and short on discretion. 'Tis why your people are under the British boot."

The arrival of three officers rescued Cutter from an indiscreet response. Warren turned to the trio and performed the introductions.

"Gentlemen, this is Abel Cutter. He has brought me a letter from Washington, who has surrendered his position on the Allegheny River and is marching back to Virginia, tail 'twixt legs." He looked at Cutter. "Sir, may I present Lieutenants Bale, Lindon and Hull."

"Abel Cutter!" This came from Jeremy Hull, who stared at the frontiersman. He took an impulsive step forward, came to attention with a clicking of heels and extended a hand. "May I shake your hand, sir?"

Cutter was startled. "Do I have reason to know who you are, sir?"

Warren was standing by, arms folded, a crooked grin on his ruddy, square-jawed face.

"No, sir," replied Hull, wide-eyed and a little breathless. "But it is a great pleasure and privilege to make your acquaintance. You see, I am..." Hull took a deep breath "I am honored and privileged to be your daughter's husband."

Cutter was struck speechless. He stared at Hull, wondering if he had misheard. Then he realized that the lieutenant still had his hand extended and reached out to shake it, much to the officer's relief.

Captain Warren looked disappointed that Cutter's reaction had not been more explosive. "Lieutenant, take your father-in-law outside while I discuss important matters with these other officers."

"Yes, Sir. Sorry, Sir." Hull looked apologetic, then gestured politely for Cutter to precede him in departing the tent. Cutter did so, and took a half dozen long strides before turning to confront the lieutenant.

"Now how the hell did this happen?"

Hull was taken aback. "I...we...well, we fell in love, sir. I profoundly regret that I was unable to ask you for your daughter's hand in marriage. But when Bella discovered that I was about to march west she agreed to marry me. A regimental chaplain did the honors. Two days later, we marched."

Cutter's eyes narrowed. "We?"

"Yes, sir, she … came with me."

Cutter's gaze was hard as steel. "You let my daughter accompany you on a military mission?"

Hull paled. "I tried to dissuade her. I swear I did. But … but, well, she's your daughter, sir. She said she would follow by herself if I forbade her from traveling with the column, and I believed her."

Cutter shook his head. "Just like her mother," he murmured. His thoughts turned to that fateful day, so many years ago, when he had ridden out of The Reach with Guy Rimbaud and his young daughter ride out of The Reach with his wife and young daughter, remembering how Bella had wept quietly as she looked back more than a few times at her home—and her mother's final resting place. With a fierce shake of his head, he brought himself back to the present. "I want to see her."

"Yes, yes, of course!" said Hull. "Please, come with me."

He led Cutter deeper into the camp. It stretched a fair distance along the river bank. Torches had been placed and lighted to dispel the gathering gloom of night. Soldiers were laying out their bedding, or had gathered around fires to eat and talk, getting swiftly to their feet as Hull strode by with the buckskin-clad frontiersman in tow. Further along, Cutter could see more cookfires illuminating the wagons and rudimentary shelters put up by the camp followers. Before they reached the wagons, Hull veered toward a tent considerably smaller than Captain Warren's. It was a simple wedge tent, the flaps pinned open, revealing the bedding already laid out.

In front of it, Bella was sitting on her heels, stirring the contents of a cast-iron cooking pot hanging on a stout metal tripod. She wore a plain brown twill skirt and jacket over a white linen chemise. She was barefoot, with her boots standing side by side at the entrance to the tent. Cutter remembered how she much she had hated shoes as a child. Her cheeks were sun-browned and her long, tangled hair was pulled back and tied in a ponytail.

As Cutter and Jeremy approached, she looked up, a warm smile touching her lips when she saw her husband. Then she her eyes moved to Cutter, and became as big as saucers. She had last seen him more than a decade ago, but she knew him instantly. A clear image of him as he had been remained clear in her memory, and he had not much changed. Still holding the long wooden spoon with which she had been stirring the cook pot's contents, she rose and only then remembered to breathe.

While Cutter stopped in his tracks several strides away, Jeremy strode to Bella and wrapped an arm around her. "Darling, look who I have found!" he exclaimed.

She clutched at Jeremy's arm, and then let it go as she stepped around the fire and moved closer to Cutter. She didn't throw herself into his arms, but rather walked up to him, wrapped her arms around his neck, rising up on the balls of her feet, and leaned into him. "Father," she whispered.

Cutter closed watering eyes and wrapped his arms around her to hold her tight. His mind went blank. He could find no words to express the way he felt at that moment, a moment that he wanted never to end.

It was Bella who moved first, her hands moving across his broad shoulders and down his arms as she settled on her heels and looked up at him, eyes bright and glistening.

"I have missed you *so* much," she said, a throaty whisper laden with strong emotion. "I hope you received all the letters I wrote you."

"I think so. I suppose you ask because I didn't always write you back. At times I didn't have much to tell you. Except that I loved you."

She smiled in a soft and loving way that assured him that he was forgiven. "I knew that. How do you come to be here?"

He gazed at her face, dirt-streaked and lovely, and was taken aback at how much she resembled her mother. It wasn't just the red hair and the cornflower-blue eyes, but mother and daughter bore a striking resemblance in build and facial features. A sharp pang of sadness lanced his heart as he saw her mother in a swift sequence of flashbacks. How she had looked on the brilliant spring day that Pastor Dunleavy had presided over their marriage, the sound of her soft and lilting laughter when they danced, how she had felt entwined with him under the quilts, and how resigned and brave—and yet profoundly sad she had been to leave him and their daughter on the terrible day that she died.

Jeremy could tell how emotionally shaken Cutter was, and tried to buy him some time by answering Bella's query, after taking a careful look around to make sure no one else was within earshot. "He brought word from Washington, who is marching back to Virginia."

Bella looked to her husband, eyes filled with hope. It was clear that the news gave her hope. "Does this mean we will not continue westward?"

"I cannot say. Geoffrey and Robert are with him now. I can only surmise that the captain is determining our next move as we speak."

Keeping a hold on her father with one hand, Bella gestured at the cookfire with the other. "You must be hungry, father. Please, share our supper. We have plenty."

"She's an awfully good cook," said Jeremy, seizing on the opportunity to brag about his wife, as he often did. "She can make anything palatable, even rabbits. And quite the hunter, too, which I imagine she inherited from you, sir. She is deadly with a slingshot."

"I could eat," said Cutter. "Thank you." He had used snares to capture his meals during the trek from Great Meadow, and on one occasion fished a stream with a long, sharpened stick, deeming it unwise to fire his long rifle in woodlands that could be crawling with Indians, many of whom were excited by the prospect of war, seeing it as a chance to gain honor and prestige, and in some cases to settle scores and wreak vengeance for past injustices.

Bella was enthusiastic in the role of waitress, filling wooden bowls with stew for her father and husband, adding some bread cut from a loaf which, she said, she had made the day before. Cutter found the meal delicious, and declared as much.

"She does everything well, Sir," said Jeremy, who jumped at any opportunity to praise his wife. "I must confess it is humbling to be around someone so perfect."

As usual, she attempted to change the subject. "How have you been, father? How are things at The Reach?"

"Fine and fine."

"I still miss the place. Many times, especially of late, I longed to come home. But Aunt Martha forbade it. She said it wasn't safe. War was coming, et cetera, et cetera." She shook her head. "War has been coming for as long as I can remember."

"Yes, well... Greed and power." His bowl empty, Cutter collected what little of the stew that remained in it with the bread. "How is your aunt?"

"She is bossy." Bella smiled warmly. "And she has been good to me. Treated me like the daughter she never had."

"I'm surprised she didn't lock you up to keep you home and safe."

"Despite all the years I lived under her roof, that was never my home, father. And, well, she didn't get the chance. I didn't tell her I was leaving. I took the coward's way and left her a letter. Are you going to scold me, father? In front of my husband?"

Cutter put the bowl aside and shook his head. "No, but when you get the chance you should write her and let her know you're alive and well. So you've always thought of The Reach as your home."

"Oh yes! Now that I have seen how children grow up in a city, I value my childhood all the more. I have missed the mountains, the forests, the rivers, all of it, terribly."

He looked at her, clearly struggling to find the words to express his feelings. Seeing this, Bella smiled softly.

"I have never blamed you for sending me away," she murmured. "I know it was my mother's dying wish that I go to Philadelphia, to become *civilized*." She made a face as she spoke the word. "A proper young lady. Now look at me. I look like a scullery maid." She laughed. "And I have never been happier than I am at this moment, here in this wild country with my two favorite men."

Jeremy was watching Cutter. "It must have been a hard thing for you to do, Sir. To send her away after losing your wife. But I confess I am very glad that you did, else I would never have met her, and my life would never have been complete."

The lieutenant and Bella locked eyes, and Cutter could tell that they were madly in love. He looked away, unable to shake a sudden melancholy, reflecting on the oddity of feeling a sense of loss on the very day he was reunited with his daughter after so many years, remembering those tragic days when he had lost both a wife and a daughter, and acknowledging to himself that he had been so consumed by grief at the former's death that he had found it so very hard to look at the latter, who looked so much like her mother. At some point during the journey to Philadelphia he had come to his senses, and multiple times a day could hardly refrain from turning around and taking Bella back to The Reach. But he had promised...

A moment later Geoffrey Bale walked up. He sat on his heels near the fire, holding his hands out to warm them, and politely declining Bella's offer of bread and stew. He put a hand on Jeremy's shoulder.

"The captain has decided we will remain here until he receives an answer to a dispatch that he will write tonight and send by messenger in the morning. So it appears we'll be here for a fortnight and more." The lieutenant looked at the wooded heights that rose on either side of the narrow winding valley carved by the Susquehanna with an expression that made it clear he was wishing he was seeing the sights on Philadelphia's Market Street instead.

"More drills and inspections, then," said Jeremy, and then turned his attention back to Cutter. "And what are your plans, sir, if I may ask?"

The question caught Cutter by surprise, and he was silent a moment as he sorted through his options. His preference would be to take his daughter home to The Reach, but under the circumstances that didn't seem to be an option.

Seeing her father at a loss, Bella spoke up. "Please, Father, stay a day or two. Tell me all about The Reach, and how Fen and Guy are doing. And all the things that have happened during my absence. And I have a lot to tell *you*."

Cutter smiled and nodded. "I'll stay." He looked up at the sky, a deep velvet blue sprinkled with stars. "It's getting late. I'll go find a place to bed down. See you in the morning."

"Stay here, by the fire," said Bella.

Jeremy took a step closer to her, took her by the arm and gently shook his head.

After Cutter had walked out of earshot he murmured, "He needs time to get used to you being all grown up ... and sleeping with your husband."

Bella nodded, but Jeremy's words did not entirely assuage her concerns, and she watched her father as he walked toward the camp made by the followers.

CHAPTER 21

Cutter found a place under one of the sutler's wagons. The followers had made their camp a short distance away from the soldiers' bivouac. Some of them gathered around a big fire. The word had come down that they would be staying where they were for at least a fortnight. Of the half-dozen whores who had accompanied the column, three of them had traveled in a wagon with their male handler. The others shared a tent. They were excited about the delay. Idle soldiers would be frequent customers. The opinions of the sutlers and the blacksmith varied from fatalistic to phlegmatic to enthused. Lying under the wagon on a woolen blanket, Cutter listened to their chatter for a while and then rolled over on his left side, his right hand resting on his long rifle, and tried not to think about Belle with Jeremy Hull in their little tent. Eventually he drifted off to sleep.

The crackle and thunder of gunfire woke him.

It was not quite daybreak. The eastern sky was brightening, but he didn't need daylight to see the pinpricks of muzzle flash blossoming in the dark woods only fifty yards away to the north. Dark figures were sprinting out of the woods toward the British encampment. He heard a ball smack into the wagon, and another. Looking toward the camp, he saw people scrambling. Then he looked west, toward the redcoats' tents. Soldiers were grabbing up their muskets and shot pouches and powder horns. Officers were bellowing commands, trying to form the enlisted men into rows, with the intent to respond with volley fire and to replace chaos with discipline.

Cutter's first thought was of Bella, and he scrambled out from under the wagon and burst into a run. Musket balls buzzed like hornets around him. From a distance he saw Jeremy Hunt burst out of the wedge hunt, saw Bella's arm reaching out through the flap to grab her husband's arm. Jeremy turned to her, gestured for her to stay down, and spoke to her, though his words couldn't reach Cutter through the cacophony of gunfire issuing from the men running out of the forest and now, in a scattered and disorganized way, from the soldiers. Jeremy ran into the midst of the disorganized troops and didn't see Cutter approaching the tent.

Bella was crawling out of the tent when he arrived. He grabbed her by the arm and held her down while trying to push her back inside. She looked up at him with wide, glistening eyes that glimmered with the onset of panic, all color drained from her cheeks, resisting him, trying to get to her feet, to run after Jeremy.

"I must be with him!" she cried out.

"No," he said sternly, and knew he had to give her a good reason if he expected her to obey. "You would distract him from his duty, and put him in greater danger. Stay down!"

As she struggled to escape his grip, he heard the blood-curdling cries of many Indian braves and looked over his shoulder. More than a few soldiers were dropping as they tried to form their lines. Beyond them, the horde of Indians were getting closer, pausing only to fire their muskets, then reloading as they ran, or discarding the long guns in favor of knife or tomahawk as they reached the encampment.

The soldiers fired a few ragged volleys. It was all they had time for.

The Indians had crept through to the woods to the forest's edge under cover of darkness, within range of the redcoats' camp, and now that they had caused fear and consternation, they were swift to close in for the coup de grace. They reached the camp of the followers first—Cutter heard a woman's scream of terror and glanced that way. The attackers swarmed the wagons and tents, slaughtering the men and one of the harlots, dragging the rest of the women away.

Then he heard Bella scream—a sound that flayed his nerves. She managed to wrench her arm free and scrambled to her feet. Cutter tried to grab her but she eluded him and began running into the middle of the fray. Beyond her, Cutter glimpsed Jeremy Hull, crumpling to the ground.

He leaped to his feet and went after her. A soldier, struck in the chest by a musketball and knocked backward, careened off Bella and she stumbled. On the run, Cutter caught a glimpse of an Indian coming at him from the side, uttering a bloodcurdling war cry and raising a tomahawk. He didn't have the time to bring his long rifle around to bear so he used it to block the downward sweep of the tomahawk and then drove the rifle's stock—particularly the brass butt plate with its sharpened ends—into the brave's face with such force that the Indian's legs ran out from under him as his upper torso was driven backward. The warrior fell, unconscious, blood spewing from an eyesocket.

Whirling, he saw that Bella had reached Jeremy, and was draping her body over her husband's, looking up at another warrior who loomed over them, a scalping knife in hand, his face twisted into a rictus of wild bloodlust. Cutter acted quicker than thought, bringing the blood-splattered butt of his long rifle to shoulder and firing. It was close range, and the impact of the .50 caliber ball lifted the man off his feet. He hit the ground limp and lifeless.

Three quick strides brought Cutter to his daughter and in those few seconds he appraised the situation. It was clear to him that the soldiers were going to be overrun. They were outnumbered and their tactics doomed them. The battle had been reduced to hand to hand combat and close-range shooting, and the redcoats were getting the worst of it. He noticed that at the western end of the camp, Captain Warren's tent was ablaze. So were several nearby wagons. There was only one possible avenue of escape.

"To the river!" he shouted over the din of battle, pulling Bella to her feet, using all the strength in his powerful frame, because she was clinging to the unconscious Jeremy, screaming hoarsely at her father.

"I won't leave him! I won't!"

Cutter didn't waste time arguing. He grabbed Jeremy and threw the lieutenant over his shoulder. At that moment he wasn't sure if the man was dead or not. His shirt and britches were covered with dirt and blood. But when he was thrown over Cutter's shoulder, he moved and moaned.

Bella was on the move, pausing only to pick up a musket that lay alongside a dead soldier, along with the shot pouch and powder horn that had been draped over the man's shoulder. Then she ran, fleet as a deer, and Cutter followed as fast as he could.

The river was nearby, but even so Cutter was astonished that they reached it without one or the other of them being struck by musketball or tomahawk. Bella hesitated at the bank, wondering if she could help, but he barked at her to swim to the other side. Wading into the river up to his waist, he pulled Jeremy down off his shoulder, put the strap of his long rifle over the same shoulder, then locked his left arm snugly around the lieutenant's waist. He turned around to face the bank from which they had come and lay back into the water, bearing Jeremy's weight on top of him. He dared to hope that they had slipped away from the bloody melee unnoticed.

He was wrong. The river was fast and strong and about eighty feet wide. He was a good swimmer but had scarcely gone a quarter of that distance when he saw two Indians arrive at the river's edge. One of them had a musket, the other a bow and arrow. The former had to reload, but the latter loosed an arrow and then another and Cutter could only surmise that it was a down-river drift as he reached the main current that threw off the Indian's aim. Even so, the arrows splashed into the river too close for comfort. With a firm grip on Jeremy's shirt, he turned his body and let the current sweep the other man off of him. Relieved of that burden, he began to swim, kicking powerful legs with his free arm sweeping through the water in a breast stroke. It was light enough now that he could clearly see Bella on the other side.

She had made a fast crossing and now stood there, re-priming the musket she had grabbed when fleeing the encampment, taking a paper cartridge from the cartridge pouch, tearing off the tip with her teeth, placing a little powder in the pan then dumping the rest, with the ball and the torn paper, into the barrel and using the ramrod to tamp it all down. Cutter had taught her how to shoot a musket but he was surprised that she did it so deftly now. She brought the long gun to her shoulder at full cock, took careful aim, and fired.

Cutter looked over his shoulder. The Indian who had been in the process of reloading his weapon fell backward, dropping the musket. The other crouched beside the fallen warrior, then rose and loosed an arrow, and then another, across the river. But Bella had stepped behind a tree trunk, and the arrows didn't even come close. With that the Indian uttered a defiant, ululating war cry, shook his fist, then grabbed up the musket and ran off.

When he reached the southern bank of the river, Cutter was spent, yet he still managed to pull Jeremy onto dry ground. He scanned the woods beyond, praying that there were no Indians on this side of the Susquehanna.

Bella dropped to her knees besides Jeremy, framing his face with her hands, her eyes glistening with tears. "Tell me he's alive," she said, in a hoarse and anguished whisper.

Cutter placed his fingertips on the lieutenant's neck, finding the carotid artery. Bella stared at her father's face and sobbed with relief when he nodded.

"His heart still beats." Cutter tore open Jeremy's blood-splattered shirt, exposing the deep and bleeding gash high on the right chest, just below the collarbone. "Tomahawk," he told her. "Deep wound. Will need to sew it up." He threw a glance over his shoulder, watching the carnage across the river.

The fight was nearly over. The ground was littered with the dead and dying, the majority of whom were soldiers of the 45th Regiment. He estimated that there had been about a hundred and fifty men in the two companies under Warren's command and at least two dozen followers. There was still a smattering of gunfire, accompanied by the triumphant whoops of the Indians, many of whom were roaming through the fallen, taking hair trophies. He grimly watched as soldiers who were not yet dead were yanked to their feet or to their knees to be killed without mercy and scalped.

The sun was about to rise above the wooded slopes to the north, but until then the last of the night gloom lingered along the river, and overhead a pall of powder smoke hovered. Angry columns of black smoke billowed up from the burning wagons in the followers' camp.

"What Indians are they?" asked Bella.

"Abenaki, I reckon. Maybe the same ones who were at Fort Necessity. Not sure about that."

She looked at him, wide-eyed. "Could they have followed you here?"

He shook his head, his dark craggy features impassive.

"I'm sorry," she murmured. "Of course they couldn't have."

"They wouldn't have needed to. I expect the word got out that British troops were on the march to reinforce Washington, and up this river was the most likely route they would take." He got to his feet and held out a hand. "Here. Carry this for me." He gave her his rifle, pouch and powder-horn. Then he bent down to get his arms under Jeremy's and then proceeded to drag him away from the river's bank, deeper into the woods and out of the view of any keen-eyed warrior who might look across the Susquehanna. He continued until they were about a hundred yards away from the river. Then he stopped, took a moment to rest and catch his breath. He told Bella he would check to make sure they had not been seen and that the Indians were staying on the other side of the river.

Returning to the Susquehanna, he paused at the edge of the woods and grimly studied the British encampment for a while. The Indians who'd had their fill of killing, scalping and looting were heading back in small groups from whence they had come, the woods to the north. Some lingered, though, and Cutter heard gut-wrenching screams of pain from a few of the soldiers unfortunate enough to survive long enough to be staked down and tortured by the handful of Indians inclined to commit such acts. He also heard the screams and sobs of at least one woman from the burnt wreckage of the follower's camp, where braves stood in a group awaiting their turn to rape her. It made his blood run cold to think that but for the grace of God that could have been Bella suffering such a horrific end. Before Cutter was convinced that the Indians would not cross the river and pose a threat to him and Bella and the lieutenant, the woman's cries abruptly stopped. He had to wonder if she had feared death or welcomed it.

When he returned to Bella she was sitting cross-legged, with Jeremy's head in her lap. She had removed his blood-soaked shirt and used it to try to staunch the blood leaking from her husband's wound. He sat on his heels and reached out to touch her dirty, tear-streaked cheek.

"It's going to be all right," he said. "We just need to stop the bleeding, and to do that I need to close the wound. While I make a fire, go collect yarrow, sumac, buck brush ..."

Bella smiled pensively. "I know what to look for, Father. I even remember that the leaves of the good sumac have a serrated edge. You taught me well."

Cutter gazed at her a moment, a vivid image of her standing at the edge of the river, loading and firing the long rifle to kill an Indian, quite possibly saving his life in the process. He had taught her how to shoot. He had taught her all the woodcraft that he had mastered. And apparently these were lessons that a decade living in a big house in a fancy part of Philadelphia couldn't take from her.

By the time Bella returned, he had a small smokeless fire crackling in a shallow hole dug into the soft woodland humus. The blade of his hunting knife lay in the flames.

Bella saw this, grimaced, and set to using a two stones one small, the other twice as large, to grind the leaves and bark she had harvested into a coarse powder. By the time this task was accomplished, the knife's blade was very hot, and she had to take firm hold of her husband and make sure he didn't move, even unconscious, while her father used the over-heated blade to staunch the trickle of blood still exiting from his ghastly wound. With the bleeding stopped, the powder was applied to the wound which was then wrapped with strips of cloth fashioned from the cleanest part of Jeremy's shirt.

This done, Cutter lay down, propped up on an elbow, and began considering their options. Bella again cradled Jeremy's head in her lap and gazed at her father a long moment before speaking.

"If you hadn't been here, Jeremy and I would both be dead. I—I haven't heard anything from the river for some time. Do you think…"

Cutter interrupted her. "They are all dead," he said flatly. He wasn't sure if all the women had been killed. Some might have been carried off. But he wasn't going to speak of such things with his daughter. He sighed deeply.

Bella was quiet a moment, tears streaming down her cheeks. Finally she trusted her voice not to break and said, "We can't just leave them for the buzzards."

"We have no choice. There are too many for us to bury. To put them on a pyre is not an option. The smoke would bring the Indians back." He shook his head. It was his opinion that every person, good or bad, deserved to be laid to rest in one way or another. But this time he had to put his daughter's and her husband's life first. "Remember them the way they were, Bella. You don't want to see them the way they are now."

"I will never forget them. All those young men, full of hopes and dreams. Why did they have to die?" She made a frustrated gesture, indicating the valleys, the forests, the mountains all around them. "Is there not enough room here for all of us?"

Cutter watched her, considering the possibility that he had done her a disservice by sending her east, to a sheltered life with her wealthy aunt, even though he had been honoring her mother's last request.

"There is," he said. "But it's human nature to want more than you need, to see that someone else has something better and want it for yourself. Greed, ambition, pride, envy. I guess we have Adam to thank for that. It's not just the kings on their faraway thrones. It's the nobility, the merchants, the land barons."

"But the folks at The Reach get along, don't they?"

"For the most part."

"It's because of you, Father."

Cutter scoffed at the idea. "They would get along just fine without me."

Bella shook her head. "No. I'm sure that's not true now, and I *know* it wasn't true when I was growing up. They depended on you then and still do. You didn't start a land holding. You don't charge them for the ground they work. You didn't promise them ground to till if they would come. They came on their own."

"I would never do that," said Cutter. "That's what the English lords did to us in Scotland before I was even born. They made us renters on our land. They charged us taxes for working the soil that was drenched with the sweat and blood of our ancestors. They took the lion's share of what we made. They said it was their right. And in a way, it was. Because they were stronger than we were. Then they convinced many of us, my parents included, to move to Ulster and even then they soon betrayed us. They said it was their right to do as they pleased, and in a way it was. They defeated us on the field of battle. That was before I was born and again after I came to the new world. Many of my relatives, valiant men and woman all, fell to English steel."

He was silent a moment. Bella thought he was reliving those grim times, and she didn't intrude on his memories. Instead, she got up and moved to his side, sitting there and resting her head on his shoulder. He put his arm around her, moved by the moment of intimacy.

"I'm sorry," he said. "You heard all that as a child. You didn't need to hear it again. And it's not my intent to impugn your husband, or those dead scarlets across the river. They aren't responsible for the generals and politicians whose bidding they do because they are good soldiers."

After a while, Bella whispered, "I want to go home. How far away is The Reach?"

Cutter looked at Jeremy. "If he's up and walking, maybe four days. Ten days, otherwise."

Bella nodded bleakly, then hung her head and began to cry quietly. Cutter didn't interrupt her. Some time later she wiped her face with the back of a hand and said, "There's going to be a war, isn't there? I don't think I ever really believed it would come to that."

Cutter nodded. "I reckon there will be. They've done it now. It's one thing to kill individuals, or colonials. But now they've killed British soldiers. The dogs of war are loosed." He couldn't get the sights and sounds of the butchery at the encampment out of his head, and wondered if he ever would. But he knew one thing for certain: his hope that somehow, some way, war would be avoided was gone now.

Conquering his weariness, he got to his feet and helped her up. Handing his long rifle to Bella, he managed to drape Jeremy Hull over a shoulder.

"We've got to get to The Reach before the war does, Bella."

She slung the both long rifles over a shoulder and he saw her transformed before his very eyes. She cast aside the sorrow, the physical and emotional distress. Head held high, she said, "We will, Father."

He smiled and led the way, heading west and deeper into the woods and she followed in his footsteps.

CHAPTER 22

They traveled for several hours, and Bella marveled at the strength her father demonstrated by doggedly carrying Jeremy all that way in that time. When Cutter decided they were far enough away from the Susquehanna to risk it, they stopped to make camp in thick woods and hard by a spring-fed creek. There was about an hour of daylight left. He bade Bella to gather more sumac, yarrow and buck bush, warned her against making a fire even though the chill of the coming night was already setting in, and then retraced their steps for nearly a mile to determine whether they were being followed. He saw no indication that this was the case. On the way back he killed a white-tail doe and carried i back to the spot he had left Bella and Jeremy.

He was pleasantly surprised to find that Jeremy was conscious. Bella had made another poultice, which she applied to her husband's wound after cleaning it. Cutter sat on his heels beside Jeremy and pressed the back of his hand against the officer's forehead.

"He has a fever," he told Bella, "but not a high one. With luck your poultice will draw the infection out of him."

"I am in your debt, Mr. Cutter," said Jeremy, his voice weak and hoarse. "I only wish we could have met under better circumstances. Thank God you were there when the Indians attacked us, else Bella would have died. Were there ... any other survivors?"

"Afraid not."

"They are all gone, Jeremy," said Bella, her eyes glistening. "Lieutenants Bale and Lindon, Captain Warren ... everyone perished."

Cutter had turned to dig a hole in the ground using his hunting knife. "Your men fought bravely, Lieutenant. But the Indians were too many and enjoyed the element of surprise."

Jeremy was mortified. "I have to confess that I feel ... guilty. That I survived, I mean."

"You wouldn't have," said Cutter, "but for Bella. A warrior was about to take your hair as a souvenir, and then he would have slit your throat. But she threw herself on top of you."

"And Father saved us both," Bella hastened to add.

Jeremy was staring at her remorsefully. "I have to tell you something, Bella. I did wonder at times if you agreed to marry me because you really loved me. I am ashamed to admit that I entertained the notion that possibly your purpose was to have protection in your return home to The Reach." He smiled faintly. "I half expected you to ask me if I would take you there, which would have put me in a difficult situation—whether to desert my regiment and protect my bride, or let you brave the dangers of the journey alone. Which, of course, would not really be a choice. I would have *had* to accompany you."

Smiling wistfully, she touched his face. "I came out here to be with you." Then she leaned forward and kissed him, a soft lingering kiss.

Cutter cleared his throat. "Bella, make a fire."

He proceeded to skin the deer, using his belt to hang it from the limb of a conifer. He cut around the bends of each leg and then made longer cuts down the inside of the legs. He worked the skin away from the hams, pulling and sometimes using the knife to separate it from muscle. Then he could pull the skin away down to the front shoulders where again he used the knife to cut the hide from the joints. Sawing the deer's belly open, he removed the organs and wrapped them in the skin. Before long, choice cuts of meat were cooking on sharped sticks driven into the ground at an angle so that the venison was directly over the flames of the fire Bella had made.

Cutter went to the creek and washed, then returned to the camp and sat near the fire. He was exhausted. Every inch of his body seemed to harbor its own ache. He began to doze off, only to be awakened by his daughter when she offered him a haunch. He was glad to see that Jeremy eagerly accepted the chunks of venison that Bella offered him. Again he began drifting off to sleep, jerking awake yet again when Bella touched his cheek.

"Get some rest," she murmured. "I'll stand watch."

Cutter nodded. "Just for a while," he mumbled as he lay down. "Wake me in a few hours." He closed his eyes and in an instant was fast asleep.

He woke to the dawn. Bella was lying down, propped up on one elbow alongside Jeremy. She had her father's long rifle cradled in her arm. When Cutter got to her feet she did likewise. He marveled at the fact that having traveled far the day before, and staying on guard throughout the night, she looked none the worse for wear. This struck him as all the more remarkable for the fact that she had spent the last decade living the city life. He found himself incredibly proud but couldn't find the words to express his pride. Instead he accepted his long rifle from her and chided her gently for not waking him so that he could take over the night watch.

"You needed to rest," she said, and left it there, as though there was no room for argument, and that made him smile pensively.

"You sound just like your mother. She was always looking out for others, but didn't take care of herself." He didn't need to tell Bella that it was her mother's selfless samaritanism that had cost her her life, and felt bad for doing so. He changed the subject, glancing over at Jeremy.

"How is he?"

"He slept fitfully. The wound is still infected. I'm afraid we need to cauterize it again."

Cutter nodded. He went to the fire and nursed it back to life. He left the blade of his hunting knife in the crackling flames and walked into the woods, then circled the camp. A few moments later he returned with three long lengths of wood. By then Jeremy was awake, and Bella was sitting on her heels beside him, dabbing his cheeks and forehead with a rag that had once been part of the hem of her dress and which she had doused with creek water.

"Good morning, sir," said Jeremy, his voice taut. "I was hoping I would feel well enough to walk on my own today but…" He gave a frustrated shake of his head. "I was telling Bella it would be best if the two of you leave me here."

"That's gallant of you," replied Cutter, "but it's not going to happen."

"You can't carry me all the way back to your settlement. It must be days away."

"It is. But I'm not going to carry you." Cutter picked up the knife and, on the way over to Jeremy, picked up a stick about three inches long and nearly an inch thick. Jeremy saw the knife and the stick and knew what Cutter intended. The latter dropped to one knee at the soldier's side and proffered the stick. He didn't have to tell the officer what to do. Jeremy bit down hard as Cutter took hold of his left arm and Bella, quite distraught, grabbed the other. They pulled him up into a sitting position and Cutter wasted no time applying the flat of the heated blade to the pus-encrusted wound. Jeremy's body jerked violently. "Hold him!" Cutter snapped at Bella, his nose crinkling at the smell of burning flesh. He kept the blade pressed hard against the wound to a count of ten. Before he got to ten Jeremy passed out.

They lay him down gently, on his side, and Cutter told Bella, "Going to need enough of your skirt to make a good, tight dressing." He plunged the blade of his knife into the ground a few times, then handed it to her handle-first. "Might want to wash what you cut off and leave it to dry before we bind him up."

Bella got busy cutting and ripping off the bottom third of her skirt, baring her legs up to the knees, then handed the knife back to her father and took the fabric down to the creek to wash it as best she could. Cutter shrugged out of his long coat and cut off six long strips of leather off the bottom of it. He used three of these to lash the two longest pieces of wood together at one end, and then to secure the third, shorter, length to the bottom of each of the longer ones. Then he tied the arms of his greatcoat to the bottom of the makeshift travois and used another strip of leather to secure the coat to the top of the travois. The last two strips of leather were tied to the top of the travois as well.

That done, they ate more venison and rested until the strips of cloth from Bella's skirt had dried sufficiently for Cutter to bind Jeremy's wound. Then, with his daughter's help, he got the unconscious man on the makeshift travois. Draping the strips of leather extending from the top of the travois across his broad shoulders, he began to pull the wounded man along. Bella walked beside the travois, carrying the both long guns. It was slow going, but Cutter didn't think about the journey ahead, focusing instead of just taking one good step after another.

Two days later Jeremy Hull was on his feet, refusing to let Cutter keep him on the travois. The latter didn't argue the point. He understood that it was a matter of self-respect for the young lieutenant. Retrieving his longcoat, he discarded the travois.

He knew the valley like the back of his hand. He was aware of the routes that Indians most traveled. They kept away from the river and stuck to the deeper woods. Even so, he saw an alarming amount of sign. News of Washington's surrender and the massacre of the British column would spread like wildfire, encouraging some Indians—the Hurons and the Abenaki to be sure—to dance the war dance, don the war paint, and take to the warpath.

Cutter was consumed with concern for The Reach's residents. He second-guessed himself for having left at all, even though he had sincerely thought he might have been able to forestall the coming conflict. That was hubris, he realized now. But if he hadn't embarked on a fool's errand, he would not have been in place to save his daughter and her husband. Still, every day that passed increased his anxiety, his fear that when at last The Reach came into view it would be a burnt ruin filled with corpses.

For this reason he pushed himself and the others to the limits of their endurance. Bella seemed up to it, and each day that passed made him ever more proud of her.

And even Jeremy Hull revealed a deep reserve of grit, especially as weak and wounded as he was, managing to keep up, sometimes with the help of his bride, who would wrap his arm around her shoulders and her arm around his waist when, late in the day, he began to stumble and falter.

In the end, Cutter thought it nothing short of a miracle that they reached their destination having been able to avoid any scouting French or prowling Indians. And when they left the woods for the last time and could see the walls of The Reach across the cultivated fields, he felt vastly relieved. He had taken the precaution of leaving Bella and Jeremy hidden in a brush-filled ravine a few hundred yards away in order to scout the forest ahead, in case there were Indians keeping an eye on The Reach. He was surprised to find no fresh sign. Retrieving his two companions, they emerged into the open and made for the main gate.

There were a handful of settlers working the fields. The nearest was Isaac Resling, a young man with a pregnant bride. Resling gave them a long look as he stopped his plow, then gave them a wave as he recognized Cutter. Retrieving the long rifle secured to the plow, he came loping toward them.

In that moment a sentry on the wall above the gate blew the warning horn. Cutter felt confident that within minutes he and his party were being examined by way of spyglasses. In short order one of the heavy gates swung open and he saw a familiar figure emerge. It was Fen MacGregor, and the big Scotsman broke into a surprisingly agile run toward them. They all converged about fifty yards from the gate.

Resling reached them first. "Welcome home, Cap'n!" he exclaimed, grinning from ear to ear. "There were some who were beginning to think you might be below snakes. But I knew you'd make it. Nothing and nobody can stop you!"

Cutter smiled faintly. After a long and harrowing journey through country crawling with enemies, he felt particularly mortal. But all he did was clap the young man on the shoulder.

"You just keep an eye out while you plow that field."

"I'm a little late doing it," admitted Resling sheepishly. "But I fell sick. Doc Lyman and my wife saw me through."

"Speaking of Doc Lyman," said Cutter, gesturing at Jeremy. "This man needs tending to. Will you run ahead and find the good doctor?"

Pensley jumped at the chance to be useful, and made for the gate with a long-loping run.

Before he arrived, Fen had already recognized that while all three of the new arrivals looked bone-weary, Jeremy Hull appeared to be on the verge of falling flat on his face. He immediately took the lieutenant's arm and draped it over his bulky shoulders. But all the while he was giving Bella a funny look. "Miss, seems like we've met before, but I canna remember when or where."

"It's 'cause you're getting old and senile," remarked Cutter, good-naturedly. "It's Bella."

Fen's eyes widened. He stared at her, slack-jawed, and Bella had to laugh softly as she fingered strands of hair out of her begrimed face.

"Jings! You've grown up! What in the world are ya doin' back here?"

"It's a long story, Fen," she said. "I'm so happy to see you!" She leaned forward and kissed his bearded cheek. "You haven't changed much."

"Well he hasn't changed his clothes or trimmed his beard since you left, anyway," said Cutter, jokingly.

"Ain't true!" growled Fen, manufacturing a menacing glower and aiming it at Cutter. "I was gonna give you some welcome news, but if you're gonna talk to me that way I just won't." He spoke then to Jeremy, who was sagging against him, looking like a man who was about to pass out. "C'mon, laddie, let's get you inside."

Fen turned toward the gate. Cutter glanced at Bella, who was gazing at the walls of The Reach, eyes bright and a warm smile touching her lips. Belatedly she realized her father was watching her and she turned her attention to him.

"I can't even find the words," she confessed. "I loved this place when I was here, loved it more when I was away."

Cutter nodded. "It was never the same without you," he murmured, his voice thick with emotion. "Every day I awoke wishing I hadn't sent you to Philadelphia. But now I'm glad I did. If I hadn't you wouldn't have met that soldier of yours. And he's a good man." Putting an arm around his delighted daughter's shoulder, they followed Fen and Jeremy.

The word had already spread that Cutter was back, as evidenced by the folks gathering just inside the gate. They greeted him with enthusiasm, and were curious about Jeremy and Bella. Cutter realized that many of them had not been at The Reach when his children were here, and expected that many of those who *had* been didn't recognize either one.

Still half-carrying Jeremy, Fen had already blazed a trail through the people, making for the blockhouse, employing a liberal use of profanity to help him make a passage through the onlookers. That passage was closing up when Cutter opened it up, bulling his way through, still holding onto his daughter. He ushered Bella inside before turning at the threshold to face the growing crowd.

"I have important news you may all want to hear. Spread the word and gather in front of The Axe'n'Ale."

Once he had closed the door behind him, he looked around the common room with the grateful eyes of one who had never expected to see home again. Then he realized that Fen was about to plant Jeremy in one of the chairs near the hearth and spoke up.

"No. Let's put him upstairs. The spare room."

"The spare room is taken," said Matty, coming down the narrow steps, an apron around her waist and a broom in hand. Her eyes were on Cutter and her expression made plain that she was so vastly relieved to see him that she teetered on the brink of joyous tears. At the bottom of the steps she leaned the broom against the stairway railing and hurried forward to throw her arms around his neck and hug him tightly. For a moment she was at a loss for words, but it was clear to all present how much she cared for him.

Cutter held her close for a moment, then glanced at Bella and said, "Matty, this is my daughter, Bella. Bella, this is Matty Armstrong. She…." He suddenly realized that he hadn't given a thought to how best to explain Matty's presence to his daughter.

"I clean and cook," said Matty, slipping out of Cutter's embrace, aware that the situation was a potentially complicated one for all three of them.

Bella smiled warmly and stepped forward to take Matty's hands in hers. "I am very pleased to meet you, Matty." She glanced sidelong at her father with a wry smile that spoke volumes, letting him know that she understood the truth of the situation and wasn't at all upset.

"What do you mean the spare room is occupied?" asked Cutter. "By who?"

Matty looked at Fen. "You didn't tell him?"

Fen shrugged as he stood beside the chair in which Jeremy, half-conscious, was slumped.

"I was gonna, but he got my dander up."

Matty smiled and glanced at Cutter. "Then I'll tell you. Your son is here. He arrived a few days ago."

Cutter was stunned. "My son..." He glanced past her and up the stairs.

"He's not here at present," she said. "I think he went to the tavern." She went to Jeremy and took a good look at him, and her brows furrowed in worry. "Help me get this man upstairs," she told Fen. "We'll put him in Abel's bed. Then you must go fetch Doc Lyman."

"Reckon he's on his way," replied Fen.

As Matty and Fen helped Jeremy up the stairs, Cutter and Bella stared at each other. Tears of happiness were glistening in the latter's eyes.

"Joshua...here," she whispered.

"Let's go find him." He took her by the arm and led her out of the blockhouse.

CHAPTER 23

Joshua was sitting across a table from Guy Rimbaud when Abel and Bella entered the Axe'n'Ale. Taney was behind the counter and a half-dozen other people were gathered around. The attention of all present was on Joshua so it was evident that either Guy had introduced him to those present, or he had identified himself. When Abel crossed the threshold, everyone fell silent.

Once inside, Abel stopped and stared at the son he hadn't seen in so many years. Joshua looked like an Indian. No one who didn't know his heritage would take him for anything else.

Bella didn't stop and stare. She walked right over to her half-brother. Joshua stood as she drew near, and she embraced him, then smiled warmly at the surprise on his face.

"I'm Bella," she said. "Your half-sister."

Guy was on his feet, turning to Abel to slap him on the back as they shook hands. "*Mon dieu!* This is a day to remember! A day I never thought I would see!" He half turned and happily gestured at Joshua and Bella, and for once was at a loss for words.

Joshua seemed to be similarly stricken. He stared at the sister he had never known, then at his father. When Bella released him, he came around the table to stand face-to-face with Abel. Then he extended a hand. Abel took it, trying to find the words. Joshua beat him to it.

"I have news I would share with you only," he said.

Abel looked at the others in the tavern, then nodded at his son. "Follow me."

He and Joshua left the tavern. The residents of The Reach were already gathering. He led the way to a door in the western wall, a door made of squared beams, framed and crossed with iron. It took all his strength to pull back the bolt and open it. Beyond was the river, not ten strides away. They stood on a high embankment that had been reinforced in places with logs standing on end and lashed together, preventing the river, when high, from eroding the river bank. Abel closed the door, glanced up at the sentry on the wall, and led Joshua further along so no one could overhear.

"My mother sent me," said Joshua. "I have news of St. Vrain."

Cutter grimaced, his eyes bleak. He had noticed that Joshua seemed to struggle a bit speaking English, which he hadn't spoken more than a half-dozen times for the past fifteen years and more. So Cutter switched to the Iroquois tongue. "So she told you about him."

"Yes. My uncle Queheg and I took furs to Montreal to trade. We had gone before and no one knew who I was. But this time I was confronted by cutthroats, one of whom tried to kill me while the others made off with the furs. I had to kill that man and so I was arrested and jailed. That's how St. Vrain found out about me. Fortunately, I have friends among the French soldiers there. One of them got me out of the city before I could be brought to trial. Queheg and I were on our way home when Hurons attacked us. St. Vrain is a friend to the Huron. He has long traded with them. I suspect he sent them to kill us."

"Aye. If they were on the warpath there would have been more of them." Cutter sighed. "Now he knows who you are and where to find you."

"Our sachem knows all this. He has sent runners to the other nations by now. The Hurons would be foolish to attack us."

"It may be that his desire to avenge his father had cooled over the years. But now..." Cutter shrugged.

"That's why my mother sent me here. To warn you." Joshua took a deep breath, gazing at Abel, his face an emotionless mask. "But now that I am here, I want to know one thing. Why did you send us away?" He gestured at the stockade. "Did you think you could not protect us?"

"When you were born the only thing standing was the blockhouse. Guy was here. Fen McGregor, a few others. When I killed the elder St. Vrain, I made enemies of the Hurons. They came for our blood. I expected them to. We survived, thanks to a French officer named Villiers, whose Indian scouts had made him aware of the Huron incursion. They don't typically come this far, so Villiers and his soldiers came to find them. They were attacking us at the time and the French helped us drive them away. I didn't expect St. Vrain to admit defeat, and I knew the Hurons would be motivated by the death of so many of their own to try again. They did, by the way, a couple of times. But after the first it seemed to me that the only safe place for you was among your mother's people, and you were gone before the other attacks"

"But you never came for us. Never even came to see us."

"Years passed before I began to wonder if St. Vrain had forsaken his desire for vengeance. Before that I didn't dare come to Onroka, even though, God knows, I wanted to. The forest sometimes hides hostile eyes. I didn't dare risk leading St. Vrain and his killers to you. By the time I thought it was safe enough, I realized you had been raised a Tuscarora. I assumed your mother had found another mate. It would have been selfish of me to come for the both of you after so much time had passed."

"My mother has never taken another man. Many have tried to woo her. But she still loves you."

Cutter looked across the river, deeply moved, his eyes glistening.

Reading the emotion on his father's face, Joshua reached out to place a hand on his father's arm.

"There was a time, when I was young, that I resented you. But Onroka is my home. I love my people and they love me. My uncle, Queheg, was like a father to me." Joshua glanced at Cutter. "If that upsets you, I am sorry."

"Don't be. I remember Queheg. I knew him when he was a young man, not much older than you. You are lucky he is your uncle."

They walked together in silence for a moment. Then Joshua said, "I understand why you did what you did, and because my mother understands, I cannot hate you."

Cutter smiled faintly. "You speak English very well."

"She taught me, as you taught her."

Cutter placed a hand over his son's, which still gripped his arm. "You've done what she sent you to do. I would like more time together but you would be safer in Onroka than here."

There was a fierce light in Joshua's eyes. "I would stay. I have a sister I never knew I had. And a father I never got to know. Your blood runs in my veins, and I don't know enough about that blood. Tell me, Father, where it has come from."

Cutter smiled and nodded. "Let's walk," he said.

He told Joshua the story of his life and of his immediate family, without leaving out anything of importance, and without skipping the parts that might cast him in a bad light.

He spoke of his father, Owen Cutter, who, with his mother, Bridget, left Galloway in 1699, fleeing a famine that had gripped all of Scotland for years, migrating to northern Ireland. They had three children with them, the youngest an infant named Abel Euan.

It was not the first wave of Scots who crossed the northern reaches of the Irish Sea to settle in Ulster. The first had happened decades earlier, a colonization of land that had been confiscated from Catholic Gaelic nobility, sanctioned by the Scottish-born king of the Three Kingdoms, James VI. Those Scots had become victims of the Irish rebellion in 1641. Thousands of them were killed.

The second wave of Scots suffered, too. The Irish were not inclined to meekly bow to the wishes of a Scottish-born king. In time the Scottish immigrants found themselves at a disadvantage, subject to the Penal laws, which gave full rights only to members of the Anglican Church—the vast majority of Scots were members of the Kirk, the Church of Scotland. The Scottish Stuarts no longer had the throne, Then came the Test laws, which discriminated against Scots to an even greater extent. The British, who had initially encouraged the Scottish colonies in Ulster, abandoned the colonizers before long, finding their fortune tied more with the ascendant Irish.

"That's why many began to seek another new beginning, this time in the New World," said Abel. "That included my father and mother, my brother Duncan, and myself. My other brother, Robert went back to Scotland."

"What happened to your family?"

"Duncan died of typhoid not long after we reached Pennsylvania, along with my parents. Returning to the land of our birth, the land I had never known, soon Robert owned his own piece of Galloway, raising cattle and horses on rolling hills overlooking Loch Ryan. He courted and wed the daughter of a Cairnryan merchant. This I know from a letter he wrote me. I have it still. I wrote back to him, several times, but never heard from him again. And then, about ten years ago, I received a letter from my Uncle Rory, who somehow had come to possess my letters to Robert. My brother had been caught up in the Forty-Five and lost his life because of it."

"The Forty-Five?"

"Aye. The *Bliadhnas Thearlaich*, the Revolution of 1745. Robert became a Jacobite. Fiercely Scottish in every way, he supported the attempt by Charles Edward Stuart to take back the British throne for his exiled father and former king, James Francis Edward Stuart, who had been overthrown during what they called the Glorious Revolution of 1688. That made Mary, James' Protestant daughter, the Queen of England. When she died her husband, the Dutchman William III, the Prince of Orange, also a Protestant, became the King of the Three Kingdoms."

"The Three Kingdoms?"

"England, Scotland and Ireland. The Jacobites wanted to return a Catholic ruler to the throne because they objected to the anti-Catholic laws that had been enforced by Mary and then William. So Robert joined the army formed by Charles Stuart. They had successes at first, but then Charles decided to march into England. That was a costly mistake. It doomed the Jacobites. There had been growing sympathy for their cause until they acted like invaders. In the end a much larger English army drew the Jacobites into a battle they had little chance of winning, at Culloden. Thousands of Jacobites were killed or wounded. Robert died there."

"The whole family…dead," murmured Joshua in dismay.

"Aye, my immediate family anyway. My father had brothers and sisters who remained in Scotland. But I came here. I had nothing to lose. And I didna want anything to do with the English. So I came west. I came with Fen MacGregor, a friend I made in Ulster. As for Guy, he was a trader like me, and I met him in these forests. In truth, at first, we were rivals, but soon enough we became fast friends. I tried to become a friend to the Six Nations, all of whom I respect. I also tried to become friends with the French. They are here for the fur trade, not so much for empire as the British are."

They walked in silence a moment. Cutter said nothing, knowing that his son had been provided a lot of information that he needed to digest.

"What about my sister. Half-sister, I suppose."

"About five years after your birth her mother arrived here, with her folks. Her name was Abigail. She preferred to be called Abbie. We were married a couple of years later. By then there was a reverend here. Six years after Bella was born Abbie fell ill with consumption. It swept through the settlement and claimed a score of lives. Including Abbie and her mother. Soon after, her father in his grief disappeared into the forest and was never seen nor heard from again. Before she passed, Abbie made me swear I would send Bella to her sister, who lives in Philadelphia and had married well. She wanted Bella to have a good life in a safe place, and I couldn't argue with that. It was her dying wish and I honored it, though I didn't think I would ever see her again." He smiled bleakly. "Expecting the worst is a Scottish thing, son."

"After what you've told me I am not surprised. And yet here she is."

"Both of you. Here. I never even dreamed that would happen."

"But why did she come back?"

Cutter related the sequence of events that had brought Bella to The Reach, which included mention of Jeremy Hull.

Joshua grunted, amused. "So you have a British soldier under your roof."

"Aye. An irony, for certain. I am glad you both are here, son. I didn't realize how much Bella loved this place, though I don't expect she'll stay. Jeremy will recover from his wounds in time and I suppose then she will have to go east with him. He doesn't strike me as a deserter."

"What about the other one under your roof? Matty."

"Her husband ran afoul of the river a few years ago. She was indentured when they met and he bought her. They were never legally wed. When he died the man who owns that tavern bought her contract, and she worked there until...until I bought her."

Joshua nodded. He seemed deep in thought, and made no reply.

"And yes, if you're wondering, she sleeps in my bed. But she is a free woman now. Free to do as she wishes."

"She is very pretty. And she seems nice."

Cutter studied Joshua's profile a moment. "I would hope you stay awhile. But the fact is you should return to Onroka as soon as possible."

"Because of the news I've brought you?"

"Aye. And it's your home. You're Tuscarora. You should be proud of it. I am. Those are your people, and they are good people. And you're a good man."

"I *am* proud of my tribe. But I have your blood in my veins, Father. And it is good blood."

Cutter smiled gratefully.

"How many men are here?"

"About sixty. Some weeks ago I explained to one and all what was coming our way. I suggested that those who wished to leave should do so. But nearly everyone stayed, it seems. I suppose debts of heart and honor keep us here. All here have given blood and sweat to make a new life. I guess they are not willing to give it up, even if it's the death of them not to."

"Now you have one more. And this time you can't send me away," continued Joshua. "This time I will stay as long as I wish. And if St. Vrain is coming with his Hurons I want to be here. One has to wonder how many of those devils St. Vrain *will* bring with him."

Cutter opened his mouth to protest Joshua's decision to stay, but in the end said nothing. He just shook his head, struck by the irony of the situation. Now, after all these years, both his children were with him again, and in a time when The Reach, and everyone in it, might be doomed.

During Cutter's absence, the preparations for a siege, which he had instructed Guy to begin prior to his departure to find Washington's little army of Virginians, had been well-started. Every man and woman at The Reach labored hard and long to prepare for an attack. Armed parties ventured into the neighboring woods to harvest young trees and fashion them into sharpened poles that were then thickly attached to horizontal logs. These frontier versions of the *chevaux de frise*, the anti-cavalry measure that dated back to medieval times, eventually ringed the perimeter wall by the dozens, slanting outward to discourage the enemy from reaching the walls. There was but one opening—this in front of the main gate—with a narrow passage through three of these, the middle one in front of a space between the other two that was barely wide enough for a pair of men side-by-side to pass.

Richard Severing's smitty had been employed day and night as the iron from many tools was melted down and fashioned into shot by individuals, since the caliber of the rifles and muskets varied greatly. Fortunately, Cutter had hoarded a half-dozen kegs of powder in the blockhouse storeroom, which he could only hope would be enough to withstand an Indian attack. He was counting on the likelihood that the Hurons were not of the temperament to endure a long siege.

Empty barrels, wash basins, buckets—and anything else capable of holding water—had been filled to the brim. Many sundry containers were placed on the parapets in the likely event that their attackers used fire arrows in an attempt to burn down sections of the wall. Fields were cultivated and harvested, with those who worked them armed and being watched over by roaming sentries. Bella and other women, along with older children, fished from the river bank. They helped Doctor Lyman by putting in a large stock of bandaging fashioned from clothing and collecting natural ingredients for ointments and such. Men hunted the nearby forest, keeping an eye out for any sign that the settlement was or had been scouted, as did Guy and Fen. Cutter and Joshua ventured further afield, taking Laddie and Bretta with them, looking for any evidence that St. Vrain's Huron allies were near. The dogs were notorious Indian hunters, but they liked Joshua.

Enough heavy chain had been found and forged together to reach across the river, secured to the stockade wall on one side and around the stoutest of the big old oaks that lined the Allegheny on the western bank. It was hoped that this would prevent attackers from coming downriver in canoes to reach the embankment at the base of the stockade's west wall.

The dreadful anticipation was a continuous cloud over the entire settlement. Josiah Taney's tavern did such a brisk business that he was soon running low on all manner of strong spirits. Pastor Dunleavy held services ever day at sunset. People tended to gather together around large outdoor fires in the evening, drawing comfort from congregating and conversing.

As for Bella, she spent a lot of time with her brother as they shared their life stories. In addition, she and Matty tended to Jeremy Hull, who recuperated in the blockhouse's spare room. A few days after his arrival at The Reach, Jeremy asked to see Cutter, with Bella present. Cutter noted the color had returned to the lieutenant's cheeks.

"First," said Jeremy, "I want to thank you again for all that you did to get me here. I don't think very many men could have done that. Secondly, Bella has told me what lies in store for your settlement. I might need some help getting on the wall but I want to fight."

"I'd rather you stayed put, and that Bella stayed with you," said Cutter.

"I am going to fight," said Bella firmly, hands on hips, "and you can't stop me!"

Jeremy smiled ruefully. "She's right. We cannot stop her. She is nothing if not strong-willed. I have a feeling she gets that from you, sir. For that reason I will not just lie here while my beloved is fighting for our lives."

Cutter studied Bella's expression and sighed. "Well, under the circumstances, in a situation where every life behind these walls are at risk, I can't stop either one of you. I'll make sure you have a good weapon and plenty of powder and shot. But you had best stay in this bed until it's time."

"What do you think our chances are?"

"Hard to say, since we don't know our enemy's numbers. But I warrant we will have a better chance than your soldiers had."

Jeremy grimaced. "I can't get it out of my head, the vision of those brave men falling by the dozens. I don't suppose I ever will. I and the other officers urged Captain Warren to double the guard. But I think he was contemptuous of Indian fighting skills."

"This will be a war unlike any the British army has engaged in. Your enemy won't fight in formations. They won't play by the rules."

"I know that now. And I will never forget."

Cutter nodded, looked at his daughter, and grimly left the room, knowing that there was nothing he could say that would keep Bella and her husband from fighting when the time came.

That evening he had supper with Joshua and Bella in the blockhouse common room, a fine feast of duck stew, fresh vegetables and bread, prepared by Matty, who ate with them at Cutter's insistence. He said little as his children conversed, each telling the other about the lives they had led. Bella spoke of the regimental ball on the night she had agreed to marry Jeremy, but left out the wild passionate coupling inside the coach-and-four. When she asked her brother if he had a love in his life, Joshua bleakly shook his head, then turned the attention to his mother, and his uncle Queheg.

It was at that moment that Guy Rimbaud appeared. The Arcadian was not his usual cheerful self.

"One of our scouts hasn't returned," he said. "Josh Halpin."

Cutter scanned the faces of the other three at the table. It was Bella who asked the question.

"Does that mean they're here?"

Cutter nodded. "Most likely. If so, they will come at dawn, from the east, the sun rising behind them. Bella, you are a fine shot, and I trust your husband is, as well. You will both use the embrasures on the second floor."

"What about me?" asked Joshua.

"You will stay at my side."

"So you can protect me?" Joshua raised an eyebrow.

"No, so you can protect me." He rose with a heavy sigh and glanced bleakly at Guy. "You haven't told Josh's wife?"

Guy shook his head. "I suspect she already knows, in her heart."

Cutter went to the door and left the blockhouse without a word.

"Where is he going?" asked Matty.

"To deliver the news to Annie Halpin. She deserves to be told."

The trio at the table were grim and silent. Guy looked them over then sat down. "I'm starving. Is that duck stew I'm smelling?" he asked Matty.

Chapter 24

Cutter was so convinced that Halpin's failure to return from his scouting meant that the enemy would attack in the morning that at first light the ramparts of The Reach were lined with men.

He was right.

As night faded and a soft pre-dawn light made the last star in the sky fade away, the Hurons began to emerge from the forest to the east. They were walking. Cutter opened a spyglass and gave them a long look. Most of them carried bows, with about one in every five carrying a firearm. Some of them carried torches. It wasn't what he expected of hostile Indians, who normally relied on speed and surprise to gain an advantage on the field of battle. Ordinarily they would have burst from the cover of the woodlands at full speed, trying to unnerve their foes with bloodcurdling screams and to close the distance as swiftly as possible. In the midst of them were a large number of *coureur des bois*, the products of French men and Indian women who usually lived among Indians, distinguishable by their height and sometimes hair color. Many of them were dressed in buckskins.

And then, the Hurons and Canadians stopped, just beyond the range of a long rifle.

"What the bloody hell are they doin'?" grumbled Fen, who stood at Cutter's side. He was disappointed that the Hurons were out of range.

"Letting us see how many they are." Cutter pondered the presence of so many foes with torches, then looked sharply at Fen. "They're going to try to set fire to the walls."

"You were right about that, Cap'n."

Cutter noted that some of the *coureur des bois* are weighed down with gourds, filled, he assumed, with tar or pitch. He looked behind him and down. Women were standing near the wall, close to big pots and barrels filled with water. Other containers full of water were already at hand on the ramparts, but if these were emptied they could be lowered on ropes and refilled by the women.

Cutter looked to his right, at Joshua, who was watching the horde across the cultivated fields of The Reach. His son was impassive. Realizing that his father was looking his way, Joshua said, "I count at least two hundred," he said calmly.

"Sounds about right." Cutter sighed with relief. He had spent a sleepless night. For a while he had been afflicted by a heart-pounding dread. Not for his own life, but rather for those of his children and everyone else in the settlement. He had even considered having Guy and Fen take Joshua and Bella downriver, by force if need be. Then he had caught himself sinking into despair, thinking there was no chance for The Reach or its residents surviving. Dread and despair—feelings that he had been able to avoid for quite a long time. But now those feelings had left him. A profound calm had come over him as the long night ended. Matty had gone off to serve as an assistant to Doctor Lyman, while he had armed himself and, with Joshua, went on the wall.

"Do you see St. Vrain?" asked Joshua.

"No. But he's out there somewhere. Has to be, since apparently the Hurons aren't going to fight like Hurons."

Suddenly the almost eerie stillness of daybreak was shattered by a war cry welling up in the throats of the Huron braves and their *coureur des bois* allies as they surged forward at the run. Not far down the wall, someone fired, and then another followed suit. Cutter put it down to nerves and not stupidity and let it be. But Fen angrily roared at them to hold their fire until they could make every shot count.

When the attackers were within a hundred and fifty yards the fifty-odd rifles on the eastern wall began to speak. A few of the men were good enough shots to hit their mark at their distance. In the time it took to reload the Huron horde was about a hundred yards away, and more of them began to stumble and fall, dead or wounded. At fifty yards many of them stopped and began loosing swarms of arrows and shot. The *coureur des bois* came closer still, up to the *chevaux de frize*, until they could hurl the gourds they carried on long ropes like they were slingshots. The gourds shattered against the palisade, spraying their flammable contents on the outer face of the wall. Fire arrows followed, and soon portions of the wall were burning, and thick black smoke billowed up to hinder the sight of the defenders.

Meanwhile, the *chevaux de frize* slowed the onslaught. They were too heavy to move, and difficult to get over or around. The gunfire from the top of the wall took a heavy toll on the Hurons and their Canadian friends. But they persisted, and some got through. Rushing to the base of the wall, they tried to climb the portions that weren't burning, using the many arrows now jutting from the logs. Some of the arrows gave way but others were imbedded deeply enough to hold the weight of those light and limber enough—and smart enough—to distribute their weight between several shafts.

While reloading his long rifle, Cutter glanced to one side and then the other, grimly taking note of those who had fallen. Others spent precious time trying to reposition out of the thick black smoke. Others poured water down the outside of the wall, or pulled up buckets refilled with water by the women below. He also glanced across the stockade, at the western wall, manned by only a dozen men, one of then Guy Rimbaud. They were firing, too, and Cutter wondered how many of the enemy were threatening The Reach from that side—and how they had managed to cross the river. Finally he looked at the blockhouse and as he did he saw the barrel of a rifle emerge from one of the gun embrasures. A blossom of fire spurted from the rifle's barrel and a Huron in the process of climbing over the top of the wall, slashing at a defender with his tomahawk, cried out and fell back and out of sight.

Finding his own view obscured now by smoke, Cutter moved past Joshua, who was loading and shooting and reloading with a tireless efficiency, just in time to see the head of a Huron warrior rise above the top of the palisade. Cutter drove the stock of his rifle into the brave's face and the Huron fell. It was then that he saw the *coureur des bois*, a half dozen of them, maneuvering around the obstacles in front of the stockade's main gate. Each one carried a powder keg.

Realizing that to shoot at them would require that he expose too much of himself above the wall, Cutter clamped a hand down on Fen's shoulder. "Hold the wall!" he shouted over the din of the battle, then turned and tugged on Joshua's arm. "They'll be coming through the gate. Come on!"

Father and son hastened down a ladder. Cutter yelled at the women below to get away from the gate as he ran toward the blockhouse, Joshua on his heels. Running around the side of the blockhouse, Cutter took his hunting knife from its sheath and cut the stout ropes that held Laddie and Bretta in check. The two big, shaggy mongrels were yipping as he did, and eagerly followed him back to the front of the blockhouse, rejoining Joshua.

A deafening explosion seemed to shake the ground beneath their feet. Cutter wasn't sure how many powder kegs had been stacked against the gate but it was enough to crack the stout timber that held the braces for the bar securing the two portals, as well as the timber bar itself. One of the portals was sufficiently shattered, to become detached from its top hinge. The other door, though suffering less damage, stayed on its hinges but was blown open.

Out of the smoke charged a dozen men, half of them Huron, half of them *coureur des bois.* Joshua and his father each dropped one in his tracks. Cutter shouted to his dogs. "Wallup 'em!" and the two beasts, already crouched and snarling, lunged at the nearest attackers, each knocking his man down and savaging the throat. Cutter took hold of his long rifle with both hands, blocking the downward trajectory of a Huron tomahawk, kicking the warrior between the legs before driving the butt of the rifle into the man's face, felling him with a cracked skull. A big and burly *coureur de bois*, snarling like a wild animal, barreled into Joshua and slammed him back into the door of the blockhouse—a door that opened a split second later. Joshua fell backward, bringing his assailant down with him as he buried his knife to the hilt inside the man's belly while keeping the other's knife at bay.

It was Matty who had opened the door. She had been watching through a gun embrasure and had seen Cutter and his son facing the rush through the broken gate. She had the old blunderbuss pistol and fired into two Hurons charging the door side by side. The dragon bucked mightily and she staggered back, but when the gun smoke stopped burning her watering eyes, she saw that both braves were down, dead or dying with their faces now just bloody messes.

Cutter heard one of his dogs cry out, turned to see that a *coureur de bois* had fired point blank into Bretta as the dog leaped at him. Bretta was dead before she hit the ground. Enraged, Cutter dropped his empty long rifle and lunged at the Canadian, driving the blade of his hunting knife into the man's neck and cutting it open as he moved past, half-severing the man's head from his shoulders. He instantly ducked under a tomahawk swing and plowed into the Huron who wielded it, gutting the brave with the long knife. Out of the corner of his eye he saw another brave coming at him, tomahawk raised, and turned to face this new threat—just as a ragged volley of gunfire reached his ears. The Huron went down, as did several other invaders. Cutter looked in the direction from which the volley had come, to see Guy Rimbaud and five other men who had been stationed on the west wall, responding to the larger threat.

Cutter saw someone coming at him and spun around to face this new threat. But it was Joshua. Cutter grimly turned toward the gate. There was no time to reload his long rifle, nor time to sort through the firearms that some of intruders had dropped in death in hopes of finding one not yet fired, knowing too that armed just with blades he and his son were most likely about to die.

But suddenly more settlers were running into the fray, having come down off the walls to help seal the breach made by the damaged gate. More rifles spoke, more Hurons and *coureur des bois* went down. An enraged Laddie leaped on a fleeing Huron, his strong jaws plunging fangs into flesh with such force that they separated the Indian's skull from his spine.

And then they were gone, the handful that had survived entering the stockade fleeing back out through the gate, most of them falling as Guy and others, including Joshua, reloading as he ran, gave chase as far as the *chevaux de frize* and fired another volley. There was still some shooting atop the wall and Cutter glanced that way.

And then his blood ran cold. He raced to the nearest ladder and climbed, and an instant later was kneeling beside Fen. For the first time in a very long time he was whispering a prayer as he desperately felt for a pulse through a river of warm blood from the wound cause by a bullet that had struck the Scotsman below the chin. Too much blood, but he searched anyway.

Numbed, Cutter got to his feet and looked over the wall at the fields beyond, fields littered with the dead and dying, some of the wounded being gathered up by the enemy left standing and now hurrying to the shelter of the distant forest. The morning sun had risen above the treeline and was in his eyes but there was no doubt that the Hurons and their *coureur des bois* allies were retreating. He looked up at the smoke rising from the fire-scorched wall and wondered if the attack was over. Or if this was just the beginning of the end.

When he turned, he realized that Guy had come up onto the rampart and was kneeling beside Fen, a hand covering his eyes, tears streaking his cheeks. Cutter tried to find words to comfort the Arcadian, but had to settle for putting a hand on Guy's shoulder a moment before going back down the ladder and making for the blockhouse. Before he reached it, Bella emerged and breathed a sigh of relief that matched his own. She came to him when he paused to kneel beside Laddie, who was lying next to Bretta's corpse, whining softly. When he rose, Bella hugged him tightly and he put an arm around her.

Joshua and a few others came back through the damaged gate.

"Looks like most of them stopped running when they got into the trees," he told Cutter.

"How many you reckon are in the fields?"

Joshua shook his head. "I didn't really count them but I would say maybe eighty. Some of them might not be dead. And we killed fourteen inside the gate."

Cutter nodded. He told the men who had come back with Joshua to help him build a barricade to block the gateway, and told the rest, some of whom were reuniting with their women, to get back on the wall, ordering them to save their ammunition by refraining from shooting at the fallen who littered the fields just to make sure they were dead or even if they moved—unless they moved in the direction of the stockade.

"Do you think they'll attack again?" asked Bella.

"I don't know. But if they do, we'll be ready."

But the Hurons and the Canadians didn't attack again. By morning there was a solid if makeshift gate in place of the ruined one, the work of many who had labored through the night. At noon the following day Cutter left The Reach to find out if their enemies were still in the area. Joshua and a dozen others went with him, and so did Laddie. They found only an abandoned camp and plenty of sign that indicated their foes were heading north. There were nine more Huron corpses at the camp, and two fresh graves, the final resting place of a couple of *coureur des bois*. Joshua volunteered to track them for a day or two to make sure they were really going home, but Cutter nixed that idea.

On the way back to the stockade, Joshua said, "I never saw St. Vrain." He scanned the bodies, which by now had attracted the attention of black vultures. "You think maybe he's out there somewhere?"

"I don't know. But if he's still alive we can hope he doesn't have the ear of the Hurons anymore. Having taken such losses, they want only to return home."

"What are we going to do about all these corpses?"

Cutter thought a moment. "We have enough of our own graves to dig. The Allegheny will take care of these."

Later that day, Pastor Dunleavy presided over the burial of sixteen men and one woman in the small cemetery located hard by the southern wall. Apart from a dozen sentries on the wall as well as Dr. Lyman and Matty, who were tending to a half-dozen seriously wounded patients, everyone was present. Cutter stood at the head of Fen MacGregor's grave, which was close by Abigail's final resting place. Joshua and Bella were beside him. Jeremy Hull was beside his wife, an arm draped over Guy's shoulders for support. Profound grief cut Cutter deeper than any physical wound he had ever endured. He couldn't imagine life without his old friend. Mourning not just for the dead but also for the widows and children, he hoped that they took some comfort from the fact that everyone at The Reach would be there for them in their time of need.

When the service was over, the residents returned to their work, and Guy made sure Jeremy got back to the blockhouse. Cutter told Joshua and Bella that he would be along but still they lingered. They visited the nearby grave of Bretta, where Laddie was lying. Sitting on his heels to pet the dog, Cutter took a long look around, at the wide Allegheny River, the tall dark forests, and the stout and stubborn walls of The Reach, then looked up at his children with a melancholy smile.

"Not too long ago I thought to leave this place, to head west again. Fen and Guy were going to come with me. One last great adventure, you could say."

"You can't leave this place," said Joshua. "You would not be whole without it, and it would not be the same without you. All those people depend on you, Father."

"Why would you ever *want* to leave this place?" asked Bella.

Cutter was silent a moment, trying to find the answer, then shook his head. He stood, and Laddie stood with him.

"Your lieutenant will be healthy enough to travel soon," he told Bella.

She glanced over her shoulder at the stockade. "Oh, I don't think we'll be leaving anytime soon."

"Why not? He will be healthy enough to make the journey in a couple of weeks. And I can see you home."

Bella looked askance at him. Hands on hips, she shook her head. "This *is* my home. Besides, soon I won't be fit for travel. You see, I missed my monthly flow. I am pregnant."

Cutter and Joshua stared at her. The latter said, "Does Jeremy know?"

"Not yet. I'll tell him tonight, since now the word is out." She smiled. "And besides, there seems to be a war on. It wouldn't be a safe journey, especially for a woman with a baby." She touched her father's arm. "I want your grandchild to be born at The Reach."

Cutter smiled warmly. He went to her and wrapped an arm around her shoulders, then extended a hand to Joshua.

"Word of the battle here will spread soon enough. You should get home so that your mother knows you are alive and well."

Joshua nodded, taking the proffered hand, and not letting go. "You're right. But I want you to come with me."

"Why? I know you're not afraid to travel alone. I don't think you're afraid of anything."

"You will be celebrated as a great hero by the Tuscarora, by all of the Six Nations. You have dealt our enemies a great blow. If there *is* to be a war, it would be a good thing for The Reach to have such allies. Besides, you *need* to see my mother, and she you. I think she is still in love with you."

"Well, I…I don't know," said Cutter.

Joshua smiled. "Whether you come with me or not, I'll be coming back. My mother is safe where she is. She sent me here to warn you about St. Vrain, and she will want me to stay with you until that man is dead. We don't know if he is. So…" He shrugged.

"So you're stuck with us," said Bella, and laughed softly.

Jeremy gave her a rare smile. "This is my birthplace, too."

Cutter put his other arm around his son's broad shoulders. "Then let's get to work and make our home right again."

Laddie trailed along behind as the three made for the gate.

THE END

About the Author

Jason Manning was born and continues to live in Texas. An avid reader and history buff from an early age, he favored the works of C.S. Forester, Jack London, Bret Harte, Ernest Haycox, John Steinbeck and William Faulkner. He started writing short stories when he was twelve. He has published over 50 novels.

ABOUT THE PUBLISHER

This book is published on behalf of the author by the Ethan Ellenberg Literary Agency.
https://ethanellenberg.com
Email: agent@ethanellenberg.com